Double Treachery

Dawnboy had Alexia in his power. The treacherous she-snake who had deceived and humiliated him was now completely at his mercy. But when his light fell on her angelically lovely face, all his vengeance melted away. He turned from the sleeping girl, ashamed and disgusted with himself.

What kind of an Apache was he anyway?

He stretched out on the floor across the cave from Alexia and drifted off into sleep. But even then he couldn't escape the spell she seemed to have cast over him. He dreamed of her. And it was such a charming dream that he hated to awaken the next morning.

Especially when he opened his eyes and saw Alexia holding a synapse disrupter . . . aimed straight at his head!

Also by Bill Starr
Published by Ballantine Books:

THE TREASURE OF WONDERWHAT

The
WAY
To
DAWNWORLD

by Bill Starr

A Farstar & Son Novel
#1

A Del Rey Book

BALLANTINE BOOKS • NEW YORK

To all the fathers and sons, mothers and daughters, who have ever stood together under a clear night sky and dreamed the stars . . .
And especially to the "other" Bill Starr.

PART I

SHOULD AULD ACQUAINTANCE BE RENEWED . . .

HISTORICAL FOOTNOTE

ON SEPTEMBER 8, 1886, GERONIMO AND HIS FOL-
LOWERS—THE LAST APACHE INDIANS TO BE AT
WAR WITH THE UNITED STATES GOVERNMENT—
WERE CAPTURED AND SENT BY TRAIN FROM THEIR
HOMELANDS IN ARIZONA TO PRISON IN FLORIDA.
AS THE TRAIN PULLED OUT, THE FOURTH CAVALRY
BAND PLAYED "AULD LANG SYNE."

1

"*Aiiii*, BROTHER GRIZZLY! Ye'll na sup on *this* lad's bones today, I think."

Dawnboy MacCochise barked an excited hunter's laugh as he wheeled his pegasus stallion, Teelget, away from the enraged bear's slashing fangs. Easing his pull on the reins, he allowed the panting beast to gain a few yards altitude above the rocky slope and circle lazily to catch his breath. The stallion gratefully expanded his twenty-foot wingspread and rode a strong thermal wave sweeping up from the verdant valley below, while both he and his rider kept a wary eye on their lumbering prey. The grizzly, a full-grown and powerfully built male, roared a furious challenge through its frothing muzzle and plunged on up the barren mountainside, its pace considerably slower than before.

It had been a long, hectic day, and now all three—the hunted, the hunter, and his mount—were feeling the strain. Most of the morning had been spent tracking down the grizzly and smoking him out of his cave in the foothills. Then, when Dawnboy's first arrow had but lodged harmlessly in the great bear's shoulder, even so young and impetuous a brave as himself realized the wisdom of exhausting his quarry with a long pursuit before trying again to finish him off.

So Dawnboy had taken to the air and had driven the grizzly up higher and higher on the jagged flank of Skull Mountain, a towering peak in the southern reaches of the Whipsaw Range that was just as naked and foreboding as its name implied. No other piece of vertical real estate on Glasgow Continent—or on the entire three-mooned world of Apache Highlands, for

3

that matter—could match the Skull's stark beauty and terrifying but irresistible fascination. Few bold climbers had conquered its sheer cliffs and razor-edged crevices to defy the icy winds that constantly howled over the glass-smooth bald dome. Many more had, on the other hand, added their own sun-bleaching bones to the Skull's sardonic fleshless grin.

"Not much longer now, Brother Grizzly," Dawnboy smiled, anticipating his triumphant coming-of-age as a hunter, yet at the same time regretting that such a noble animal must die to make this possible. He had always had that strange quality in his nature: a shameful womanly softness that tempered his strength and courage even when he outstripped the other youths of his clan in the rough games that prepared them for the brutal masculine glories of raiding and hunting. Many a wrestling match and mock combat he had lost through fear of injuring an opponent he didn't hate. Such a weakness might have gotten him branded a coward, had not even the most aggressive bullies learned to fear and respect his raging temper when it blazed forth.

"Soon your fence-breaking and sheep-killing days will be ended," the boy promised the bear and circled for a final, harassing dive. Steering the airborne steed with his knees, he raised his steel-backed bow and notched the last arrow from his quiver. Already a half-dozen feathered shafts pincushioned the massive brownish-yellow back, smearing the bear's shaggy coat with patches of clotted and still flowing blood. But even though the animal was visibly weakened by its wounds and exertion, Dawnboy knew better than to expect an easy kill. There was still ample strength in that quarter-ton of predatory fury to provide its slayer with a well-earned reputation for valor.

Driving his final arrow into the grizzly's flank, Dawnboy sheathed his bow and took up his lance. He noted with satisfaction that the additional pain had urged the bear on toward a small hollow a hundred yards up the boulder-strewn slope, a hollow he had spotted at the height of Teelget's soaring climb. Good.

That, Dawnboy thought, would give him some level ground on which to maneuver when he dismounted to meet his adversary in honorable face-to-face combat.

Spurring the pegasus on ahead of their shambling quarry, he glimpsed a small waterfall—now shrunken by late summer to a mere trickle—at the upper end of the hollow. That was even better—a skilled hunter always tried to bag his game near water.

He leaped from the saddle even before Teelget's foreclaws touched down, impatient for the bear's arrival. He hopped about happily, limbering up joints grown stiff from hours of riding. Teelget breathed an excited hiss and showed his own eagerness to fight. But Dawnboy snapped a stern command, and the pegasus obediently flew off to perch on a tall upthrust granite slab, where he would at least have a clear view of the approaching showdown.

Poised on long, twig-thin legs, the saddled mount more closely resembled a flying snake than the winged horse of ancient Earth myth whose name had been given to his species. But the early human colonists on Apache Highlands had possessed more old-time romance than creative imaginations in classifying the myriad native life-forms they found, and in time the appellation had become so commonplace that few of the planet's inhabitants ever thought of the original Pegasus's greater similarity to their pitifully surface-bound horses.

Teelget's slender twelve-foot tube of a body stiffened as the grizzly topped the lower rim of the hollow and caught sight of Dawnboy. The sky serpent's nervous gaze flicked from hunted to hunter, and his long, hollow tongue fluttered out to taste their scents on the light breeze. Lacking true eyes and unable to swivel his head, the reptile nevertheless achieved 360-degree vision through a band of light-sensitive cells around the top of his skull, a survival device provided by evolution for a species that had been both predator and prey during much of its world's violent prehistory. For Teelget came of a flesh-eating breed whose diet had, for a time, included the exotically succulent bipeds who had dropped from the stars to claim this planet as their own. Even now only the bravest clansman dared to capture and saddle-break a wild, high-spirited pegasus; and few of them did so without acquiring the scars to prove it. At thirteen, Dawnboy had won much honor by taking Teelget as a yearling colt from his mother and gradually winning him over with a combination of gentle patience and stubborn dominance. By now the reptile's small, primitive brain even cherished a measure of affection for his young master—as long as he was fed regularly enough to keep his rapacious appetite in check. Just now, Teelget was too hungry to be particular whether man or beast emerged victorious from the hollow, as long as enough leftovers remained for him to feed on.

Dawnboy stood warily as the grizzly bellowed insanely and charged across the narrow field of glacier-polished stone. Adrenalin pumped into his bloodstream like electric shocks, setting every nerve in his body on edge. Staring spellbound at the onrushing bear's powerful shoulders, great slashing teeth, and pain-maddened small red eyes, he knew that moment of gut-wrenching terror so familiar to all hunters of truly dangerous game—including man. For a split second, he wished he had paid heed to his concerned kinswomen's arguments that sixteen was too green an age for a lad to seek so demanding a test of manhood. Even Grandsire Angus had cautioned him to bide a wee time more, although the old patriarch hadn't been able to conceal his pride when the apple of his eye had insisted upon riding out after the marauding bear. How grown-up and scornful of their anxiety he had felt then! And how fearfully aware of his childish unreadiness he felt now! If only he could wipe out the day's activities and be back in the safety of the tribal keep, playing frivolous games with Kathleen Red Deer, his favorite girl cousin, and the other younger children ...

But even if such an option had been open to him, he knew he wouldn't have taken it. He had chosen his course of action, and now personal honor and "family" demanded that he follow through to its final conclusion—however punishing or rewarding that might be. *"Live Free or Die!"* he shouted the MacCochises' ancient motto into the bear's murderous face, taking strength from the proud tradition it had inspired.

In a thousand-year sojourn on this savage globe, the clan had fiercely clung to its independence and property. Not one of the rival chieftains, or even a long succession of self-appointed world-unifiers—kings, dictators, elected leaders-of-the-people, or whatever they chose to call themselves—had ever forced a MacCochise to bow under his yoke or pay a farthing of tribute. Dawnboy and his kin breathed the same air of freedom as their first ancestors, thanks to the fighting courage of MacCochise men and the fertile loins and staunch domestic support of their women. Now it was time for him either to join that illustrious company or add his gnawed bones to Skull Mountain's grim collection, when few tears would be shed to mark his passing. It was a harsh code they lived by, but a necessary one of a clan who had long ago determined to savor life's fullest joys by dint of teetering on the brink of annihilation, rather than trade liberty for the dull, mechanized security that had become firmly established in the planet's other societies.

Dawnboy gripped his lance. He felt the warrior's pre-contact calm settle over him, assuring either clear wits for victory or a serene acceptance of death. He was as ready as he ever would be to prove himself fit for the company of men. Big for his age, he stood nearly six feet in moccasins, leggings, and breechclout. His wiry bare torso and arms would in time fill out with muscular roundness, but even now they were rawhide-tough from long hours of farm and ranch work. His shining black braids and thin, high-bridged nostrils attested to his Old Earth Scots-Indian ancestry, but his wide-set gray eyes and handsome, long-jawed features hinted at something else—an off-world gene-pool that seldom made intimate contact with his close-knit people.

The grizzly's first wild rush was easily evaded by the steel-spring resiliency of the young body the animal attempted to bowl over with speed and brute force. Dawnboy waited till the last possible moment, then sprang lightly aside and thrust his lance point at the bear's throat. But the bear had instinctively kept its head low, so the keen-edged spearhead opened only a superficial wound on its left shoulder.

Dawnboy whirled in midair and alighted flat-footed to face the bear as it halted and came about snarling. But the grizzly did not instantly renew his attack. The animal had fought men before, and dim memories of their superior cunning warned it to curb its passionate anger. Cautiously it hesitated, sizing up the situation, then rushed in again with head low, as if making another bull-like charge. Then, as Dawnboy prepared to sink his lance into the thick neck in hopes of severing the animal's spinal column, the bear suddenly reared up on its hind legs, swinging its foreclaws in powerful blows that could easily have disemboweled a horse.

Caught off-guard, the hunter could only stumble backward dodging the murderous claws and struggling to keep his balance. The bear's gaseous breath and foul scent of filthy mud wallows nearly choked him as he glimpsed the temptingly exposed soft underbelly and throat. But before he could bring his lance into play again, the grizzly had dropped back on all fours and closed in, snapping at his ankles in an effort to trip him up. Dawnboy continued his dancing retreat, too desperately preoccupied with defense to think of an effective counterattack.

Abruptly Dawnboy's feet skidded on loose gravel, and panic gripped his guts at the sensation of falling. His legs churned wildly. Catching sight of a low, flat-topped boulder, he leaped toward it with all the skill and strength of his acrobatic reflexes, just barely made the edge of the rock, and scrambled onto it, never taking his eyes off the bear, which stopped and squinted curiously at the boy as if not quite sure what to make of this strange enemy's puzzling behavior. Then, as if he had decided to quit the contest in disgust, the grizzly turned and ambled away toward the opposite rim of the hollow.

Dawnboy nearly shouted with pleasure: he had put his quarry to flight again, and in its exhausted state he would now be able to run it down even without Teelget's help. He jumped down from the boulder and hurried in pursuit, thinking that if he could draw alongside and slip his lance under the bear's left armpit, he had a good chance of striking the heart. A more experienced bear hunter would have recognized the grizzly's ruse and proceeded cautiously. But Dawnboy, exhilarated by the thought of an easy kill, trotted eagerly up to the lazily moving animal that now seemed oblivious to his existence.

When the hunter was nearly upon him, the bear's astonishing speed exploded into action again as the animal pivoted and made a second attempt at its opponent's ankles.

Once more Dawnboy was forced to beat a hasty withdrawal. He had profited from the previous clash and was less frightened and more guarded now. But the bear seemed to have learned to anticipate the hunter's movements, too, for the grizzly wisely kept himself between the boy and any boulder he might take refuge on. He drove the boy back several yards, alternately rearing up and striking low to keep him on the defensive and prevent him from inflicting more than a few shallow wounds in the thick hide of his back.

Dawnboy was gasping drily now, and sweat bathed his aching muscles. At this rate he would tire sooner than the bear, and he could not even hope to reach his pegasus to escape. Though not normally very devout, he sent out a swift prayer to Jesus Yéoltoi, hunting god of the Highland Apaches, to send a miracle to save him—or at least a clever stratagem that the bear wouldn't be expecting.

Almost at once the prayer was answered, as Dawnboy glimpsed a low gray shape about a dozen yards off at the left rim of his vision. At first he thought it was a boulder, but a quick glance revealed it to be a lightning bush—one of the rare vegetable life-forms adapted to survival at these all but lifeless higher altitudes. With no soil to provide support or nutriment, the plant's weblike roots crept over the naked rocks to find anchorage in the most minute cracks, while its brittle needles waited for a passing insect, bird, or small animal to trigger their deadly electrical charge. Then the roots patiently dined on the decomposing corpse and stored up enough energy for another charge.

Dawnboy estimated that a bush this size would throw a shock strong enough to stun a man and only irritate something as big as the bear. But the irritation might divert the grizzly's attention from him for the moment it took to cast a spear. That is, if the bush hadn't been discharged recently ... Well, such gambles were what made hunting an interesting pastime, as his Uncle Ravenslayer Lochnagar would have remarked philosophically. And since no better opportunity seemed likely to present itself, Dawnboy decided to chance it.

Waiting for the grizzly's furious assault to falter for a moment, he turned and ran at top speed to the bush and slipped behind it, not daring to look back at the pursuer he was sure would be on his heels. When he did stop and spin around, it was just in time to see the bear's tender snout slam full tilt into the deceptively fragile-looked bush.

Blue sparks flew and the air smoked with scorched-fur stink, as the bear recoiled, screaming with fear and rage. The animal needed but a second to recover; then he rocked back on his haunches to slash furiously with fang and claw at the now helpless bush.

The grizzly's chest was exposed. Dawnboy concentrated his full strength into his right arm as he sent his lance flying at the great animal's heart. His aim was true, but years of dozing on den floors and riverbanks had worked gravel and small stones into the bear's matted chest hair until it was almost the equivalent of armor plating. The spearpoint penetrated only deeply enough to prick the bear's flesh, and the haft dangled down like a fifth leg that the grizzly's paws brushed at in annoyance.

Dawnboy's heart sank, but he drew his knife and

watied impassively for the bear's next—and probably last—charge.

Suddenly he heard a *whistle-zip!* sound behind him, and ducked reflexively as a blurred streak shot past his head and slammed into the ground. For a moment even the bear was too startled to do anything but stare at the object that went bounding and rolling over the rocks.

Dawnboy identified it more by its sound than by its shape: an ironbeak, the most dangerous predatory bird on the planet. Though no bigger than a man's head, the bird's fantastic diving speed could drive its hard needle-point bill through flesh and bone like a hot knife slicing butter. In olden days the bird's larger and now extinct cousins had even preyed on pegasuses, killing them in the air and voraciously devouring the falling bodies before they hit the ground.

But a diving ironbeak had never been known to miss its target, unless . . . Dawnboy chanced a quick glance around and saw a man floating in the air near Teelget's perch.

The sight surprised him, but only because he had thought himself completely alone on the mountain. He had seen travelers from more advanced worlds using antigravity packs before. Apache Highlands had never been much of a tourist attraction, but the starships of scientists, traders, and other star rovers did call there occasionally. He even had a vague knowledge of the raytube weapon the man was holding and had evidently used on the ironbeak. Dawnboy owed him his life for that; but when the visitor took aim at the bear, the young brave cried out: "Nay! He's mine. Don't interfere!"

The stranger looked surprised, but held his fire. Dawnboy turned back to the bear, who seemed to understand that it was still a one-to-one conflict. Roaring triumphantly, the animal dropped to all fours for another charge—his first and last mistake. The butt of the lance now lodged firmly against the rock, and the bear's weight driving down on the spearhead finished the job Dawnboy's throwing arm had not been able to accomplish. The grizzly uttered a surprised whimper

11

and took a few uncertain steps forward, then sank slowly down on his right side. Blood spurted around the grooves in the spearhead, and the animal weakly pawed the air, then was still and quiet.

Dawnboy stared at the huge lifeless body, too numb-witted with fatigue and disbelief to realize that it was all over. Then he moved forward slowly and knelt to lay a hand on the great noble head, feeling close to tears.

"Rest now, my brother," he whispered hoarsely. "Before starting thy long spirit voyage to the gods, to sing to them of him who slew thee and who now takes thy strength and courage unto himself. May I be worthy of what thou hast died to give me."

Dawnboy heard a flutter of wings as Teelget alighted, drawn by hunger and the scent of fresh blood. He rose and roughly ordered the pegasus back, just as the stranger drifted down to stand a few paces from him and smile slightly.

Dawnboy felt something oddly disturbing about him, although he seemed quite normal and unmenacing in appearance. The man stood a few inches taller than the Highland Apache, even allowing for the latter's sturdy spaceboots; and his build was rangy but well-muscled under the snug-fitting shirt and trousers. Dark lenses concealed his eyes, but what could be seen of his long face and close-cropped blond hair looked manly and handsome enough that even a MacCochise would not be ashamed to greet him as an equal.

Dawnboy didn't know if the man was acquainted with local custom, but still the etiquette of the hunt required that he render full honors to a guest. With a nod of greeting, he squatted over the bear again and deftly cut out its liver, carefully dividing it in two equal shares. The stranger watched expressionlessly as the youth stood up and walked over to him, holding out half of the slippery, dripping organ. "I thank ye, gentlemen from afar, for saving my life. 'Tis pitifully little I can offer ye in return, but if ye'd care to do me the honor . . ."

" 'Tis you who do me honor, young chief." The

12

man's voice was a deep rich baritone with just a hint of amusement in it. He solemnly took the liver. "The life-debt was incurred not at your asking, and therefore requires no payment. But I accept your hospitality with deepest thanks."

"I am na chief yet," Dawnboy laughed, wondering at the stranger's knowledge of good manners among Highland Apaches. If he had any reluctance to tasting raw meat, he managed to conceal it well as he began to eat the liver and smack his lips appreciatively. "I am but Dawnboy MacCochise, a brave of the Skull Mountain tribe and grandson of Angus MacCochise, Grand Laird of the Clan."

"I know. I just spoke to your grandfather. He told me where I could expect to find you."

Dawnboy shot a piercing glance at the man's eyes but saw only his own reflection in the dark glasses. So this mysterious void-crosser had come looking for *him* personally? For what reason, when the two had never— to his recollection—set eyes on one another before? Curiosity made his tongue a taut bowstring. Had this meeting taken place a few hours before, he would have shot off probing questions in boyish eagerness to learn what the stranger wanted of him. But he was a man now, and men didn't offend one another's dignity by prying like thoughtless children or gossip-mongering women. If the man had business with him, he would get around to it in his own good time.

They slowly ate the liver, the young warrior-hunter apologizing for the poor quality of game animals nowadays. It was almost an insult to offer a guest such unpalatable meat, he said, but one must comply with tradition.

The stranger countered by saying that the meat's toughness attested to the bear's great strength, and he complimented Dawnboy on besting so great an adversary. He was sure the deed would be sung far and wide, bringing much honor to the hunter and to his tribe.

Dawnboy concealed his growing pleasure at the man's praise by dismissing the hunt as mere exercise.

13

He thought he detected a faint smile from his companion when his voice cracked a bit, but he was proud that his limbs had ceased trembling and he could look at the bear's corpse without shuddering at the memory of how fierce it had been in life.

When they had finished their meal, Dawnboy quickly skinned the grizzly and made a compact bundle of its pelt. Then he permitted Teelget to feed on the carcass while he went to the stream to drink and wash.

The spaceman grimaced at the pegasus's uninspiring eating habits and quickly looked away. The reptile had no teeth, but its rasp-rough tongue tore off and sucked up bits of flesh and bone with the mechanical ardor of a meat grinder.

Dawnboy crouched on the streambank, splashing cold water over his sweat-sticky chest, when the man's shadow darkened the ground beside him. A broad hand rested on his shoulder, and then reached out tenderly to stroke his braids. The young Apache froze, then exploded into action like a venomous spitcat, knocking the man sprawling on his back and whipping out his knife. Though revulsion turned his stomach, his mind was calm with icy contempt. He was almost sorry, for the stranger had seemed to be a man. But not even the laws of hospitality protected *that* kind.

The stranger's sunglasses were knocked off in the fall, and when Dawnboy sprang on his chest he was startled to find himself staring into wide-set gray eyes much like his own. When his blade was at the unresisting throat, he forced himself to think of this creature as just another pest to be gotten rid of, like the bear.

"Have ye a name, mon?" he gritted through clenched teeth. "I'll see 'tis carved on yer stone, when I have Shamam MacDuff at the Brotherhood of Geronimo Monastery do the decent thing by yer miserable remains!"

The other's gray eyes peered back unblinking; and then the stranger smiled fully for the first time. It was a good smile, from a wide mouth full of even white teeth, expressing strength, courage, pride, good humor—and

14

something else that Dawnboy could not understand but instinctively liked.

"They call me Ranger Farstar," the man said quietly. "Out along the spaceways, where a man's good name and reputation are as important as here among your own people. I'm your father."

2

TEELGET WAS SLUGGISH with a full belly, so Dawnboy let him glide slowly back down the mountainside under the double load of himself and the bear pelt. The now familiar stranger drifted alongside them, but the youth carefully avoided glancing at him. His thoughts were so confused and puzzled that he was reluctant to express himself until he had time to sort them out.

What was he to make of this abrupt reunion with a father he hadn't seen or heard from in over ten years? He still had a few dim memories of the two godlike creatures with whom he had spent his early childhood, while they hurtled through time and space on a strange quest that he'd never fully understood. But his busy, happy years of growing up on Apache Highlands had made his previous life seem no more than a dream. Nowadays only his Aunt Evening-Sadness Red Deer—who had reared him as her own—ever mentioned his mother, Gayheart MacCochise, and the dashing spaceman who had won her girlish love away from dozens of other eager suitors.

Those had been wonderful times, Aunt Eve had told him, when she and Gay were the most beautiful maidens in the clan. Old Angus had cherished them with the same love and pride he had lavished on their nine stalwart brothers. Then Ranger Farstar had come among them, and nothing was ever the same again.

He was a free-lance space trader and explorer, a proud captain-owner of his own ship who roamed the universe, blazing trade routes and seeking new market worlds for the burgeoning commerce of industrial civilizations that were all but incomprehensible to people accustomed to the primitive barter-economy of Apache Highlands. His business on this planet was with the city folk down in Londonburg, and he probably would never have come in contact with the rustic clansmen had not a raingrouse hunting holiday upcountry given him a chance to exchange flirting glances with the ripe and bold Gayheart. After that, there had been no keeping the two young hotheads apart. Even Old Angus had reluctantly consented to a formal wedding, fearing that otherwise his headstrong daughter might shame him by eloping—or worse.

Scarcely had the honeymooning couple departed the planet when tragedy struck the clan. First, Eve had been carried off by a raiding band of the barbarous Mongol-Sioux and forced to become a wife of their fierce war chief, Genghis Red Deer. That was when her virgin name, Evening-Joy, became Evening-Sadness. Her ordeal lasted five years, until her cousin, Ravenslayer Lochnagar, had dueled her savage husband to the death and brought her back to her own people, along with her daughter Kathleen and a sickly infant son who soon died.

Her father had aged visibly during Eve's absence, and she learned that this was because five of his sons had fallen in battle and none of the survivors showed promise of proving worthy to succeed to his title. Old Angus took his losses stoically, as befitted a warrior and Grand Laird. But it was rumored that he secretly agreed with the medicine men and soothsayers, who attributed his ill-luck to his having offended the gods by giving his firstborn girl-child to an off-worlder.

Meanwhile, Dawnboy had been born in deep space and rapidly learned to toddle curiously about in the electronic wonderland of his parents' traveling home.

Both Ranger and Gay had wanted desperately to keep him with them constantly, but they agreed it wasn't fair to make him spend all his formative years out of touch with other children his own age. So, when he was five, they made the agonizing decision to send him to Apache Highlands for his early schooling, since little danger existed that he would grow up to be a sissy there. After that, they planned for him to go on to a university on a more advanced world and eventually to join them in the growing family business.

Four years later, however, Old Angus received word that Gay had been killed and Ranger seriously injured by a destabilized light-energy converter on their ship. Afterwards, there had been no further news from or about Ranger, so Dawnboy had gradually assumed that he too must be dead, and fully accepted his mother's world and people as his own. It was a good, hearty, man's life that he had here; only sometimes, on lonely nights, he would look up dreamy-eyed at the so-near-but-so-distant stars that might have been his . . .

And now here was the man who held those stars in his hands, bringing back all the old dreams and yearnings that Dawnboy had thought he could live without. Oh, damn Bridget Natséelit, the fickle goddess of men's destinies! Why couldn't she have left well enough alone?

Ranger also felt awkward and uncertain of how he should relate to his son. But unlike Dawnboy, he was not at all shy about drinking in the sight of the lad with glowing eyes. Great God of Space! Look at the size the kid had grown to! And the cool, confident way his son sat his mount—which must be like straddling a whipsaw—with his fine-chiseled features thrust haughtily into the wind, gave Ranger the eerie sensation of seeing Gayheart again for the first time. How proud she would have been to see her son like this; for although Ranger had helped her gain much scientific knowledge and sophisticated polish, at heart she had always remained a wild, freedom-loving Apache squaw.

He could picture her laughing excitedly at the bold way Dawnboy stood up to the grizzly, even as his own

17

stomach twisted sickeningly with fear for the lad's safety. He couldn't have asked for a better display of the manly strength and courage that they had sent their son to this semi-savage environment to acquire. Now, if only he hadn't adapted *too* well to the clansmen's unique life-style and become unable or unwilling to experiment with others . . .

But thinking of the bear reminded him of its liver, and that sharpened the bitter taste of bile on his tongue. He popped a dentifrice capsule into his mouth and savored its clean, minty effervescence as he thought of all the exotic food he had choked down with a smile during his travels throughout the universe. Sometimes a strong stomach and diplomatic sensitivity were more valuable assets to a star trader than all his astronavigational skill or bargaining shrewdness. And something told him he was going to need all the diplomacy and persuasiveness he possessed to get what he had come to Apache Highlands for. Some of the things he would probably have to swallow to win back his son's love and respect might even make raw liver taste good by comparison.

"My grandsire's prize flock," Dawnboy said, waving to a shepherd boy in the foothills below them. They were passing over high pasture lands covered with snow-white masses of grazing elephant-sized hybrid sheep. "I used to tend 'em meself, when I was but a stripling."

Ranger kept a straight face at the youth's condescending tone. He complimented the animals' weight and richness of fleece, adding that he hoped they weren't prone to stampede.

"La, nay," Dawnboy scoffed. "A babe could herd 'em, so gentle they are."

Ranger nodded as they flew on toward the patchwork-quilt pattern of cultivated crops in the lower valleys. He had taken refresher courses on Apache Highlands' history and culture during the cruise here, using the subliminal Sleep-Teacher in his ship's computer to save time. Now he mentally reviewed the pertinent facts to make sure he had them right.

The planet was fifth in a solar system of seven major satellites and a thick asteroid belt. Though smaller than Old Earth, it had an Earth-style gravity and atmosphere and had evolved enough to support human life. It had been discovered and settled about twelve centuries ago, during what had come to be known historically as the "Ethnic Migrations," one of the strange, inexplicable periods in the developing story of *Homo sapiens* when large numbers of people were seized with a lemming-like compulsion to surge out into new territories. On that particular occasion, the compulsion flared up just when much of humanity was experiencing a renewed interest in Old Earth races and cultures. The startling results were that adventurous space pioneers established a New Rome, a New Atlantis, a New New Zealand, and other experiments in revived nationalism on countless wilderness worlds. There was even a New Black Harlem and a New South Africa, which were wisely located at opposite ends of the galaxy.

One of the most unusual leaders in the Ethnic Migrations was Irving Kersch, a brilliant visionary poet and mystic who was convinced that mankind had reached the zenith of its evolutionary and cultural advancement in the Scots Highlander and Apache Indian of the eighteenth century. He theorized that blending the two races' extraordinary physical toughness, brave fighting spirits, cunning intelligences, frugal and honest personalities, richly artistic imaginations, and other characteristics would produce what he conceived to be the ideal human being. The fact that Kersch himself was a myopic 130-pound weakling may have had something to do with his becoming a euthenics and eugenics fanatic. But that didn't prevent him from attracting several hundred followers of Scottish and Indian ancestry who pooled their resources to charter a starship to bring them to this isolated but savagely beautiful setting for their new-old way of life.

Kersch, like most romantic dreamers, was totally unsuited for survival in a harsh, primitive environment that taxed even the endurance of a robust practical-minded activist like the original Angus MacCochise, who served as his second-in-command. But even after Kersch's swift demise, his dream lingered on and became the clan's spiritual bedrock foundation and unbreakable code of behavior. Later arrivals on the planet and discontented offspring of the original colonists drifted away from the clan to establish independent tribes and villages which—as the growing population developed a fairly industrialized civilization —expanded to the size of cities, nations, and empires. But for the clan, and a few even wilder groups such as the Mongol-Sioux, technological advancement did not necessarily promise progress, and they clung stubbornly to Kersch's ideals. Though they numbered no more than four hundred thousand out of a planetwide population of fifty-odd million, their more pushy neighbors had learned the danger of trying to force change upon them. Within their borders the clock stood still; and though various religions had captured their fancies over the centuries, freedom remained the one eternal god to whom they sacrificed all else—that is, if you could call living in an almost constant state of warfare "freedom."

But the tribesmen thrived on it. And, as if fighting among themselves and hunting the deadly native predators wasn't exciting enough, they had even imported some exotic man-eaters for sport—such as the North American grizzly bear and the Rigelian Screamforhelp. The latter was a mean-tempered monster of about the size, strength, and swiftness of a tiger. It somewhat resembled a cross between a shark and a giant spider, with six-inch fangs and poisoned claws at the end of its eight legs. About the only good thing about it, Ranger had been relieved to learn, was its extreme rarity. The clan reserved the special title of Master Hunter for the few braves who has successfully stalked the Screamforhelp. They also had a special name for city folk who tried it; they called them suicides.

"Yonder the castle," Dawnboy announced, pointing with his lance.

Ranger followed his gaze and adjusted the controls

of his antigrav to keep pace with Teelget as the beast put on speed at the sight of the home. They were passing over outlying farmlands with their sturdy cottages of stone and thatch. Further on were the first small villages, pinpointed by the tall spires and crosses of their parish kirks. Everything looked neat and clean; and the fat farm animals and healthy-looking peasants reflected the clan's present security and prosperity.

Several of the workers in the fields paused to exchange waves with Dawnboy and to stare curiously at the stranger with him. Ranger peered beyond them and over the rolling hills to make out the grim gray towers of Castle MacCochise. The River Glasgow ran past its front door, forming a natural moat; and its rear walls rose from the sheer cliffs overlooking Loch Anadarko, a narrow, twisting arm of the Sea of Brown-haired Fish. In olden times the clan's Viking tribe had often sailed down the loch to raid the less warlike settlements along the southern coast, until the reinvention of gunpowder had made such ventures too risky.

Ranger studied the castle's defenses with interest as they drew nearer. Although his considerable military experience would not have judged it entirely impregnable, he still wouldn't have relished the mission of capturing it with only the weapons and technology available on this planet. But fortunately he didn't have to worry about fighting a major battle to get what he came here for—he hoped.

"What in the name o' Saint Geronimo is *that?*" Dawnboy muttered, squinting at a dark object hanging motionless several thousand feet above the castle. The rays of the setting sun struck silvery glints along its underside, obscuring the rest of its shape. " 'Tis na raincloud, in this clear sky . . ."

"That's my ship," Ranger explained. "As I'm sure you know, clan law forbids any vehicle more modern than a stagecoach from traveling on clan territory, so I had to leave her parked up there. But don't worry about her falling on anyone. The antigrav drive unit would hold her in position for longer than both of our lifetimes, even if I never got back to adjust it."

"A starship with wings?" the boy puzzled, getting a clearer view of the boomerang-shaped craft.

"She was made to be maneuverable in atmosphere as well as in the vacuum of space. Actually, she's nearly *all* wing, except for the rudder and stabilizer assembly at the rear. Her builders on Newtonia, the Science Planet, wanted to give her the maximum of airfoil surface, so that she could glide to a safe landing in case of an overall power failure. But there's not much chance of that ever happening, with the three separate propulsion systems she carries."

"*Three* machines to make one vessel go?" Dawnboy laughed. "Is that na like the skinny mon who wore a belt and suspenders and gripped his waistband with both hands, for fear his kilt would fall down?"

Ranger laughed with him. "Yes, it does seem overly cautious. But in my line of work, the result of an equipment failure can be more than just embarrassing. That's why we have rockets for planetary takeoffs and landings; an antigrav drive for flights within solar systems; and a light-energy converter for long hops between stars. By the way, 'antigrav' is a commonly used but inaccurate term. There really isn't any such thing as antigravity. What it refers to is the process of using the gravitational field of one body to overcome the gravity of a closer or stronger body, just as this pack I'm wearing amplifies the gravity of Apache Highlands' largest moon to counter the planet's pull on my body."

"I think I ken what ye mean," Dawnboy said. "But what about the light-energy converter? That must be a fair puzzler."

"That's a fascinating device, but not too difficult to understand," Ranger said. "It's based on the Jarles Effect, named after the half-crazy genius Harlington Jarles, who discovered it on my own homeworld of Old New America nearly fifteen centuries ago. Before then, all star travel was at sub-lightspeeds and passengers could die of boredom during the generations it took to get to some of the more distant systems. Jarles was an amateur sailor and he became interested in the way a light-hulled boat with a big spinnaker could be made to move even faster than the actual speed of the wind. He theorized that the same principle could be utilized in space, if a way could be found for a ship to catch light rays from stars and turn them into thrust that would push the vessel in the opposite direction. Once a ship had broken through the light barrier, its momentum would keep driving it ahead at increasing velocities, until it was squaring the speed of light every few seconds."

"That's all there is to it?" Dawnboy asked in astonishment. "Why, even a stone-witted fool like myself could have thought of that."

"Yes, as with most really important scientific discoveries, the basic principles are deceptively simple. The hard part comes when you try to find a way to get practical results out of them. That often requires a high level of science and technology that can take an intelligent race millions of years to achieve. As it was, Jarles himself was long dead before the transuranic element luxium was discovered on Aldebaran Two. Using refined luxium for fuel made it possible to convert light to energy in a safe, economical manner. But even so, flitting about the universe is an expensive pastime. So I have to make it worthwhile for my backers by finding ways to earn them good profits on their investments."

"Aye, every mon must work to earn his keep," Dawnboy said sagely. "As Grandsire Angus keeps reminding me."

"Your grandfather is a very wise man," Ranger said sincerely. "I have always respected him greatly. But if you want to know more about the ship—"

He abruptly found himself speaking to thin air, as Teelget went into a steep dive. Ranger looked down and saw that they were nearly over the castle courtyard, where a crowd of people was gathering to welcome his son's triumphant return from his hunt-for-manhood. As usual, when he became absorbed with his favorite subjects of starships and star-voyaging, he had become oblivious to his surroundings and not noticed that they had reached their destination. He

23

sharply reminded himself to be more attentive, as he descended in the wake of the landing pegasus.

3

RANGER ALIGHTED A few paces behind Teelget just as his son was dismounting. The crowd, composed largely of youths and maidens of Dawnboy's age and younger children, pressed close to admire the bear pelt and fire excited questions at the proud hunter. One pretty girl of about fourteen even threw her arms around his neck and kissed him boldly on the lips. Then she danced teasingly out of reach as the crowd roared and the blushing Dawnboy tried to cuff her. The family resemblance was strong enough for Ranger to recognize her as Kathleen Red Deer, even before her mother pushed through the crowd to stand before Dawnboy.

The years had treated Eve kindly, with only a few streaks of premature gray in her long black hair and light lines about her eyes and mouth to mark her ordeal as a captive of the Mongol-Sioux. She was still a strikingly beautiful woman, with the full, firm-fleshed figure of a lass attending her first mate-choosing festival. A sharp pang of loss and longing cut through Ranger as he realized that he was seeing what Gay would have looked like if she had lived this long. Less than a year separated the two sister's ages, and they had been almost twinlike in appearance.

"Well done, lad," Eve said, placing a firm hand on Dawnboy's shoulder. "Ye've brought no discredit on yer clan and kin this day. Now get to yer room and bathe and dress for dinner. I've had the kitchen staff working like devils to prepare a feast that'll give ye a bloated belly to match yer swelled-up head."

"Ye ordered a victory celebration even before ye knew that I'd return successful from the hunt?" Dawnboy demanded. "Ye take a lot on yerself for a mere woman, Aunt Eve."

"Tish! Hear the big brave warrior vaunt himself over us poor mortals, will ye," Eve scolded, playfully twisting his right ear. "Dare ye rebuke me, who only yesterday it seems would pull up yer kilt and smack yer bare backside for sneaking sweets between meals? And I can still do it, me fine overgrown papoose, if I hear anymore of yer sass!"

"And if she canna do the job proper alone, I'll add me own big hand to it," a deep voice thundered from above.

Everyone in the courtyard turned to look respectfully up at the laughing face of Grand Laird Angus MacCochise, as he stood on a balcony with his gentlemen-at-arms and other important functionaries. Ordinarily his white-bearded and deeply wrinkled face made him look older than his sixty years, but his glowing pride and love for his favorite grandchild seemed to rekindle that inner flame that had enabled him to lead his tribe and clan to countless victories in his prime.

Ranger, looking up at the grand old man surrounded by his adoring followers, almost wished that he could have been a part of this enchantingly semi-barbaric life that was his son's. Then he caught sight of another old man standing beside Angus, and remembered the opposite side of the all-too-human character of the Apache Highlander.

Chatto MacNair stood with his arms folded over his chest in an attitude of calm dignity that not even his sightless eyes could diminish. All over the planet, troubadours had sung his tragic story: of how he had challenged Angus for leadership of the clan, of the bloody battles fought between MacCochise and MacNair warbands. Then, when it looked as if neither side would ever gain a decisive victory, young Rincon-the-Pegasus-Tamer—Angus's eldest and most able son—fell in love with Chatto's daughter and agreed to betray his own people for her hand. When the lad was caught in his treachery, Angus was bound by clan law to execute him with his own claymore. Chatto was taken prisoner and Angus, in a mad fit of revenge, ordered him blinded with hot needles. It was an ignoble act that Angus had instantly regretted. To make up for it, he swore a vow of eternal friendship with the MacNairs and named Chatto as his chief adviser. Now the two men had become as brothers, as they grew old together and realized the stupid wastefulness of their early enmity.

Ranger reflected on that bit of recent history as he gazed up at the two old men. What made it especially poignant was the realization that such things had happened here so often before and would doubtlessly happen again and again in the future, because that was how life was on Apache Highlands.

"Grandsire! Wait till ye hear o' the grand hunt I've had!" cried Dawnboy, once more an excited adolescent anxious to boast of his deeds.

"And how can these deaf old ears hear of it with ye so far away down there?" Angus retorted. "Get yerself on up here, lad."

"Aye, sir."

Dawnboy paused only long enough to ask one of his friends to take Teelget around to the stables and to give the bear pelt to a tanner, who promised to turn it into a first-rate rug for him. Then he rushed through the castle's tall front doors as Angus and his retinue went back inside.

The crowd began to disperse and Eve followed her nephew into the castle. She had not once looked in Ranger's direction, nor had anyone else, except for a few shy, curious glances. The significance of the snub was not wasted on the spaceman. He was well aware that no member of the MacCochise family had much love for him, with the possible exception of Dawnboy—and that still remained to be seen. Only the clan's ironbound code of hospitality prevented them from openly showing their hostility toward him, and he thought he could even have accepted that. What made him really uneasy was not knowing what to expect from the one leading member of the clan whom he had not yet seen: Ravenslayer Lochnagar.

The Raven—as he was known to all in fear and respect—was the greatest of the clan's warchiefs. When barely twenty, he had vanquished the renegade Aberdeen Raven tribe and killed so many of its best warriors in personal combat that the survivors had been cowed into returning to the clan as vassal subjects. The Raven was second cousin to Angus, but because his line of the family was far less influential, he had tried to make up for it by distinguishing himself in battle and also by marrying Gayheart. In fact, the two were about to be betrothed when Ranger had arrived on the scene. The Raven had jealously challenged his rival to an honorable death duel for the lady's hand, but then had mysteriously withdrawn the challenge and made no further attempt to interfere with her marriage to the stranger. Not until years later did Ranger get Gay to reveal that she had pursuaded Ravenslayer to give her up by swearing that she could never love anyone but Ranger and that she would emasculate any man who harmed him. Ranger did not suppose a man with a grudge like that would likely have forgotten it even after all these years, despite the fact that he now had three wives and countless mistresses, according to the gossipy part of the clan's recent history he had reviewed.

Suddenly Ranger felt the familiar creepy-spine sensation of being watched by unseen eyes. He spun around sharply, nearly knocking over Kathleen Red Deer, who was standing nearly at his heels and staring at him in wide-eyed wonder.

"Hello there, lassie," he smiled, to calm her frightened expression. "Something I can do for you?"

"Excuse me, sir," she said in a small, awe-stricken voice. "But are ye truly my uncle?"

"Well, there's no blood kin between us." He used the clan's term for her convenience. "But I was married to your aunt, and your cousin Dawnboy is my son. So I guess you're entitled to call me Uncle Ranger, if you want to."

"And will ye be taking Dawnboy away wi' ye in yon ship?" She gazed longingly up at the motionless craft that still gleamed in the last rays of a sun that had now sunk below the horizon.

"Only if he chooses of his own free will to go with me," Ranger answered. "Why, are you afraid you'll miss him too much when he's gone?"

"'Tis na that so much," Kathleen said, and looked him boldly in the eye. "I want to go wi' ye, too!"

Ranger was startled by the intensity of this remarkably lovely child-woman. She wore the loose-fitting knee-length tunic of all the clan's unmarried girls and early adolescence made her slim figure seem awkward in all the wrong places. But she showed definite promise of developing into a real beauty, and he was sorry that she and Dawnboy were first cousins. It would have been interesting to see the children that a marriage between them might produce. He tried to laugh off her request by saying: "I don't think your mother would be much in favor of that."

"Oh, please, Uncle Ranger!" She gripped his right hand with both of hers. "Take me wi' ye! I promise I'll be nay extra trouble and mind ye like a slave. To Dawnboy it may na be so important, because he's a mon and can make whatever he wants o' his life here. But this is the only chance I'll ever have to get into space—something I've always wanted more than anything else in the world, ever since I learned it's possible to travel between the stars!"

"I know how you feel." He gently patted her shoulder. "It was the same on the backward world where I grew up. When I wasn't too much older than you, I was desperate enough to pay any price to get into space. But sometimes the price can turn out to be far greater than we imagine."

"I do na care!" the girl cried heatedly. "I have to—" She broke off abruptly and stared past his left shoulder.

Ranger turned his head and saw an attractive girl of about nineteen walking toward them. Masses of golden curls framed her heart-shaped face, and her tunic was belted high to show off a goodly portion of her shapely

28

thighs. He judged her to be a brazen wench—with much to be brazen about.

"Kathleen, your mother wants you in the kitchen," she said, and continued to smile pleasantly as the child glared at her and slunk away. Then she curtsied deeply to Ranger. "I'm Tessie, one of the upstairs maids, m'lord. I was sent to show you to your room. This way, please."

Ranger had planned to spend the night aboard his ship, but he saw no reason to refuse the laird's hospitality. He followed Tessie into the castle. They went through the enormous entrance hall and visitors' gallery, up a long curving staircase, and seemed to walk down miles of richly carpeted and tapestried hallways before finally coming to a stout wooden door. The maid opened it and ushered him into a large high-ceilinged room sparsely furnished with a canopied bed, some chairs, and a dresser-commode holding a washbasin and pitcher.

"I hope you'll be comfortable here, m'lord," Tessie said, crossing the room to close the balcony doors against the approaching evening chill. "Though these be a far cry from the fine lodgings that a gentleman like yourself is accustomed to, I'll wager."

"I've had worse," Ranger assured her. "You're not a native here, are you? I don't detect the clan's burr in your speech."

"No, sir. I was born in Londonburg, of a prosperous merchant family. But my father was bankrupted by the unfair taxation laws of King Larry the Louse's corrupt officials, so he had to sell his children to save them from starvation. I went to a farm in New Cornwall, where I was captured by a raiding band from the Mescalero-Stuart tribe."

"So now you're a slave of the clan. Do you mind it very much?"

"It's not so bad," she said philosophically. "Better a well-fed slave than a starving free citizen. Besides, there's always the chance a brave may buy me to be his concubine. And if I give him healthy sons, he may even raise me to the status of a legal wife."

That was about the most any woman in the clan could look forward to, Ranger thought sympathetically. But what right had he to criticize the system, if the women themselves were content with it? That is, all of them except his niece Kathleen. Something about the child's burning determination, as compared to Tessie's languid acceptance of her fate, made him suddenly decide to help her fulfill her dream, if it was possible. But first he had to take care of his business with Dawnboy. And before he could think any more about that, he had to find out just what Tessie was up to.

She had gone to turn down the bed, and she was making such a production of it that it became obvious that she was giving him an opportunity to view her ample charms from all angles. He was still male enough to be impressed, even though he had not thought much about women since his wife's death. He became especially distracted when Tessie sat on the bed and ran her hand sensuously over the mattress.

"This is a very soft, yielding bed, m'lord," she purred. "I'm sure you will spend a very satisfying night in it."

"I don't care for soft beds," he told her. "I prefer to have something with more resistance under me."

"That can be arranged." She lounged back on one elbow and crossed her legs, smiling invitingly at him. "Come here, m'lord, and I'll show you what I mean."

Ranger gave her a tight smile and gripped the hilt of his Artelian synapse disrupter. "Good try, Tessie, but I've been set up like this before—by experts. Now, who ordered you to do this? Ravenslayer? Or Old Angus himself? No, I don't think he would stoop that low."

"Why, I don't know what you mean," Tessie simpered with dewy-eyed innocence. "I just happen to find you a very handsome and desirable gentleman, m'lord. And I thought you'd like a bit of fun before supper."

"Don't try to—"

The sound of rapidly approaching footsteps outside the door jerked his attention away from the maid. But he kept a wary eye on her as he brought his weapon up to meet the danger he felt certain was imminent.

A drastic transformation overcame the girl as she, too, heard the footsteps. She ripped open the front of her dress with both hands and whipped her head wildly from side to side, crying out in terror, "Oh, please m'lord, don't hurt me! Help! Help! He's gone mad! Someone please help me!"

Ranger thought she was overacting terribly, but the charade was convincing enough to give a legal excuse to anyone who wanted to hack off his head. Since that was just the sort of intruder he expected to burst in on them, he was rather surprised when Eve Red Deer thrust open the unlocked door and stepped into the room. Evidently Tessie wasn't expecting her, either, because she suddenly fell silent and gaped bugeyed at the woman.

Eve took in the scene with a quick glance, as she closed and bolted the door. "I thought it would be something like this," she said flatly, "when Kathleen told me about ye being led off by this slut of Ravenslayer's."

"Please, ma'am, I—" Tessie began fearfully.

"Shut yer foul mouth, slave," Eve snapped. "I ken ye were forced to do this, but that makes ye no less guilty in my eyes. A whipping ye'll get for sure, but if ye vex me further, I vow I'll have yer scalp for a dust mop!"

Tessie shut her mouth obediently, as other and heavier footsteps were heard outside on the balcony. Ranger started to turn in that direction with his disrupter, when Eve warned, "Put that toy away, fool! Ye'd only get us all killed that way."

Ranger decided to trust her, and holstered the weapon as the balcony door crashed open and a half-dozen brawny men rushed in. They were armed with a variety of hand weapons including broadswords, lances, and a tomahawk. He recognized the handsome scarred face of Ravenslayer in the lead, and although the famous warchief was a good two inches taller than himself, the others towered even over him. There was a lot of solid flesh on those tall frames with thick chests, and shoulders bulging out of leather doublets, and powerful hairy calf muscles below colorful kilts. Obviously Eve had been right: they would have torn him to pieces before he could have knocked down more than two or three of them with his disrupter.

The men poured angrily into the room, then milled about uncertainly as Ravenslayer came to an abrupt halt at the sight of Eve. He seemed puzzled, but still determined to play out his little melodrama. "What's the trouble here?" he demanded of Tessie. "We heard screams and—"

Eve cut him off with a scornful laugh. "So this is how the high and mighty Raven dishonors his clan—by trying to murder the laird's guest on a false charge of attacking a strumpet slave! Have ye no shame, mon?"

For a moment Ravenslayer was completely abashed by her bold assault, as he flushed and dropped his gaze guiltily. But he recovered quickly and snapped, "Hobble yer tongue, woman! This be mon's business."

"Anything that affects the clan's good name is the business of all of us," Eve retorted. "Think ye that my father would na banish even his foremost warchief for so base a crime as this?" That brought a worried expression to the Raven's face, and she went on in a softer tone. "Oh, do na worry—I shan't tell him, seeing's there was no real harm done. But get ye and yer henchmen out o' here before all this commotion attracts looser tongues than mine."

"I'll leave because there's nay good reason for me to stay," Ravenslayer said haughtily. "Nor do I relish the company." He started toward the balcony door with his men at his heels, then turned back to Ranger and said: "But do na think this is yet finished between us, mon. Only blood can wash away the injury ye've done me. And I vow I'll have yers if ye stay much longer on Apache Highlands!"

He strode swifty out of the room before Ranger could reply. His men followed him, each of them giving Ranger a menacing glare as they went. Tessie cast a frightened glance at Eve, then jumped off the bed and ran out.

Ranger heaved an inward sigh of relief and turned to

Evening-Sadness. "Thanks for your help, Eve. I don't think I could have—"

"Thank me for nothing, ye misbegotten scum of a space rat!" she spat viciously. "What I did was for the clan. Otherwise I'd be delighted to dance on yer grave. How I've cursed the day I ever laid eyes on ye! Ye've brought nought but trouble and misery to my life. First, ye took my dear sister away to die far from her kith and kin; and now ye've come back for her wee bairn, that I've raised up and come to love as my very own. Oh, damn ye, Ranger Farstar! Were I a mon, I'd kill ye myself!"

"I understand how you feel," he said softly. "Sometimes I almost hate myself that much. I've never set out to hurt anyone, but it seems that everything I touch turns sour. Even after I recovered from the accident that killed Gay, I couldn't get anything to go right for me again. No one would trust me in a position of responsibility, and I had to take whatever jobs around the spaceports I could get—cargo loader, ordinary deckhand, steward on a cruise liner. It's taken me all these years to work my way back up to command level, and it was only by good luck that I was able to find enough financial backers to enable me to get my own ship again. But you're mistaken in thinking that I'm here to take Dawnboy away from you."

Eve stared incredulously at him. "Then why . . . ?"

"I've only come to visit my son. Surely a father has that right."

Hope flickered across her lovely face, then she frowned skeptically. "Nay, that's too pat a denial. Yer playing the sly-boots, I'll wager."

Ranger held out his open hands to her. "No tricks, I promise. I promised Gay on her deathbed that I'd let the boy live his own life. So all I'm going to do is offer him the opportunity to come with me when I leave. Of course, I'll be happy if he says yes; but if instead he decides to stay here, well, I won't try to pressure him into changing his mind."

"I wish I could believe ye," Eve said sincerely. "But

it seems too unnatural an attitude for a parent to have for his own flesh and blood."

"It might be, if I were in another line of work," he agreed. "But it takes a very special kind of individual to make a good spaceman—only a handful of us out of a universal population of trillions of human and other intelligent beings. If Dawnboy doesn't have that special talent—and the stubborn determination to make the grade—then I would only be hurting him if I tried to push him into a career of star-voyaging." He hesitated as he considered telling her about her daughter's fervent interest in space travel. Deciding this wasn't the proper time to mention that, he only said: "But I should also tell you that if a person is definitely cut out to be a star-rover, then he'll find a way to become one, no matter what barriers stand in his way."

Eve nodded fatalistically. "Aye, none of us can escape the destiny that the gods have in store fer us. So, if I've your word not to try to influence the lad unduly, I'll promise the same." She held out her right hand. "Agreed?"

"Agreed." Ranger pressed her strong, work-roughened hand and was again uncomfortably reminded of Gay. Eve's hair also had the strong scent of heather and warm summer wind that he had been unable to bury along with the old memories.

She briskly pulled away from him and flashed an almost friendly smile. "Now get washed up for dinner, and be sure to bring a big appetite. Ye'll have to stuff yerself like a hog to do honor to yer son's hunt-for-manhood celebration."

"I'm already hungry enough to outeat ten of your biggest braves," he assured her. "As long as raw liver isn't on the menu."

4

"I PURPOSELY ASKED that ye be seated next to me," Chatto MacNair said as Ranger took his assigned chair at the huge horeshoe-shaped table in the castle's vast Festival Hall, "because I wanted to question ye about yer travels. I hope ye do na mind the prattle of a foolish old mon."

"Not at all, sir," Ranger replied respectfully, looking toward the head of the table where Dawnboy occupied the guest of honor's seat beside Laird Angus. The lad certainly cut a striking figure as he sat stiffly in his finest coat and kilt with a single ironbeak feather in his tam to mark his debut as a full-fledged hunter. "But I trust you'll overlook my ignorance on many subjects. I'm just a trader and explorer, not a dedicated scholar like yourself."

The old Highlander's sightless eyes glowed at the compliment, but he modestly brushed it aside. "Nay, sir, credit me na wi' the wisdom o' a true intellectual. I grew up learning neither to read nor write, but when my fighting days were o'er I had to find some useful way to fill me time. So I acquired a vast library and some educated slaves to read to me. And that's gien me a consuming interest in distant worlds and peoples. For example, I hear ye've been to Nonith in the Praesepe Cluster. Is it true that the humanoid race there has *three* sexes?"

Ranger's attention had shifted from his son to his father-in-law, who was also garbed in the full ceremonial splendor of the clan's scarlet-and-gold tartan, hairy goatskin sporran, and long trailing war bonnet of eagle feathers. All around them tribal chiefs, ambassadors, important religious leaders, and others who ranked high enough to be invited to the laird's table tried to outdo each other with their fanciness of dress and decorations. Ranger, who knew something about the cultural accoutrements of the different Scottish and Indian groups of Old Earth, had to suppress a smile at some of the strange combinations that time and evolution had produced on this planet. About the only one present—besides Ranger—who didn't seem to be showing off his finery was Ravenslayer, who could afford to put on a true hero's display of modest self-depreciation. While the others had ostentatious means of accounting for their military achievements—enemy scalps on the belt, medals for valor, a feather for every raid participated in, etc.—Ravenslayer wore only a simple necklace of Screamforhelp teeth, one for each major war he had won. There were an even dozen of them.

"Excuse me; I was distracted," Ranger said, coming back to his blind neighbor's question. "You asked about the Nonithians? Yes, in a sense they are trisexual. It's an evolutionary means of improving the species through natural selection, as I understand it. The females outnumber the males by two to one, so each family consists of a husband and two wives, at the beginning. But only the stronger wife mates with the male, after having beaten off the weaker wife."

"That seems a bit unfair to the poor lass," Chatto observed.

"Yes, but nature manages to even things out in the long run, even on Nonith. After the husband has fertilized the stronger wife's eggs, she deposits them in the womb of the weaker wife, who gestates them, gives birth, and cares for the young. Once the husband and other wife have fulfilled their part of the reproductive cycle, their sex organs gradually atrophy and they become neutered hunters and warriors. The weaker wife needs two such "husbands" to provide for and protect her and the children because of the planet's extremely harsh living conditions."

"Fascinating!" Chatto exclaimed, adding wistfully, "Ah, how I envy ye yer young years and freedom to go a-roving about the galaxies. If only I had me own life to live over again—" His nose suddenly twitched as he sniffed a faint breeze wafting through the hall. "Hark! The kitchen door was just opened. The food'll be coming soon. Before it arrives, let's have a wee dram to whet our appetites."

He snapped his fingers, and the body servant who stood attentively behind Chatto's chair leaned forward to fill their glasses from one of the many bottles on the table. Ranger knew that the clan's traditional beverage—a blend of Scotch whisky and mescal—was highly potent stuff, so he cautioned himself to go easy on it. Raising his filled glass, he politely touched it to the old chief's. "To your health, sir."

"Nay, lad, do na waste a good toast on the burned-out likes o' me," Chatto responded, raising his own glass. "To space, and the brave men and women who dare to challenge it! And may yer own good fortune continue wher'er the cosmic tides carry ye."

"So long as they carry ye far from here," a deep voice at Ranger's right muttered. Ranger turned his head to the previously empty chair and saw that it was occupied by a huge Highlander whom he recognized as one of those who had been with Ravenslayer in his room.

The body servant quietly identified him to Ranger as a member of the MacCarthy tribe, which had been named after one of the man's ancient Earth ancestors believed to have been a famous warrior: Charlie Mac-Carthy. Ranger guessed that the Raven had ordered the big brute to try to provoke a fight with him, and he resolved to ignore anything he might say.

Fortunately Charlie had a Highlander's overpowering interest in good food and he rapidly lost interest in Ranger as the serving wenches trooped into the hall bearing large platters heaped with steaming beefsteaks, mutton chops, roast port, and other plain but solid filling fare that pleased the unsophisticated tastes of fighting men. Eve, her dusky cheeks flushed from the kitchen heat, supervised the wenches and saw to it that every dinner guest's plate was overflowing with thick, rich meats and vegetables before taking her own seat at the women's section of the table. For, although the Highland Apaches strictly believed in keeping women in their place, the female members of the clan had—as women everywhere somehow manage to do—subtly made their place equal to menfolks'.

Before the feasting could begin, Old Angus stood up and proposed a toast to welcome his grandson to the company of men. Ranger was pointedly ignored, but he supposed that was only fair enough, since he had contributed little except a few chromosomes toward making Dawnboy's achievements possible. Then the Grand Laird, with a true Scot's perverse humor, kept his guests salivating over their dinners while the clan's leading troubadour played and sang a new hunting ballad that he had composed especially in Dawnboy's honor. And after that there were more toasts, until Ranger's head was spinning from the fiery Scotch-mescal. He was glad to see that Dawnboy drank only light wine; the boy's nervous laughter and shining eyes indicated he was becoming intoxicated enough on the flattering attention he was receiving. But finally the old laird took pity on his guests and, by sinking his fork into a thick steak, gave the signal for them to fall on their food like ravenous wolves.

"Look at the women's section," Chatto said softly to Ranger as he gnawed a mutton chop with his few remaining teeth, "and tell me if ye see a pretty red-haired lass of about twenty-five, with a rather obvious disfigurement."

Ranger obligingly searched among the chattering women and girls and soon singled out the one in question. It wasn't difficult—the tip of her nose had been cut off. It was pathetic the way she tried to hide the scar by shyly turning her face away from the company or holding a hand over it.

"Did her husband catch her with another man?" Ranger asked, knowing that type of mutilation was the common Apache punishment for unfaithful wives.

"Aye. She's Sage-hen, Ravenslayer's third wife. But *he* didn't do it to her. She was married to a Duncan-

Chiricahua brave when the Raven took a fancy to her. The husband found out about their affair and took appropriate action, thinking that she was just another easy conquest for the Raven, who would soon leave her alone. But Ravenslayer happened to be deeply in love with this particular lassie, so he killed the brave and married her. He still suffers a deep sense of guilt for her mark of shame. It's the only weak point in his character. Ye may want to remember that, for whatever 'tis worth."

Ranger thanked him and tucked the information away in his memory, although at the moment he couldn't imagine any possible use he might make of it. As the meal progressed, Chatto continued to ply him with questions about the far-flung intelligent races he had visited. Ranger was impressed by the old chief's knowledge, and he even began to relax and enjoy the feeling of warm friendliness that the liquor and good food spread around the table. These men never knew when they might find themselves locked in mortal combat with each other, so they had learned to take their pleasures where they found them.

As bellies filled and spirits rose in boisterous laughter, a troop of wandering entertainers moved into the open space between the table's curving flanks. For a while the warriors good-naturedly applauded the musicians, dancers, acrobats, and jugglers as they worked hard to earn the handsome fee Old Angus was paying them. But such tame stuff could not hold the attention of rugged men of action for long. When they began to jeer and whistle and stamp their feet restlessly, the laird understandingly gave a signal to his major domo. The performers were herded out, then a blaring fanfare from a doorway at the opposite end of the hall announced the entrance of the clan's own music-makers.

First came the bagpipers of the Black Watch tribe, their instruments squealing full-blast and their booted heels stomping to a lusty battle march. The men at the table roared appreciation at the sight of the flowing dark tartans, tall bearskin busbies, and stern-eyed concentration. After them came a fife-and-drum company, and several husky men struggling under the weight of great war tom-toms. They paraded up and down before the dinner guests; then the pipemaster halted at the head of the table and saluted the Grand Laird.

Angus solemnly unsheathed his broadsword and took another from one of his gentlemen-at-arms. Then he walked out into the cleared space and laid the two crossed blades on the floor.

"Show us ye can still shake the old stumps, Laird!" a voice called from the ranks, and others shouted encouragement.

"Nay, this be the lad's night," Angus replied, beckoning to Dawnboy. "Come on out here, ye frisky young puppy, and we'll see if ye can dance like a mon as well as ye hunt grizzlies like one!"

A loud cheer went up as Dawnboy, blushing self-consciously, was pulled from his chair and pushed out onto the floor by laughing comrades. He took his place at the crossed swords, and the pipemaster raised his baton. At the first wheeze of the pipes, the tom-toms began to throb. The boy quickly caught the beat, leaping and twirling to alight on his toes between the swords, then twirling again with a force that whipped his kilt between his legs. The rhythm picked up and so did his speed, until his feet were a flying blur and his lean body was like a twisting candle with his flushed face its flickering flame.

Ranger looked on with a mixture of fatherly pride, fear that the boy might cut off a few toes, and mounting excitement at the gracefully brutal ritual. He had seen ceremonial war preparations and victory celebrations among dozens of races and nonhuman species, but none had ever been quite as exhilarating as the martial spirit that he felt now vibrating around him. Even the women were caught up in the savagely stirring rhythms as they leaned forward with tapping feet and enviously followed Dawnboy's movements. But they would have to restrain their fun-loving hearts tonight, for the sword dance is a war dance and strictly for men only. No self-respecting clanswoman would dare to degrade the dance by taking part, just as none would dream of disgracing herself by donning a kilt—which everyone knows is masculine garb and totally unsuited to the feminine figure.

"Would ye like another steak, sir?" a small voice asked in Ranger's right ear. He glanced down at his plate and was surprised to discover he had cleaned up all but a few scraps of his meal. Turning to accept another portion, he found himself looking into Kathleen's twinkling eyes as she held a heavy platter of meat.

"Begone wi' ye, lassie!" Chatto's manservant scolded her. "I be seeing to these gentlemen's wants."

"Watch how ye speak to yer betters, ye baseborn son of a stablehand!" the girl shot back. "Or I'll have the hide flayed from yer worthless carcass, as I often saw my father do to his enemies in the Mongol-Sioux camp."

"I doubt that ye have any clear memories of that early period in yer life," Chatto smiled. "However, ye may stay and help Rob Roy serve us, since ve're so anxious to be near yer void-roving uncle that ye begged yer mother to let ye be among the serving wenches tonight."

Kathleen stared at him in astonishment. "How did ye know . . . ?"

"Have ye na heard that the blind are possessed o' second sight?" the old man said mysteriously. "Now do na make a nuisance o' yerself, or I'll reveal all yer secrets to the world."

"Aye, sir," the child said in a cowed whisper, then turned her worshipful gaze back to her uncle.

Ranger wiped away his smile with a mouthful of beefsteak and looked back at the dance just in time to see Dawnboy finish his performance and stumble panting and sweaty to his chair, amid thunderous applause.

The pipers and drummers struck up another tune, and several men rushed out onto the floor to fling themselves into warlike dance steps. The music's blood-stirring inspiration touched the men at the table, too; but since fighting at the laird's board was frowned upon, they had to content themselves with loud arguments, drinking bouts, arm wrestling, knuckle-tug, and other tests of strength.

Ranger and Chatto continued their conversation, drifting from one topic to another as the mood struck them. Ranger was making what he thought was a significant comparison between ancient and modern social customs, when a heavy hand fell roughly on his right shoulder.

"What's that?" a slurred voice demanded. "Ye say we are na true to the Highland Apache way o' life?"

A sudden silence spread around them as Ranger turned and peered into the angry, drink-flushed face of Charlie MacCarthy. "I merely pointed out how any human tradition can gradually change over the centuries until it becomes the opposite of what it was originally," Ranger said calmly. "The example I gave was how the term 'clan,' among the primitive Scots and the Indians of Old Earth, referred to a social unit consisting of a number of families who traced their descent from a common ancestor. And a 'tribe' was composed of several clans. But in your culture it's just the other way around—with the tribes being subgroups of the clan."

"Ye're a filthy liar!" Charlie snarled viciously. "Our life-style is that o' the Old Earth Apaches and Highlanders, as laid down for us by Irving-the-Founder, and we've never strayed an inch from it. There can be but one answer to such a foul insult to the clan's honor—this!"

Ranger's head snapped back, and he momentarily blacked out, as the hulking giant's ham-sized hand smashed across his face. When his vision cleared, Ranger saw that Dawnboy had leaped to his feet in alarm.

Old Angus was watching the scene intently, as was nearly everyone else in the hall. The music died away to leave them all frozen in a thick silence.

"If I had offended the clan, I would gladly apologize," Ranger told the clansman with all the self-restraint he could muster. "But obviously you're just trying to use any excuse you can find to pick a fight with me. I beg you not to push me any further, as this is a special occasion for my son and I would not want it to be spoiled by violence."

"Ye beg me, do ye?" Charlie threw back his head and roared with scornful laughter. "Hear that, lads? This yellow dog of space *begs*, instead of taking what he wants, like a real mon would. All right, dog, if ye want to beg, then get down on all fours and do it proper."

"Ye leave my uncle be, pig!" Kathleen cried, snatching up a knife from the table and flinging herself at Charlie. "I'll cut yer stinking heart out!"

Ranger caught the girl and pushed her into the safety of old Chatto's arms, as Charlie laughed even louder. "Now he's hiding behind the skirts o' a wee lassie! Do they na ken how to fight where ye come from, dog?"

Ranger rose to his feet and dropped his weapon belt in his chair. He saw Ravenslayer watching them impassively and thought briefly of appealing directly to him to settle this. But that would not accomplish anything. "Very well," he said to Charlie. "Since I am the challenged party, I have the right to choose the weapons. Let it be bare-handed combat, with no quarter."

"That suits me," Charlie grinned, rising and flexing his huge biceps. "If ye've a mind to commit suicide, I'm just the lad to satisfy your wish."

"Now that'll be enough o' that," Grand Laird Angus said in his stern voice of authority. "I'll permit no bloodshed at my table."

"Let the two o' them have it out, Angus," Chatto spoke up. "This party needs a bit o' entertainment to liven it up."

Several of the gentlemen-at-arms had started forward to separate the two combatants, but Angus was so surprised to hear his old friend disagree with him that he called them back and gave his consent to the contest. Ranger and Charlie walked out onto the floor as the pipers cleared a space for them where the crossed swords had lain. They halted and faced each other, as a tight-pitched voice cried out, "Don't do it, Father! He'll kill ye!"

Ranger chanced a quick glance at the white-faced Dawnboy, thinking that hearing his son call him that almost made this foolishness worthwhile.

"Now, lassie, tell me exactly what happens out there," Chatto whispered to Kathleen. "Describe every move yer uncle makes, and do na leave out a single detail."

"Aye, sir," the girl said. But a few moments later she gasped, "Oh, my word! I canna believe it!"

"What happened?" Chatto demanded impatiently. "Tell me, ye silly little snip!"

"But nothing happened," Kathleen protested. "Nothing I could see too clearly. One instant Uncle Ranger was just standing there; an' the next Charlie is down on his back groaning and squirming and spitting blood. He only seemed to touch the big lout with his open hand—in the throat, the pit o' the stomach, and some other places I could na see, because he moved so fast. I guess 'tis all over now. Charlie can't get up, and Uncle Ranger's turned his back on him."

"I suspected as much," Chatto chuckled, "when I shook yer uncle's hand and felt the hard calluses on his fingertips. That's the mark o' a Logar't finger-duelist— a Perfect of the Third or Fourth Degree, probably. Aagh, if only I'd thought to place a good-sized bet on him, with these uneducated braves who think muscles are everything!"

The spectators recovered from their shock and started to chatter excitedly as Ranger walked to the head of the table. He heard the terms "witchcraft" and "black magic" whispered in frightened tones as he halted before Dawnboy. For a long moment the youth stared uncertainly at his father; then a slow smile lifted the corners of Ranger's mouth, and Dawnboy answered it with a broad grin.

Old Angus fully understood the exchange between father and son, and he glowered his displeasure even while he was admiring Ranger's skillful self-defense.

Ranger turned to face him and the still expressionless Ravenslayer. He picked up Dawnboy's half-empty glass and said loudly, "Laird Angus, I thank you for the hospitality you've shown me, and for the excellent care you've given to the boy for whom we both have such high hopes. Now I ask everyone here to join me in a toast—to my son. May he always know what he wants out of life, and may he never lack the courage to go after it."

"I'll drink to that!" Chatto cried, raising his glass. "And the rest of ye'd best do likewise, if ye do na want to get what Charlie got."

Every man and woman present raised his or her glass. Even Ravenslayer, despite the hate-filled look he gave Ranger.

5

RANGER WALKED OUT into the castle garden and gratefully inhaled the cool night air. Behind him the great hall still echoed with sounds of wild revelry, but he had felt he had to get away for a while to clear his head of the strong drink. He never consumed alcohol in space, and this sudden overindulgence was too much for him. Besides, he had noticed Dawnboy slipping out through the garden entrance a short time before, and he was anxious for an opportunity to speak privately with him.

He looked around curiously at the maze of walkways through the array of strange flowering plants. The garden was dimly illuminated by the softly twinkling sparkleberries on domesticated lightning bushes, which had been grafted and crossbred for several generations to make them discharge all of their electricity in the form of light. No one was in sight, but an occasional giggle or happy sigh told him that some of the more serious of the flirting couples from the party had reached the garden ahead of him. He picked his way carefully through

the concealing greenery, to avoid embarassing anybody
—which he very nearly did when he suddenly came
upon an embracing couple in a secluded corner of the
garden. Seeing that his arrival was unnoticed, Ranger
started to back away discreetly, when the male figure
roughly broke off the kiss and pushed the female away.
He halted just out of sight of them as he heard Dawnboy's voice grate harshly: "Nay, woman. Do na tempt
me! Ye ken 'tis wrong for a brave to take a mate before
he has honorably won the right to call himself a mon."

" 'Tis not wrong, young lord," Tessie's voice came
soft and pleading. "You've proved your manhood by
killing the dangerous bear single-handedly. That enti-
tles you to choose your adult name and have a woman
and enjoy all the other privileges of a warrior."

"Nay," Dawnboy insisted. "Hunting is but sport.
Killing a game animal is na the equal o' slaying an enemy warrior. Only when I have demonstrated my valor
in battle will I have truly come of age, according to
clan law."

"But no one except you and I need ever know about
it," Tessie wheedled, swaying toward Dawnboy with
enticing movements. "It isn't as if I'd expect you to
marry me, or even make me your concubine. I just
want to have the honor and pleasure of being the first
woman to please the brave who is surely destined to
become a great leader of the clan."

The youth was obviously moved by her flattery and
sensuality. His voice quivered with passion; but his
body remained sternly unyielding as he again pushed
the girl away. "Nay. I canna do as ye ask. Now be off
wi' ye, afore I lose me patience and give ye the beating
an insolent slave deserves!"

"All right, be a stiff-necked prude, for all I care!"
Tessie snapped as she whirled and flounced away.
"You'll regret it later, when I've found myself a man
who isn't afraid to act like a man!"

Ranger had to admire Tessie's determined ambition
to raise her status in the clan. And, having been himself subjected to her considerable charms, he also ad-
mired his son's self-control. Not that he would have ob-

jected on moral grounds if Dawnboy had surrendered
to an entirely natural and understandable demand of
the flesh. But he still didn't think it was good for such a
young sensitive lad to get involved with an older and
obviously far more experienced female. A woman like
that could make or break a good man, but neither al-
ternative seemed to promise the sort of future that
Ranger deemed best for Dawnboy.

Deciding to give the youth a little time alone to
recover from Tessie's overstimulation, Ranger remained
in the shadows while Dawnboy gazed moodily up at
the star-flecked sky. The hovering spaceship glowed
faintly in the light of Jock, Usen, and Tso-ay, the
planet's three moons. According to ancient legend, Jock
and Usen, the two larger satellites, were the spirits of a
male and a female of a race presumed to have inhabited Apache Highlands long before humans arrived.
Tso-ay was their son, a lively, inquisitive child who was
always running off to explore and poke about in strange
places. One day he failed to return home at supper
time, and his parents searched and finally found him,
dead from the venom of a spitcat. The heartbroken
mother and father died of grief; and the gods, taking
pity on the family, placed their love-illuminated souls
in the night sky. But even there the unruly child still
tries to run away from his parents, rising and setting a
good ten minutes ahead of them.

"Oh, hello, Son," Ranger said, rustling some shrubbery to announce his presence. "I didn't know anyone
was back here. I just stepped out for a little fresh air."

"Me, too," Dawnboy said. "The party was getting
too hectic for me."

"I know what you mean. I hope I don't have too
great a hangover tomorrow morning."

"Ye won't feel nearly as bad as Charlie MacCarthy
will, I'll wager," Dawnboy grinned. "That was a grand
thrashing ye gave him. Could ye teach me to fight like
that?"

"Sure, if we had enough time together."

The boy caught the drift of his thinking and looked
back at the sky. " 'Tis a big universe out there, isn't it,

47

Father?" The word was still strange and uneasy on his tongue.

"Too big for mere words to describe," Ranger replied. "Uncounted billions of stars in a limitless ocean of space, and of them at least a million in this galaxy alone are thought to have Earth-type planets. But only some thirty-five thousand of those are known to be populated by human or other intelligent life-forms—in all stages of development from pre–Stone Age to a few civilizations so far advanced that even the scientists on Newtonia appear to be helpless primitives to them. You'll find all kinds of beings out there—from the giant Brainsponges of the Denebola System to the semi-gaseous Chemo-Gypsies who wander through the cosmos without ships and draw nutriment directly from solar radiation. And as for their systems of society and government—my God, what haven't they thought of? Patriarchies, matriarchies, democracies, kingdoms, dictatorships, religious theocracies, worlds ruled by poets or business corporations; others with no visible ruler at all, totalitarian empires and confederated republics embracing several different star systems—you name it, and chances are such a system is or was in existence somewhere among the races of the universe."

"And that does na include the uninhabited worlds that haven't been discovered yet," Dawnboy said with a dreamy faraway look in his eyes. "Those are the planets ye most want to find, aren't they? So that ye can sell them at great profit to land-hungry colonists from over-populated worlds."

"Yes, that's the grand prize that every space trader and explorer dreams of making his fortune on. But few of us ever actually do it, because such finds are extremely rare and searching for them is a risky, expensive gamble. As a matter of fact, I plan to embark on just such a voyage of discovery when I leave here and head for an unexplored sector of space that I have good reason to suspect might contain one or more planets fit for human habitation that aren't as yet claimed by other intelligent species."

Dawnboy looked at him sharply. "Ye're telling me that to tempt me to go wi' ye, aren't ye?"

Ranger laughed, and shrugged helplessly. "Guilty as charged, your honor."

Dawnboy smiled with him. "'Tis na crime, and I confess I'm sorely tempted to go wi' ye. But I'm equally inclined to stay here and become a warchief o' the clan. Aagh, if only the two prospects were na so strongly appealing! I can well see how a mon could devote his whole life to space, as ye've done."

"Just having you understand me that well makes this trip worthwhile," Ranger said. "You know, I wasn't much older than you are now when I joined the Space Rangers and became a part of the exclusive company of men and women who roam the void."

"The Space Rangers?" Dawnboy spoke the words distastefully. "But they're *mercenaries*! I've heard that no honorable mon trusts them."

"Yes, most patriots and noncombatants have contempt for those who fight only for pay, but that doesn't prevent them from hiring the Rangers when they need help defeating their enemies," Ranger said drily. "But at that time, on my homeworld of Old New America, civilized progress was in a regressive slump and the Rangers were my only hope of getting into space. One of their recruiting ships stopped over on the way to the civil war between the planets of Castor and Pollux, and so I lied about my age and enlisted under an assumed name. I called myself Farstar, because that was my ambition: to travel to the farthest star and learn all the secrets of the universe. It didn't take me long to find out that interplanetary war isn't the best way to achieve that goal. But at least that got me into space and enabled me to learn the skills to become a starship captain. When my four-year enlistment was up, I had the knowledge and money to buy my own ship and go into business for myself, a business which eventually brought me to Apache Highlands and your mother. So even if you don't like the Rangers, you can thank them for playing some small part in making your existence possible."

"Well, then I guess they canna be all bad," Dawnboy relented. "What was your original name?"

"Maybe I'll tell you sometime, when I think you need a good laugh."

"That bad?"

"Worse. That's why I let your mother follow the Apache custom of giving you a childhood name and allowing you to take one of your own choice when you come of age. Not that names are terribly important, but a man shouldn't be made to feel a complete fool when someone addresses him."

"Farstar has a nice ring to it," Dawnboy mused. "Perhaps I'll take it for meself, when I've earned my full manhood."

"I'd be very proud to have you accept even that much of me," Ranger said feelingly. "But I think it's more suitable for a spaceman than a warchief."

"Aye, we keep coming back to that, don't we?" Dawnboy peered thoughtfully up at the ship again. "There's no denying I have a strong lust for the stars, while I'm standing here safe on my own home ground. But how would I react out *there*? Do I really have it in me to become a good spaceman? Or would I just be a disappointment to ye and make a misery of my life?"

"You'll never know for sure if you don't try it. But at least I can give you a sample of what space travel is like, by taking you up to visit the ship."

"Ye mean right now?"

"Why not? They won't miss us at the party."

Dawnboy hesitated for a moment, then shrugged. "All right, let's go."

"Good. I didn't bring along an extra antigrav pack for you, but that's no problem." Ranger turned his head away and said: "Send down an elevator for us, Lulu." Then he explained to Dawnboy, "I can communicate with the ship's biocomputer and autopilot through a tiny transmitter planted under the skin at my larynx. And I have a receiver in my left ear. The range is limited, but it's more convenient than carrying a radio unit around. I think you'll enjoy meeting Lulu; she takes good care of the *Gayheart* when I'm not aboard."

50

"The *Gayheart*?" Dawnboy raised his eyebrows.

"What else would I have named my ship?" Ranger asked simply.

"I see what ye mean," Dawnboy said solemnly. "I've often wished I could remember Mother more clearly. What was she like? Aunt Eve says she was even more beautiful than—"

"She was a great deal like your aunt in many ways, but a unique individual in her own right," Ranger broke in. "I'm sorry, but I'm not the one to give you an objective description of her."

"I know, but I wish I'd gotten to know her better."

"So do I. I've alway felt guilty for not insisting that she go along with you when we sent you here. But we were so happy together that we couldn't bear to be separated. Sometimes parents don't realize how selfish they are with their children, until it's too late."

"That's all right, Father. I understand."

"No, you don't," Ranger told him. "That is something you can't possibly understand fully until you experience it yourself—until you find that one special woman whom you must have, even if you have to fight all the demons of space to make her yours. But I'm glad that you forgive me. Now here comes our transportation."

An object of shiny plasti-steel that was box-shaped and about the size of a stagecoach came drifting down out of the sky. Finding no cleared space in the garden big enough to land in, it hovered ten feet above their heads and extended a ladder to Ranger. "It's powered by an antigrav unit and has a two-ton lifting capacity," Ranger told Dawnboy. "Not much for speed or maneuverability, but it's handy for picking up cargo in remote areas and for other planetary chores."

"It doesna look safe to me," Dawnboy said uneasily. "But if ye say so, I'm game to try it."

"Wait! I want to go, too!" a shrill voice cried, as a figure burst through the shrubbery to join them.

Ranger spun about in a defensive posture, then relaxed. "Kathleen! What are you doing here?"

"Spying on us, weren't ye?" Dawnboy growled,

roughly grabbing the girl's arms. "I'll give ye the hiding o' yer life, ye little sneak!"

"If ye do, I'll scream bloody murder and bring everybody running," Kathleen threatened. "Then Grandsire won't let ye go up to the ship."

"She has a good point," Ranger said, freeing her from her cousin's grasp. "No one is going to hurt you, dear. But you'd better go back to the party. Your mother will be worried about you."

"She knows I can take care o' meself," Kathleen said confidently. "Please, Uncle Ranger, take me up wi' ye. I might never ever have another chance to see the inside of a starship."

"Oh, do na be such a pest!" Dawnboy snapped. "I vow I'll never ken what bothersome females like ye are good for."

"I think that's something you'll learn in due time," Ranger smiled. He peered thoughtfully into Kathleen's pleading eyes, then playfully rumpled her hair. "Oh, I guess it won't do any harm for you to come with us, since we won't be gone very long."

Kathleen clapped her hands excitedly, then hurried up the ladder at Ranger's instruction. The two men followed her through the car's open hatch, which slid smoothly shut behind them. The youngsters peered out the portholes and gasped as they were lifted rapidly away from the castle's dwindling lights. The dark countryside spread out below them, lighted here and there by village bonfires. But before they had much time to study the view, their car docked gently with the ship and the hatch opened into an air lock.

"Hello, children. Welcome to the *Gayheart*," a deep, motherly female voice said as Ranger ushered them through the air lock and into a narrow corridor.

The voice seemed to vibrate from the bulkheads, causing Kathleen to utter a frightened little squeak and grip Ranger's hand. Even Dawnboy, playing the nonchalant brave, couldn't resist glancing around nervously.

"That's just Lulu," Ranger assured them, pointing to a loudspeaker in the bulkhead, with a photoelectric cell above it. "There's one of her eyes. Well, what do you think of my boy, Lulu? Chip off the old block, huh?"

"Luckily he seems to have gotten his good looks from his mother," Lulu replied. "And if he didn't inherit your intelligence, I just might be able to make a spacehand out of him."

"You sure know how to give a man a good buildup in front of his son," Ranger grumbled. "The next time you get overhauled, I think I'll have a flattery circuit installed."

"Is that yer computer?" Dawnboy whispered. "She sounds almost . . ."

"Almost human?" Lulu's voice supplied, with a trace of amusement. "That's because I was a human being once. Now all that's left of me is my poor old brain, floating in a tank of cerebrospinal fluid and wired to the computer memory banks and other mechanical parts of the ship."

"A disembodied human brain?" Dawnboy looked at Ranger in horror. "Father, ye didna . . . ?"

"For cosmos' sake, Lulu, explain it to him," Ranger cried. "Don't make me out to be a monster to my own kid."

"No, your father didn't crack my skull and pick out my gray matter like the goody from a nutshell," Lulu said. "You see, I was a native of New Tokyo, in the Altair System, where medical science has been able to extend the human life span to nearly two centuries. But when I was a hundred and twenty-six I contracted Hirosaki's Disease, which results in rapid physical deterioration. I was sent to Newtonia for treatment, but even the scientists there couldn't prevent my body from becoming a withered, useless hulk. With only the prospect of a vegetable-like existence to look forward to, I chose instead to volunteer for a new experiment in biocybernetics. So now I have this brand new body—the ship that you're standing in. It may not be as attractive as my first one, but it's far more practical for my work."

"It . . . it must've been a sore sad thing for ye to lose yer body and all physical contact with life," Kathleen said sympathetically.

"Don't waste your pity on me, child," Lulu responded serenely. "I was nearing the end of a long, full life, anyway. My husband was dead, my children and grandchildren had grown up and no longer needed me, and I probably would not have done anything for the next sixty-odd years except twiddle my thumbs in enforced retirement anyway. Now I have a far more stimulating and fulfilling existence of star-voyaging and performing useful work for humanity."

"Aye, that's the kind o' life I want!" the girl exclaimed.

"And I hope you get it," Lulu said. "But not in the way I did."

"Come on, I'll give you both a quick tour of the ship," Ranger said, leading his charges down the corridor. They rounded a bend and he pointed to a stairway leading to a lower level, from which they heard a low-pitched, vibrationless hum. "The engine room is down there. The machinery is pretty extensive and far too complicated to explain, so we'll skip it for now. Up ahead is the lab, where he computer's memory banks do most of the work of analyzing data gathered by luxium laser probes of stars, planets, and other celestial bodies we encounter."

"What do you mean, giving the memory banks all the credit for that?" Lulu protested. "They couldn't do anything without my natural intelligence to direct them."

"Don't give me any back talk, or I'll pull you out of your tank and spank your cerebellum," Ranger threatened.

Their good-natured bickering continued as Ranger guided the youngsters through the communications center, the gym and recreation compartments, the galley and messroom, the sewage-recycling system, and the "farm"—where hydroponics-grown plants provided food, decoration, and fresh oxygen. From there they went into the sick bay, where Dawnboy stared curiously at a long, weaponlike object that was encircled by electronic coils and suspended over the examining table.

"That's a gadget that I was afraid I might have to use on you," Ranger said, "when I saw you tussling with that grizzly. It's called a protoplasm regenerator, and it can heal flesh wounds and simple fractures in a few hours, without even leaving a scar."

"That would be of no use to the clan," Dawnboy scoffed, "because a warrior who lacked the scars to prove his battlefield valor would only be a laughing-stock."

They passed on to the library, where Kathleen was enchanted by the flickering images of the entertainment tapes. The men left her absorbed in a story about a little girl and her pet silk tree on Hut-no's Revenge, and moved on to Ranger's tidy, compact cabin. From there they stepped through a connecting doorway into the ship's bridge.

Dawnboy gasped in amazement as he looked through the transparent forward bulkhead at the castle, which appeared to lie only a few dozen yards below them.

"The entire bulkhead is the lens of an electron telescope," Ranger explained. "It's capable of bringing in scenes from up to five light-years away, if there's no radiation or atmospheric interference."

"Makes a handy tool for peeping toms," Lulu added.

" 'Tis even more wonderful than I'd ever dreamed," Dawnboy sighed. He sank into the pilot's chair and ran his gaze over the rows of instruments on the control panel. "To think that just ye and Lulu can handle the whole ship. 'Tis a miracle!"

"The miracle of automation," his father said. "Some captains prefer to carry a full crew, anyway, just in case. But I've always worked better alone, or with just my family."

"Oh, Ranger," Lulu said, "I forgot to tell you that we received a sub-ether message from Capitalia. The cipher-lobe has just finished unscrambling it."

"Okay, pipe it into my earphone. Excuse me a minute, Son." Ranger turned away and stood in silence for a few moments, then muttered angrily under his breath.

"Bad news?" Dawnboy asked.

"I'm not sure. You remember I said I was going

planet hunting when I left here? Well, it appears that another explorer ship is headed for that same sector. My principal backer wants to talk to me about it in person, so I'll have to leave here much sooner than I'd planned."

"How much sooner?"

"Within twenty-four hours. Come on; I'd better get you and Kathleen back to the castle while I think this over."

6

ON THE TRIP down, the two young people chattered excitedly about the marvels they had encountered aboard the *Gayheart*. Ranger, distracted by the news he had just received, absent-mindedly answered their queries with brief comments. His thoughts were in a turmoil: he was pulled in opposite directions by two equally strong desires.

The planet-hunting expedition was something he had planned for and dreamed about for years, and he was in agony to think of someone else snatching the prize out from under his laser probe at the last moment. On the other hand, he hated to leave Apache Highlands just as he and Dawnboy were starting to get reacquainted. How could he expect the boy to reach a decision that would affect his whole future, on such short notice? He thought of all the bright, hopeful plans he and Gay had made for their son as he grimly recalled his promise to Eve that he would not try to influence Dawnboy's decision. Of course he would have to accept the bitter disappointment if Dawnboy chose not to go with him, but he did not think he would be a very good loser about it.

Ranger looked out a porthole as the car settled down in the castle courtyard, and braced himself at the sight of Eve, Old Angus, Chatto, and several others awaiting their landing. As soon as the hatch opened and the three stepped out, Eve rushed forward to grab her daughter in a protective hug.

"Where have ye been, ye empty-headed little goose?" Eve demanded furiously. "Have ye na enough consideration to tell me where ye're going? Instead of leaving me to search high and low for ye, worried half out of me mind that some drunken brave had dragged ye off to take advantage o' ye."

"Oh, do na be foolish, Mum," Kathleen laughed. "Uncle Ranger was just showing us his ship. Ye should see what a grand and wondrous thing it is!"

"So ye disobeyed my orders to stay away from this tribeless space drifter?" Eve accused. Then, when the girl tried to protest, she silenced her with a light but meaningful slap on the cheek. "I'm in no mood for more o' yer cheeky answers, lass. Get up to yer room, and I'll deal wi' ye later for this."

Kathleen stared at her mother in shocked humiliation, her bright eyes dimming with tears. Then she turned and ran sobbing into the castle.

" 'Twas na her fault, Aunt Eve. She only wanted to tag along because I went up to the ship," Dawnboy said pleadingly, for although he was often aggravated to the point of murder by Kathleen's merciless teasing, it always hurt him deeply to see his cousin punished.

"Don't be too hard on her, Eve," Ranger put in. "It's only natural for kids to be curious about new things."

Eve turned the full force of her anger on him. "I might have known ye aren't to be trusted, ye promise-breaking paleface! Not only do ye try to sneak behind my back and win Dawnboy over, ye even try to turn me own child against me to get what ye want from us!"

"That will be enough, Daughter," Old Angus said firmly. He was obviously upset by her use of the vulgar and insulting word "paleface"—something even a warrior in the heat of battle would hesitate to call his worst enemy. "The young ones have been returned safely, so there be no reason to break the laws o' hospitality." He turned to Ranger. "But hereafter, sir, it would be advisable for ye to obtain the proper permission before taking any o' our people aboard yer vessel."

Ranger bowed his head slightly. "I accept your rebuke as being deserved, Laird. I apologize for any unnecessary worry and inconvenience that my thoughtless actions may have caused, and I promise to be more considerate of clan protocol in the future."

The Grand Laird accepted his apology with a curt nod and turned away. Chief Chatto MacNair, holding his body servant's arm for guidance, cried out: "So all's well that ends well! Now let's get on wi' the party. The night's yet young, and there still be dancing to be done and bottles to be emptied!"

That broke what was left of the tension, and the group made a laughing rush back to the hall. Eve, with a final angry glare at Ranger, strode stiff-backed after them. Dawnboy started to follow, but hesitated when his father didn't go along.

"I still have some things to think out," Ranger said. "But you go ahead and enjoy the rest of your celebration. We'll talk some more in the morning."

"All right. Good night, Father, and thanks for showing me yer ship."

Alone in the courtyard, Ranger thrust his hands into his pockets and paced about aimlessly, deep in thought. When a half-hour of pacing had got him nowhere, he decided he might as well go to bed and tackle the problem with a fresh mind in the morning. He had a little trouble finding his way back through the cavernous corridors to his room, but when he finally reached it he noticed a faint sliver of light under the door. Warily he shoved open the door and peered inside at the hulking form of Charlie MacCarthy slumped in a chair with a nearly empty bottle on his lap.

Charlie's head jerked up at the sound of the door, which creaked despite Ranger's care, and he yawned as the spaceman moved cautiously into the room, looking around to make sure no one else was there. "Leash yer war dogs, m'lord," he grated with vocal cords that still ached from the finger-jabbing Ranger had given them. "I come alone and in peace."

"I gladly welcome you in peace," Ranger said, closing the door. "But with a touch of skepticism, recalling our last encounter."

"Fear not. I be mon enough to own that I was bested in a fair fight by a superior warrior. Nor am I so lowborn as to deprecate the fact that ye spared my life, when I fully intended to kill ye if I had won. 'Tis to repay that debt that I be here now."

"How do you propose to do that?" Ranger asked interestedly.

"By warning ye that the Raven is planning a murder before the morrow dawns," Charlie answered. When Ranger only smiled, he went on: "Nor be *ye* the victim. Ye already know that yer na safe so long as ye and Ravenslayer are alive on the same planet. 'Tis yer son he plots to do away with."

That shook Ranger out of his complacency. "Dawnboy? Why would Ravenslayer want to kill him?"

"To slay two birds wi' one stone. First, he kens full well that the lad's death would cause ye more grief than yer own. Second, he has his heart set on becoming Grand Laird when Angus dies. Until today he felt confident the tribal elders would elect him. But Dawnboy is in a more direct line o' succession, and if the lad goes on to fulfill his promise o' becoming a great warchief . . ."

"I see what you mean. Do you know the details of the plot?"

"Nay, only that he canna act so long as the lad remains at the party, which likely will go on till the wee hours." Charlie stood up and moved to the door. "Ye have that long to do what ye can wi' this information, for 'tis all I can give ye. I canna stand wi' ye agin me own tribesmen, and 'tis worth me life if the Raven even learns I've been here. So do na count on me as a witness if ye decide to bring charges agin him."

"You've already done plenty for us, and I thank you for it," Ranger said, seeing him out. When he was alone, he flopped into a chair, rubbing both eyes with his fists in anguish, and said to Lulu, "Talk about problems coming in bunches! What am I going to do now?"

"Since you asked me, I say grab the boy and run like hell," his biocomputer suggested matter-of-factly from her vantage point above the turmoil.

"No, that wouldn't be practical. If Dawnboy goes into space, it must be by his own free choice. If I told him about Ravenslayer's plot, with no proof, he might think I was lying to trick him into going with me."

"You could go to Laird Angus to get special protection for Dawnboy."

"Same problem—no evidence to support my story. Oh, that might save Dawnboy's life this time, but what if he decided not to go with me? Ravenslayer will have plenty of opportunities to kill when I'm no longer around."

"Then your only logical solution is to kill Ravenslayer first," Lulu said. "You have weapons powerful enough to wipe out him and any of his bully boys who are in this with him."

"That option certainly has appeal," Ranger conceded. "But then I'd probably have to go on and annihilate a few entire tribes, to forestall the blood feud that their deaths would surely start. No, the ideal solution would be to find a way to neutralize Ravenslayer. I can't hope to ever win his friendship, or even to reduce his hatred toward me. But if I could just think of some way to put him in my debt, as with Charlie, then his savage pride would not let him dishonor himself by harming someone to whom he was beholden."

"Sounds good," Lulu agreed. "But as you say, it's the *ideal* solution, and ideals are notoriously unattainable."

"Ravenslayer is a tough target to get a fix on, all right, but still there must be something ... Wait a minute!" He sat up straight, scowling thoughtfully. "Hmm, it's a long shot, but just maybe ..."

Ranger was silent for so long that Lulu demanded: "What is it, for cosmos' sake?"

"Yes, I think I'll chance it," Ranger muttered, reaching for the bell cord to summon a servant. "I don't have time to explain, so be patient and keep an elevator car ready near my balcony. I may be bringing a guest up very shortly."

The chambermaid who answered his call was not Tessie, but for a bribe consisting of one of the semi-precious meteor jewels that Ranger carried for such purposes she agreed to fetch the buxom blond slave girl.

When Tessie arrived, she entered the room reluctantly and stood before Ranger looking like a timid wild animal; she was poised to flee at the first sign of danger.

Ranger dismissed the other chambermaid and smiled reassuringly at Tessie. "Don't be frightened," he said. "I'm not angry with you for what happened earlier. In fact, I was rather flattered by your attention. Perhaps, if we had met under different circumstances . . ." He let his voice trail off suggestively and watched her features soften into an expression of pleased satisfaction, as he had expected. Experience had taught him that even a highly desirable woman likes to be told that she *is* desirable.

"You're most kind to forgive me, m'lord," Tessie murmured.

"What's done is done. Now I have another sort of business proposition to offer you. How would you like to earn enough gold to buy your freedom and have enough left for a sizable dowry to attract even a war-chief's marriage proposal?"

Tessie's blue eyes widened with greedy eagerness. "And what would I have to do to earn so fabulous a reward?" she asked breathlessly.

Ranger told her, and watched her eyes grow even wider with fear. "Oh, no, not that," she groaned. "It could cost me my head!"

"Freedom doesn't come without risks," he informed her. "Wouldn't it be worth a gamble with death to be able to hold your head up proudly in front of the clanswomen who have ordered you about and treated you with contempt? Perhaps you could even hire some of them to be *your* servants."

It didn't take much persuasion to convince Tessie. Terrified but determined, she left him and went down to the banquet hall. Ranger strolled out to the garden to wait for her.

Thrity minutes later Tessie walked out into the garden, leading another female figure. As soon as the second woman saw Ranger she turned away in alarm, but a stun-charge from his synapse disrupter ended her retreat. Ranger picked up the now still figure, called down his waiting car, and carried the woman aboard. As Ranger started up to his ship with his unwilling passenger, Tessie was already running to find herself a secure hiding place for the next few hours.

Dawn's first dim light had not quite reached the planet's surface when Ranger again descended to the castle courtyard. Below him a hundred or more torch-flames moved about jerkily like angry fireflies.

As his car touched the ground, an ominously muttering crowd pressed close around it. The hatch slid open and Ranger peered out at the flint-eyed glares of Laird Angus and his gentlemen-at-arms—all of them fully armed and spoiling for a fight. Behind them he glimpsed Chief Chatto, Dawnboy, Eve, and a few other familiar faces, now taut with anxiety.

Ranger had little time to exchange glances with them before Ravenslayer shouldered his way forward, his cruelly handsome face twisted into a mask of murderous fury. His right hand gripped a wicked-looking war club and his left was tangled in Tessie's golden curls; he dragged the girl along roughly in spite of her weeping pleas.

"So, ye decided ye had not previously given me ample reason to kill ye!" the mighty warrior raged, waving his club at Ranger. "Yer traitorous accomplice here has confessed everything, and not e'en the clan's hospitality laws can protect a wife-thief!"

The mob roared in agreement and started to push forward, but Ranger halted them by raising his disrupter threateningly. "Control your temper, Chief Raven-slayer," he said calmly. "I have done you no injury."

"Ye have the gall to say that, after kidnaping my favorite wife and keeping her aboard yer ship all this time?" The Raven laughed bitterly. "What do ye expect me to do—pay ye for the service ye've done her?"

"I'll let you decide that after you've examined the results of my work." Ranger stepped out of the car, leading Sage-hen by the hand.

At the sight of her, the mob's fury disappeared in a gasp of amazement. Ravenslayer's club fell forgotten from his hand and he made a sound that was half-curse and half-sob as he stared incredulously at Sage-hen, now smiling radiantly to show off her pert, upturned, and newly regenerated nose.

7

RANGER GAZED MOODILY down at the sun-drenched countryside as he rode the car back up to the *Gayheart*—this time alone. He spotted two horsemen riding away from the castle toward the western grazing lands and thought they were probably Dawnboy and his grandfather; but Ranger wasn't interested enough to peer closely at them.

When he reached the ship, he went directly to the bridge and dropped into the pilot's seat, his right hand fiddling absently with the now powerless control switches.

"Time's getting short, Boss," Lulu's voice announced. "If we don't get under way for Capitalia soon—"

"I'm aware of the situation," he snapped. "Let me worry about it."

"Yessir, Your Majesty. Please forgive me for speaking out of turn."

"Aw, I'm sorry, Lulu," he growled in a gentler tone. "I shouldn't take out my mad on you, just because you're the handiest target to hit at."

"Oh? Are you anything but your usual sweet-natured, lovable self?" she asked innocently. "I hadn't noticed."

"Sarcasm has never been your best form of expression," Ranger said. "I guess what I feel isn't so much anger as emotional letdown. After all the excitement of the past eighteen hours, I suddenly have nothing to do but wait and worry. And not having gotten any sleep last night doesn't help matters very much."

"Then why did you agree to let Dawnboy spend some time alone with Old Angus? You know he'll just try to talk the boy into staying here."

"You've been eavesdropping again?"

"If you don't want me to hear what's going on, you can always tune me out."

"No, it doesn't make any difference. There wasn't much I could have done to keep Dawnboy away from his grandfather, anyway, without losing what little favor I've gained with the clan so far. The boy has to make up his own mind, and if a few words from Old Angus can turn him against me—well, it's better to find out now than later that he cares so little for me."

"You don't really mean that," Lulu said softly.

"Of course not. I'd give an arm or leg to win him over. It's just that . . . oh, I don't know. Things don't seem so definite in my mind anymore. During all the years I dreamed of having him with me again—working and saving and finagling to get back on my feet and have another ship of my own—it never occurred to me to wonder if what I wanted would be best for both of us. I guess I never stopped thinking of him as just the little child I used to bounce on my knee. So I naturally assumed that he would need and want me. But now I see that he's almost a man, and he seems well adjusted to his life here."

"You think it might be best to leave him here, to

grow up to be a half-savage warrior who will spend most of his time fighting and looting and bragging about it—and will probably meet an early, violent death?"

"Come on, Lulu, you know the life of a space explorer is no less dangerous than that. Besides, it isn't important how a man dies, as long as he was able to choose the way of life that was most fulfilling for his talents. One thing my career of star-hopping has taught me is not to pass moral judgment on any society's values. But as for Dawnboy—is he really well suited for a lifetime in space? And what about me? Am I still capable of being a good father to him? Are the two of us compatible enough to spend months cooped up together in this tub without wanting to tear each other apart? It scares me to think that I could ruin his life, when I only want to help him."

"It seems to me you're doing a lot of unnecessary worrying about problems that may never come up," Lulu said. "After all, you made a good adjustment with his mother; and the differences between your background and hers were far greater. Anyway, that's the impression I got from what you told me about her."

"The two cases aren't quite the same," Ranger smiled. "Or have you forgotten how things are between a man and woman?"

"Unfortunately I still remember that too vividly for my own good," Lulu said wistfully. "But I think the principle is the same in this case. If you and Dawnboy like each other enough, you can work things out together as you go along. And if not—well, why fret about something that can't be helped? You already have enough problems to overtax that underdeveloped organ that we computers laughingly refer to as the human brain. Now why don't you get some sleep? I can keep watch on the situation below, and wake you if anything important comes up."

"That's the best suggestion you've made so far."

Ranger yawned, stood up, and made his way to his cabin. He wearily undressed and started toward his bunk, then paused and touched a button on his desk. A panel in the bulkhead above the desk slid back, revealing an eighteen-by-twenty-four-inch compartment containing the 3-D image of Gay as she had appeared a short time before the accident. He peered into her warm, smiling eyes and sighed deeply. "If only you were here now, my darling. You would know how to handle that wild son of ours, if anyone would."

"I'm sure she'd offer a lot of useful advice," Lulu said. "For one thing, she might ask why you haven't told Dawnboy the truth about her."

"All in good time. He already has enough to digest for now."

"Maybe, but I think—"

"That's the trouble with you—you think too much."

"What else can I do?"

Ranger had long ago learned the futility of trying to get in the last word with either a woman or a machine, let alone with a combination of the two, so he just closed the 3-D compartment and stretched out on his bunk. "Keep a scanner on things, Lulu, and wake me in about three hours, if nothing happens before then."

"Aye, aye, Cap'n. Sweet dreams."

He was halfway there the moment he closed his eyes.

The two riders topped the final ridgeline enclosing Loch o' the Winds. Dawnboy's thirsty pony, scenting water, trotted ahead of Laird Angus's plodding mare.

Dawnboy started to pull in his mount, but the old man called, "Let the poor beast ha' his way, lad. I'll be along to join ye in good time."

Dawnboy gratefully urged his horse to a mild gallop down through the sparse forest of spore palms and slenderstems, which somewhat resembled forty-foot dandelions. When his grandfather had proposed this outing to the lochshore for just the two of them, Dawnboy had looked forward to a soaring flight on Teelget's back. But Angus had begged off, saying that his stiff old joints weren't up to controlling a high-spirited pegasus. So they had ambled along on horseback for nearly two hours, and now the youth was glad to have some speed under him again.

He savored the cool, moist wind as he left the trees behind and rode over grassy meadows to the small but exquisitely beautiful body of fresh water cupped in a bowl of velvet. The pony halted fetlock-deep in the loch and dipped his nose to drink. Dawnboy slipped down and sprawled flat on his belly beside him, pressing his face into the cool liquid. He could have used his half-full canteen or the jug of buttermilk his grandfather had purchased at a roadside farmhouse, but water always tasted better when drunk from its natural source. At least it did to a Highland Apache.

Out in the loch a rainbow trout made a high, splashing leap that spread ripples over the calm surface, and Dawnboy watched minnows dart about the shallows. The so-called "brown-haired fish" for which the sea was named were, with its other native aquatic life-forms, actually varieties of marsupial mammals. Although many of them were edible and provided good sport, several clansmen—Angus and Dawnboy foremost among them—derived special pleasure from landing the loch's trout, salmon, and other imported game fish. Technically Loch o' the Winds was part of the Grand Laird's private game preserve, but Angus had always good-naturedly turned a blind eye toward poachers, as long as they weren't too greedy. He was a shrewd enough leader to realize that if he strictly punished every brave who violated game laws, he would have precious few warriors left to fight for him.

His thirst quenched, Dawnboy hunkered on his heels and idly plunked pebbles into the water while his horse nibbled the rich grass along the shore. It had been a stimulating ride, but now fatigue from the exertions of yesterday's hunt and the night-long celebration was catching up with him. He yawned drowsily under the warm mid-morning sun as his grandfather reined up and dismounted beside him.

"Ye look nigh done-in, laddie," Angus said, untying his casting rod from the saddle horn. "Lie back and catch a few winks, while I see if I can catch our lunch. A nap'll improve yer appetite."

Dawnboy belched painfully and rubbed his still-

67

swollen abdomen. "Please do na make me think o' food again, after last night. But I think I will get a bit o' sleep. What about ye, Gran? Ye must be tired, too."

"I'll ha' rest enough when I'm dead," the old laird grunted. "When a mon reaches my age, he must spend even more time than ye youngsters at enjoying what little is left o' his life. Luckily, fishing is one form o' pleasure that does na require much hard work, nor is it sinful enough to trouble the conscience overmuch. So get ye to sleep, and leave an old fool to play out his second childhood."

"Aye, sir, if ye insist."

Dawnboy smiled fondly after the old man as he finished assembling his rod and moved off along the water's edge to find a suitable casting spot. He would have loved to wet a hook with him and thrill to the struggle of a hard-fighting game fish on the line, if only his eyelids weren't so heavy . . . Instead, he stretched out on the grass and put a hand over his eyes to filter out the sunglare from the sky, where clouds like gobs of whipped cream stood out against the otherwise clear blue. He knew his father's spaceship could be seen from here, if he just turned his head to the left. But he was too relaxed to make the effort . . .

He was on Teelget again, racing hell-bent after the grizzly. No, that wasn't quite right: he was a warchief, spurring his mount at the head of a raiding party, with lance and claymore held high. But as he opened his mouth to shout a battle cry, the scene changed again. He was still flying, but up higher and higher above the clouds and through the stratosphere into free space. This wasn't at all the way he had thought conditions would be out there; he could breathe in the cold cosmic winds that stung his cheeks even as his hair was scorched by blazing comet tails that streaked past like sparks from a campfire. The exhilarating ride filled him with both ecstasy and terror, until he nearly screamed for relief. But an Apache brave does not cry. And besides, he was too curious.

He looked down and saw that Teelget had somehow become the original Pegasus, a winged horse speeding him across galaxies on a mysterious quest whose purpose he could only guess. What was their destination? Why were they going there? For what sensible reason would anyone voluntarily leave a comfortable home on firm ground and risk the dangers of star-voyaging? Pondering those questions stirred up old memories, and from far back in his mind a strange procession of words came marching rhythmically—words from "The Star-going Heart," a famous song-poem by his teen-age idol Johnny Orpheus. Since its introduction nine years ago, on the artists' planet of Musendowment, the poem had become popular on nearly every human-inhabited world that starships and communications beams could reach. In five hundred inspiringly beautiful stanzas, the poet had summed up mankind's age-old yearning for the stars as few other artists had done. Often, under a clear night sky, Dawnboy would breathlessly recite portions of the poem to himself, until he heard them in his sleep. But why did they come back to him now?

"Time for lunch," his grandfather said, and Dawnboy awakened to the tempting aroma of freshly cooked salmon.

He sat up and rubbed his eyes. The sun was past its zenith. The old man squatted over a firepit where he had baked his catch—wrapped in palm leaves—to mouth-watering tenderness. To his surprise, Dawnboy was hungry again and needed no urging when Angus told him to get a move on before he ate the entire meal himself.

Dawnboy went to the loch and washed his face with cold water. Then, wide awake but with the dream still vivid in his mind, he joined his grandfather. They went to work on the salmon with their knives, eating it with the bread and cheese they had brought from home and washing it down with cold buttermilk.

The meal finished, Angus lit up his pipe and Dawnboy leaned back with a satisfied feeling under his belt once more. Ah, this was more like it: a simple, lazy day with the old man he had come to love so much— doing simple, satisfying, and manly things, free of the pressures of decision-making and the frilly, nagging re-

strictions that womenfolk imposed on a man. What
more could he ask for? A man would have to be a
cussed-out fool to want to leave this kind of life. Then
why did his gaze continue to wander restlessly back to
the silvery speck of the *Gayheart* in the distant sky?

" 'Twas a grand hunt ye had yesterday." Old Angus
broke the long silence between them. "Not even a sea-
soned warrior could ha' done better. I'm exceedingly
proud o' ye, grandson."

Dawnboy was too pleased by the compliment to do
more than nod his appreciation. He was also impressed
by the change in character that the old man's warm
tone conveyed. A hearty slap on the back, a bawdy
jest, a generous gift gruffly offered—those were the
laird's usual means of bestowing praise on strangers
and kinsmen alike. He had to be in a rare mood indeed
to show his softer side; and the boy was desirous of
seeing more of it. Nor was he disappointed.

" 'Twould be false for me to say I've not watched
with great satisfaction the sort of mon yer developing
into, for it's been my secret hope ever since ye first
came to us that ye might grow up to replace the able
sons I lost and someday to take my place." He brushed
aside the boy's protest. "Do na waste time on modesty.
That's a children's game. A mon must squarely face his
strong points as well as his shortcomings, and then
learn to make the best o' them. And do na think I'd be
doing ye any great favor by recommending ye as my
successor to the tribal elders. Ye'd ha' yer work cut out
to gain and hold the lairdship, wi' so many other qualified and ambitious leaders in the clan. Ravenslayer—to
name just one—could fill me moccasins in many ways
when I'm gone, though he lacks that touch o' human
compassion that can make a *great* leader."

"We've a long time yet to think about replacing ye,"
Dawnboy scoffed. "All the braves say yer such a tough
old bag o' bones and gristle that ye'll outlive us all."

Angus grinned back at him, then grew sober. "I pray
the gods will spare me that fate, for I've already buried
too many o' those dear to me. Do ye recall the story
the bards used to tell—about the Old Earth warrior-

hero named Achilles, and how his gods offered him a short life full of action and glory, or a long one of dullness and obscurity? Well, I seem to ha' been given both glory and longevity—but at a great price that had to be paid by those around me: the loss o' my best sons, yer mother's death, Eve's ordeal with the Mongol-Sioux, even poor Chatto's eyesight." He closed his eyes briefly to ease the pain of remembering. "The gods must be cruel, indeed, to make so many suffer for my sake! Still, I canna say I would ha' had it any other way, if it meant changing the way things are for the clan. For all it has cost in blood and hardship and sorrow, we have a good, free, manly life here."

"The best in the universe!" Dawnboy said with patriotic fervor.

"The best for us, at any rate, though others may be happier doing things differently. Even the life of a spaceman has its rewards, I suppose." He smiled at the guilty look Dawnboy cast toward the spaceship. "Do na be ashamed to show that ye ha' a normal, adventurous yearning to go wi' yer father. Ye're na the first to be pulled by two mutually exclusive desires. But na many ha' yer opportunity to fulfill one or the other o' yer ambitions to such a great extent."

Angus raised his lined face to the sky, and for a moment his years seemed to fall away as his blue eyes glowed with childlike wonder. "Aye, 'tis easy to guess how ye feel. Out there is a vast infinity o' discoveries waiting to be made, an excitement-filled universe where ye can learn and grow beyond the narrow confines o' this backward world. What lad worth his salt wouldna be tempted, when yer father can give all that to ye? And yet . . ." He lowered his gaze and looked around at his own world with an air of contentment.

"And yet ye'd rather I stayed here?" Dawnboy ventured.

"Aagh! How could I be expected to give aught but a prejudiced answer to that? O' course I want ye to stay, but 'tis na my decision to make. 'Tis ye who must play Achilles and choose one path to travel, forever turning yer back on t'other."

"Must it be that way?" Dawnboy wondered aloud. "Could I na possibly ask my father to let me go with him on just one cruise, to see how I liked it? Then, if things didna work out for me in space, I could come back here and take up the clan's ways again."

Angus frowned thoughtfully over the new proposition. "I do na know if that would be possible. A year in space might change ye so much that ye could never fit in here again, even if ye wanted to. But then, who can say what the gods ha' in store for ye? If only they'd send us a sign!"

"Maybe they have," Dawnboy said slowly, and told his grandfather about his dream. Angus listened silently, age creeping back into his face with every word the boy spoke. When the tale was finished, his expression was as bleak and hopeless as the grin on Skull Mountain. "Do ye ken what the dream signifies, Gran?" Dawnboy asked fearfully.

"Aye," the old man said. "It means that ye want to go home."

"Home?" Dawnboy stared at him as if he were mad. "But *this* is my home: Apache Highlands. This is where I've lived all my—" He stopped abruptly, remembering, and Angus nodded grimly.

"Starborn ye were, lad, and now the stars are calling ye back. I should've known that yer father's space lust was in the seed ye grew from and would someday spring forth as surely as any growing thing bears its fruit. I reckon I did know that all along, but I didna want to admit it."

"But maybe that is na the dream's true meaning." Dawnboy searched desperately for some way to ease the old man's anguish. "Ye could be reading it wrong. Maybe if we consult a good soothsayer . . ."

Angus shook his head slowly. "Do na attempt to dodge the arrow wi' yer name on it, lad. That only makes better sport for the gods. And, seeing as how this was what they had in mind for ye all along, I guess I should thank 'em for letting ye be wi' us this long. But somehow I can't feel much gratitude just now." Then he forced a cheerful smile, knocked the ash out

72

of his pipe, and stood up. "But I'm damned if I'll let that spoil the rest of our day here. Come along now, while we've still time for a bit o' fishing. Half-crown wager on who catches the most?"

"Ye're on!" Dawnboy smiled with him.

8

THE ENTIRE CLAN seemed to be crowded into the castle courtyard that afternoon, to see Dawnboy off. They watched with mixed emotions as the young brave walked, between his father and grandfather, toward the waiting elevator car. They were followed by Eve, Kathleen, Chatto, Tessie, and other friends and kinspeople.

Dawnboy was solemn, but Angus laughingly replied to greetings called out to him from the crowd. Like most men of war, he was a gambler at heart and had learned to take his losses philosophically while keeping up his spirits with carefree bravado. Or at least he had learned it was best to give that impression to the world.

Ranger wore a relaxed but somewhat distracted expression. He naturally had been delighted by his son's decision to go with him; but now that the matter had been resolved, his practical mind had moved on to the details of their journey to Capitalia and to the problems that awaited them there. Like Angus, he did not waste time dwelling on past victories or defeats.

Ravenslayer, Sage-hen, and most of his followers were conspicuously absent. But Charlie MacCarthy was there, his roguish gaze thoughtfully appraising Tessie's trim figure and newly acquired air of proud independence. But as they came to the car, the shadow of the waiting *Gayheart* seemed to cast a pall of silence over all of them.

Ranger, seeking a way to keep their leave-taking on a light note, glanced down at Dawnboy's bow, quiver of arrows, and small bundle of personal belongings.

"You sure that's all you want to take with you?" he asked his son.

"Aye, sir. As ye said, the ship contains everything I'll need, and what little I require to remind me o' home is in here." He touched his heart.

" 'Tis na good for a mon starting a new life to burden himself wi' too much o' the old," Chief Chatto remarked approvingly.

Ranger glanced at the car's open hatchway, then looked around at the sad, friendly faces turned longgingly at his son. He tried to imagine how hard it must be for Dawnboy to tear himself away from the world he had come to love and to feel so much at home in. His own unhappy childhood and the years of wandering, rootless, from star to star had left him with little feelings of homesickness or desire to settle down in one place. But now, strangely, even he felt a powerful emotional bond with these often tragically foolish semi-barbarians who, for all their crudity and violence, seemed to have developed such humanizing traits as family love, friendship, justice, honor, and loyalty to a far higher degree than many of the supposedly more civilized societies. They certainly had a more uninhibited zest for life and a greater capacity for happiness than any other people he had encountered; that was probably a major reason he had fallen in love with Gay. There was as much truth as poetry in the old saying that every man secretly desires a touch of the passionate savage in his woman.

He broke off that line of thought, remembering that time was short, and exchanged warm handshakes with the two old men. "I can't begin to thank you for all you've done for both of us," he began. "But if there's ever anything I can do in return . . ."

"Think ye even need to say it, lad?" Chatto laughed. "What would be more natural than for us to seek our clansman's aid, if ever we need it?"

Ranger wasn't sure if that was intended for himself

or for Dawnboy, but he thought it best not to question so great a compliment.

Angus, gripping his hand longer than necessary, leaned forward to whisper confidentially, "Ah, about the machine that ye used to fix Sage-hen's nose—could it perhaps restore someone's ... Uh, that is, if a mon had lost his sight ..."

"No ... I'm sorry." Ranger shook his head sadly. "The protoplasm regenerator hasn't been developed enough to handle anything as complex as the human eye. But there are some worlds where surgical techniques—"

"Quit yer whispering like gossipy old women," Chatto grumbled. "I can hear every word ye say. For what would I want me sight back after all these years? To see the stupid foolishness o' the world around me? Nay, I prefer to remain blind to the clan's destruction, which is certainly coming, though perhaps not in our lifetimes."

"There ye go again, playing the future-seer," Angus growled impatiently. "I should've cut off yer wagging tongue, instead o' yer sight."

"It requires no magic, just common sense," his old companion insisted, "to realize that someday King Larry the Louse or some other despot will succeed in reuniting the empire of William the Odd. And when that happens, the clan will be crushed in the superpowers' war of expansion."

"The clan has survived such conflicts before," Angus retorted.

"Aye, when fighting agin weapons na much more advanced than our own. But ask the spaceman here what chance bows and lances stand agin machine guns and artillery. Face facts, ye stubborn old blockhead, the clan has had its day and 'twas glorious while it lasted. But now we're destined to become the victims o' progress, the same as every other race that ever struggled upright to live like men. Dawnboy is wise to be looking to his future, when all we can offer him is a great past."

Angus started to reply, but Ranger—suspecting this

was a long-standing argument between them—cut in: "I'm afraid we'll have to say good-bye now."

"Nay, na good-bye, Uncle," Kathleen piped up. "Remember yer promise to come back for me in three years' time, when I be grown-up enough to go into space wi' ye."

"I only said we'd come back for a visit then, if we can't manage to return sooner," he corrected her. "Meanwhile, you study the books and tapes I gave you, and learn all you can about space-voyaging. Then, if you're still this keen on becoming a starbum, I'll see about getting your mother's permission for you to make a cruise or two with us."

Eve looked up at him with weary resignation in her eyes. "And what ha' I to say about it? Apparently the gods ha' ruled that I'm fated to lose all o' my loved ones to ye. I guess I'll just ha' to accept that, though I won't stop praying for a miracle."

"I hope you understand that I never meant to hurt you or anyone else here, Eve," Ranger said, gently touching her arm.

"I understand that." She smiled faintly. "But it does na ease the pain o' seeing my bonnie lad go from me."

"Do na be so downhearted, Aunt Eve," Dawnboy said cheerfully. "Maybe ye can go wi' us, too, when we return for yer pesty daughter here."

Kathleen stuck her tongue out at him, and Evening-Sadness shook her head. "Nay, son. I lack yer mother's adventurous spirit, and besides I'm too old to make such a change. As a clanswoman I've lived and as a clanswoman I'll die, when my time finally comes."

"And so will I," Tessie said, stepping up to Ranger. But her usual bold flirtatiousness was missing, and when he looked at her she demurely dropped her gaze. "I . . . I wish you were staying longer. Some of the braves have already shown new interest in me, and I'd like to have you here to give me away at my wedding. You've become almost a second father to me, the way you've given me a chance for a new life."

"Please, I already feel old enough with a strapping son of my own!" Ranger chuckled. "And I'm sure

Laird Angus will be happy to do the honors for you. He's had plenty of experience marrying off his own children."

"Aye, we'll fix her up wi' a good mon," Angus promised, restraining an urge to slap Tessie good-naturedly on her backside, out of respect for her new status as a freewoman of the clan.

"Well, I reckon 'tis time we departed," Dawnboy said. His throat was suddenly tight with emotion and he tried to think of some distraction to keep him from going all mushy-soft like a silly woman. "Ho, Charlie," he called out to the big Highlander in the crowd. "Ye be sure to take good care o' Teelget now. He'll make ye a fine war mount, wi' the proper training."

"Do na worry, lad, I'll nurse him along like a babe," the warrior promised. "And thanks again. 'Tis the finest present I've ever had."

Ranger shook hands all around again, while Dawnboy was warmly hugged and kissed by his tearful kinswomen. Tessie, catching Ranger at an unguarded moment, threw her arms around his neck and gave him a quick smack on the lips. Then she turned and hurried away, dabbing her eyes.

Ranger found himself face to face with Eve again and was trying to think of something comforting to say to her, when Kathleen impishly pushed her mother into his arms.

"Go ahead and kiss 'im, Mummy," the child giggled. "Ye ken 'tis what ye want to do!"

The crowd roared with laughter and called out ribald encouragement, as Ranger and Eve peered deeply into each other's eyes for a brief moment. Then Eve pulled away, blushing, and Ranger quickly ushered Dawnboy into the car and touched the control stud.

The two men stared silently out the porthole at the waving clanspeople until they dwindled away to a shapeless blob of colors in the castle courtyar Dawnboy sniffed unashamedly and Ranger reflected on the mysteries of the human heart as he studied his own reluctance to leave Apache Highlands. Out of all the more comfortable and attractive worlds he had visited, why did this particular one seem so much like home to him? Oh, well, maybe someday, when his star-going days were finished, he would come back here to retire. There were far worse places where a used-up space-hand could live out his declining years, and at least life with the clan would never be dull.

This time the car didn't dock at the air lock, but instead headed straight for the ship's belly. One of the cargo hold hatches opened, and the car floated in and clamped into its berth alongside the other small vehicles.

Ranger led the way up a ladder to the engine room, where he checked several rows of dials and gauges, making a few adjustments. "Everything secured for blast-off?" he asked Lulu.

"Aye, aye, Cap'n," the biocomputer answered. "We're all squared away and programed for Capitalia, as soon as you give the order."

"Good." Ranger beckoned to Dawnboy. "Come on, I'll show you to your cabin and you can stow your gear."

"Why were ye so rough wi' Aunt Eve?" Dawnboy asked as he followed his father up the stairwell to the main deck. "I kind o' thought maybe ye and she—"

"Well, don't think things like that!" Ranger said sharply. Then he paused amd smiled at the youth's puzzled expression. "I'm sorry, Son. I didn't mean to bite your head off. I guess, from your point of view, it would be a good idea for your father to marry the woman who's been like a mother to you. And I have to admit that Eve appeals to me in many ways, what with her strong resemblance to your mother. But it's just impossible for me to consider her as a wife."

"But why?" Dawnboy persisted. "I've heard that on some worlds a mon canna marry his dead wife's sister because the law says that a sister-in-law is the same as a blood sister—"

"No, that has nothing to do with it. I can't explain it to you right now, so you'll just have to take my word that there can never be anything more than friendship between your aunt and me."

"All right, if ye say so," Dawnboy said uncertainly.

"Good. I'm glad we have that settled."

Ranger took him to the cabin next to his own and showed him how to pack his bow and other belongings securely in the locker. Then they went to the bridge and strapped themselves down on the pneumatic acceleration couches.

"By the way," Ranger turned his head to smile at the boy. "Welcome aboard, Son. I'm very glad to have you shipping out with me."

"And I'm glad to be going wi' ye, Dad." Dawnboy squirmed nervously on his couch. "At least, I hope I will be glad about it."

"There's only one way to learn for sure if you're cut out for space," Ranger said philosophically. "Okay, Lulu, let's burn atmosphere out of here."

"Yessir." Lulu seemed to purr with anticipation as her computer relays clicked and green lights flashed on the go-system panel.

Dawnboy felt a slight tilting sensation as the *Gayheart* turned her tail to the planet, and a dull roar filled his ears when her aft rockets fired up. Then his body turned to lead and was crushed down into the folds of the couch as the ship shot out into a widening orbit around Apache Highlands. His chest tightened convulsively and he labored for breath, then lost consciousness for a few minutes when they broke away from the planet's gravity field. He revived in silence to his normal weight, as his father unbuckled his straps.

"I should have warned you about that," Ranger said. "Our antigrav unit relieves most of the pressure of blast-off, but it still takes some getting used to. Take it easy for a little while and you'll be all right. There won't be any further sensation of motion, even when we get beyond this solar system and go into star-drive."

Dawnboy sat up and looked through the forward bulkhead telescope at the at the blazing kaleidoscope of lights-on-black-velvet that stretched out to infinity before them. As he stared entranced at the dazzling display, his grandfather's final words on the shore of Loch o' the Winds echoed in his mind: "Go wi' yer father, lad. He can give ye the stars." That was true; but he also vaguely realized that old Angus had given him something that was in its own way of equal value. He turned his face to the blank bulkhead behind him.

"Is there some sort o' rear window? I wanted to ha' a last look at home, as we left it."

"I'm afraid you can't look back," Lulu said. "Starships aren't built that way."

"You can only look forward," Ranger said. "You'll find that's the best way in the days to come."

PART II

APPRENTICE TO THE STARS

9

FOR MANY PEOPLE two weeks of interstellar travel can become intolerably boring, once they have exhausted the novelty of poking about their ship and gazing out at the star-punctured void. But for an energetic adolescent with above-average intelligence, a lively curiosity, and a burning desire to learn as much as possible about his newly chosen profession, such an experience can be the most fascinating and stimulating adventure imaginable.

Nearly every moment of his first space cruise provided Dawnboy with thrilling new discoveries about the universe and about his own rapidly expanding interest in it. While he rested, his hungry mind gobbled up information from the Sleep-Teacher; and his waking hours were spent in frenzied efforts to make enough well-organized sense out of the information—by questioning his father and Lulu—to conduct learning experiments with the assorted apparatus and materials the ship contained. So zealous was the boy's pursuit of knowledge, in fact, that Ranger was often embarrassed by the extent of his own ignorance of some of the subjects with which Dawnboy became passionately intrigued. And even Lulu's machinelike patience, acquired from her long life and freedom from physical distractions, was strained by the boy's endless questions and demands for more detailed explanations.

He had received little formal education in the clan, whose customs decreed that even a potential Grand Laird required just the bare fundamentals of reading, 'riting, and 'rithmatic. Clansmen and -women were mainly concerned with living their lives to the fullest; and the most important life skills were best taught by experience. So they considered heavy book-learning of less importance than keeping an open, inquiring mind to cope with any new and unexpected problems that might arise. That mental habit gave Dawnboy a charming, childlike sense of wonder that set his eyes aglow at every new thing he encountered abroad the *Gayheart*. His lack of the usual teen-ager's blasé know-it-allness made his incessant questing for more and more data bearable to his elders.

Another trait he had absorbed from the clan also helped make him an exceptionally keen student. Like most primitive and semi-primitive peoples, Dawnboy's people tended to see the world more as an integrated whole than as being fragmented into the various specialized fields civilization invariably produces. That spared them the specialist's frequent error of rigidly dividing his thinking into different compartments and failing to observe correlations between them. For example, a member of some highly advanced society—however bright or stupid he may be—has definite opinions about science, religion, art, politics, business, and any other activities of interest to him. He is not apt to worship a volcano or expect a tree to turn into a beautiful woman or find much entertainment in the routine day-to-day workings of most human occupations. But to the primitive, anything is possible: the universe is new to him, and his mind has not yet been cluttered by the molecular structures of organic and inorganic substances—the "pictures" of information—that make it so hard for his civilized brothers to think straight. This all-in-one, non-compartmentalized outlook is, of course, a characteristic shared by every young child, but unfortunately most of them outgrow it as they mature and take on the thought patterns of their cultures. The only exceptions, among developed peoples, seem to be great artists and eccentrics such as Jor'lex the smog-weaver of Hitttyl. Such individuals manage to gather vast amounts of knowledge in various fields and blend it in novel creations that are occasionally valuable, often pointless, and always startling.

Dawnboy's peculiar ability to think on several different levels at once was sharply brought home to Ranger by the lad's reaction to the ship's light-energy converter. The smoothly humming contraption fascinated him, and he would spend hours puzzling over its operation—something Lulu assured him would require several advanced science degrees and half the information in her computer banks to fully understand. But that didn't relieve his frustration—until he found his own way of dealing with it. Though he had never been especially religious, his aunt had always insisted that he join in the morning family prayer to Father Sun and the other leading Apache gods. Now he continued the practice on his own, to fight homesickness and retain at least one spiritual tie with the clan. Ranger, passing the open door of Dawnboy's cabin one morning, was surprised to hear him mention the converter in his prayer.

The experience left Ranger somewhat disturbed, until he had a chance to talk it over with Lulu in private. She said Dawnboy was probably not actually praying to the converter as a deity. But since he was so overawed by the machine's great power, he had to associate it with another, more familiar power source to translate it into terms that he could begin to cope with. She guessed that as the boy came to understand the converter for what it really was, it would lose its supernatural aura.

Ranger accepted her advice to let Dawnboy work this out for himself. Sure enough, in a few days he stopped mentioning the converter in his prayers and started treating it with almost friendly contempt.

Ranger remembered now—and he wondered how he could ever have forgotten—that Gay had also been wildly eager to learn all about spacefaring. But she had been primarily motivated by a desire to adopt her husband's way of life. Dawnboy, on the other hand, seemed to have actually fallen in love with knowledge, and this had set off a learning explosion in his mind that at times left him literally dazed and speechless. Although Ranger frequently cautioned him to go slowly and not try to learn too much at once, he had enough normal parental pride to be delighted with his son's enthusiastic progress. He was especially pleased with the boy's great talent for astronavigation and other basic spaceman's skills, which indicated that he was indeed well suited for life in space. Within a week Dawnboy was in the copilot's seat, putting the ship through simple maneuvers with minimal instruction from Lulu or his father.

Despite his growing sophistication, Dawnboy remained enough of an Apache warrior to be fascinated by the wide variety of weapons in the *Gayheart*'s arsenal. After being told that as businessmen they traveled to far-flung worlds for peaceful commerce, he had been puzzled to learn that his father was an expert at many different kinds of armed and hand-to-hand combat—until he heard about some of the dangers that a visitor might encounter on some of those worlds. Even more puzzling was Ranger's obvious disdain for the various martial arts that he constantly practiced—and thoroughly taught Dawnboy—in daily gym workouts. Any clansman would have traded his soul for Ranger's fighting abilities, which would have earned him much honor and envy from friends and foes alike. But Ranger said only that he was in business to make profits, not enemies; and that while the law of survival demanded that a man be prepared to deal with any challenge that might come his way, it did not require him to be stupid enough to enjoy conflict more than friendly intercourse with his fellow-beings.

The probable reason for Ranger's attitude, Lulu confided to Dawnboy, was that the large-scale slaughter he had witnessed and participated in as a youthful Space Ranger had permanently disillusioned him regarding the glamor, adventure, and idealism that war supposedly possesses. Dawnboy thought he could understand that. Even in the clan, occasionally a highly renowned warchief or brave would grow weary of a life of endless battles and would turn instead to the quieter world of a religious order. But even Ranger admitted that his years of mercenary soldiering had been a valuable experience in many ways.

In addition to learning to be an ace star-combat pilot, Dawnboy's father had acquired the Rangers' cool-headed, no-nonsense attitude toward life and death. The clan on Apache Highlands and other famous warrior races might glory in the blood-stirring thrill of war, but because the Rangers fought only for pay they had become the most professional and least excitable fighting force in the universe. When they took up arms it was to go to work, and the sooner the job was done the sooner they could collect their wages. Untroubled by patriotism, ideological convictions, or excessive loyalty to one side or the other, they were free to give their full attention to the business at hand. Only rarely did an individual Ranger find himself pitted against his own homeworld or countrymen, and by then, as likely as not, he would come to identify so wholeheartedly with the Ranger organization that little conflict of interests troubled his mind. "Never salute a flag you can't spend" was the Rangers' cynical but practical motto, handed down by their founder, the swashbuckling, sometime space pirate Captain John Paul Drake of Freedonia. According to the records, very few members of the force have ever failed to follow that advice to the letter, mainly because they've seldom received a better offer.

Such was the hard school in which Ranger Farstar had learned his early lessons about war, survival in space and on hostile planets, and all the other vital problems of existence.

Dawnboy realized that his father had much valuable knowledge to give him, and he quickly developed a severe case of hero worship that was not diminished even by the older man's stern demand for excellence in everything he did. Time after time he would arise aching and exhausted from the gym mat to receive more bruising instruction in finger-dueling, karate, free-fall wrestling, and other exotic disciplines of unarmed self-defense. He came to enjoy the giddy weightlessness of zero gravity, once he got the hang of flitting about the ship without colliding painfully with bulkheads and other hard objects. But Ranger also insisted that he become accustomed to functioning normally under the various gravities of the worlds they were most likely to visit.

The generally acceptable range of gravity pull for *Homo sapiens* was from 0.75 to 1.25 of Earth's. Anything less than that couldn't hold a dense-enough atmosphere for optimal human survival; and too strong a gravity overtaxed the heart muscles and dangerously restricted the blood supply to the brain. There were, of course, a few striking exceptions to that rule. Gargantua, in the Antares System, was Neptune-sized and had a gravity nearly twice as strong as Earth's. Yet a handful of humans shipwrecked there in the thirty-first-century had managed to survive and multiply to form a population of over a million squat, muscle-bound caricatures of their parent species. Ranger drily advised Dawnboy not to pick a fight with a Gargantuan, should he ever meet one. Then he added the reassuring information that they were among the most friendly and easygoing people in the universe. The struggle against their harsh environment had forced them to develop their cooperative instincts to such a high degree that it was all but impossible for them to take violent action against any intelligent being.

Dawnboy dutifully staggered through his grueling training under improvised heavy gravity. But he couldn't hide his relief when the ship's antigrav unit was set back to normal—that being a space-going euphemism for Earth standards. Because the Jarles Effect of hyper–light speed played havoc with the usual concepts of space and time—a condition made even more confusing by the different sizes, masses, and rotational and revolutionary periods of the varied human-inhabited planets—it had been agreed early in the era of star travel to adopt Earth terms as the universal measuring standard. The method was not very scientific, but at least it enabled the peoples of different worlds to communicate and work together with a fair possibility of understanding one another. At first, therefore, Dawnboy had trouble adapting his sleeping habits to the shipboard schedule, because an Apache Highlands day was nearly an hour shorter than an Earth day. But he quickly adjusted to the change.

After those hard sessions on the mat, Dawnboy welcomed the comparative ease of weapons drill. His first favorite from the arsenal—because it was so closely related to the primitive armament of his previous experience—was the comeback blade of New Aussieland. It had the shape and airfoil of an ancient boomerang, but was made of razor-edged steel with a wooden handle for throwing and catching. Ranger said that a veteran New Aussie warrior could cast the blade so deftly that it would lop off an enemy's head at fifty yards and return to the precise spot where his hand waited to grasp it. Dawnboy found that hard to believe, when his first efforts with the weapon left it twanging unnervingly in the shield that was a valuable accessory to its use.

Among the highly advanced energy weapons, Ranger favored the Artelian synapse disrupter that he had used to kill the ironbeak on Skull Mountain and to stun Sage-hen for her nose-restoration operation. Although its full charge could be lethal to any creature with a chemical-electrical nervous system up to the size of a sperm whale, its ability to inflict paralysis or unconsciousness made it a most humanitarian form of self-defense. But the disrupter—like the laser dirk, the photon torch, and other such implements—had the serious drawback of limited range and required frequent recharging and maintenance by sophisticated equipment. The same held true of individually protective force-fields, which were just then beginning to be produced in compact-enough units for a man to carry on his person.

But for a space frontiersman's basic, dependable and all-round useful survival tool, technology had yet to come up with a substitute for the old-fashioned firearm. With a good gun and an adequate supply of ammunition, even shipwrecked or marooned explorers had managed to get along comfortably for years in highly inhospitable surroundings. Of course, many improvements had been made on the early muzzle-loader and the Colt six-shooter models, which impressed Dawnboy as fascinating playthings. The best of the newer models, in the judgment of most sportsmen and star-rovers, was the Berlix .057 Magnum needle rifle with a self-adjusting infrared sight. Its telescoping barrel and stock made it easy to carry, along with several hundred cartridges whose self-cleaning, smokeless charges could drive their tiny projectiles with great smashing force and accuracy to targets a mile away. It was, among other things, a gunrunner's delight, so the Protectorate Patrol teams of the SSA (Sentient Species Association) often had their hands full trying to prevent unscrupulous traders from selling the weapons for their weight in precious elements on backward worlds where the natives' favorite pastime was slaughtering one another. That was one form of commerce—along with slave-catching and transporting dangerous drugs—that Ranger frowned upon, despite his businessman's aversion to government restrictions on free trade.

At first Dawnboy felt uneasy with the new arms, because clan tradition deemed it unmanly for a warrior or hunter to use any weapon that involved more than his own physical strength. But soon he came to accept them as necessary tools in his new vocation. He even got over his fear of the ship's heavy armament—energy beams, nuclear cannon, and space-depth charges—when he learned that their operation was keyed exclusively to Ranger's voice print. Lulu, for all of her power and control over the *Gayheart*, was strictly programed against taking any action that might have been harmful to humans or other intelligent beings. Man's old fear that his creations might turn against him had become reality often enough for scientists to have made a habit of installing fail-safe devices on all of their thinking machines.

But for all of the young spaceman's growing education, one thing about his father and other businessmen remained a complete mystery to him: their dedicated pursuit of great wealth. He could pretty well follow Lulu's explanation of how the profit motive of peaceful industry and commerce naturally followed the barbaric

war-plundering period of a race's climb up the ladder
of civilization. It seemed to be merely good sense for a
star trader to seek a good return on his transactions in
order to cover the expenses of his ship, fuel, equipment, merchandise, etc., and still have enough left over
to pay himself well for his work. But beyond that,
Ranger expressed a desire to amass a fortune large
enough to make him independent of all further need to
labor for his livelihood.

Such acquisitiveness was shamefully greedy and totally incomprehensible to Dawnboy's clan-oriented
sense of values. Among his mother's people, individual
merit—expressed in martial excellence by men and in
domestic proficiency by women—was far more highly
regarded than material possessions. Of course, a triumphant warrior would bring home all of his vanquished foe's property that he could carry. But that was
in the nature of collecting victory trophies, tangible
proof of one's superior valor. Far from keeping the
booty for one's own use, it was established custom for
the returning hero to use it to give a lavish victory feast
for as many guests as he could afford to feed. The generous hospitality he thus displayed won him as much
honor and prestige as his performance on the battlefield. What could be more important to any man than
bringing great honor to himself and his tribe?

When Dawnboy finally asked Ranger why he wanted
to become rich, his father smiled and answered: "The
reasons for having a lot of money always present themselves; the money doesn't." Then, observing Dawnboy's bewilderment, he tried to explain further.
"Frankly, I don't understand it too well myself, because money has never been all that important to me.
But in business it's the object of the game, just as it's
victory in war, and in art it's creating a masterpiece,
and in science it's making a new discovery. Whatever a
man's work is, he has to have some goal; although I
guess greed and personal ambition have a lot to do with
it, too. I learned early that I don't have much talent for
anything except this crazy business of star-voyaging, so
I may as well try to do it the best way I can. A lot of

people seem to feel, as you do, that there's something morally wrong with wanting to be a successful businessman. But I don't see why I should feel guilty about it as long as I play by the rules and try not to hurt others while I'm going for the grand prize. Anyhow, if I ever do make a fortune, I'll probably just give it away to charity. Or on the other hand, I may decide to become a high-living, free-spending playboy. But what's the use of worrying about it? For now let's concentrate on getting money, before we decide what we'll do with it."

That sounded like good advice, but Dawnboy still couldn't resist puzzling over the enigma of money, and the strange spell it had cast over most men's minds throughout history—or anyway for as much of human history as he had been able so far to learn from the Sleep-Teacher and the library. Disagreements over money, or different economic systems, apparently even influenced mankind's earliest ventures into space, though recorded details of that period were incomplete. The first interstellar flight held special interest for Dawnboy, because it had been from Old Earth to Ranger's homeworld, Old New America, in the Alpha-Centauri System.

It seemed that Earth in the twentieth century (B.C. or A.D.?—he would have to look that up) had been shaken by an interhemispheric conflict between two powerful and radically opposite ecopolitical structures. The eastern superstate, called either Rus-China or Sov-Nazi (historians disputed whether the names applied to the same or different nations, due to the difficulties of translating from dead languages), was a sort of tribal-collectivist society. Descriptions of living conditions there were most confusing—either everybody owned everything or nobody owned anything; either the people were free and starving or they were well fed and cared for in slave compounds; either the government had become total or had withered away entirely; and they all seemed to be religious fanatics who didn't believe in God. As Lulu said, that period evidently had an intoxicating effect on scholars' minds, so the best a student

92

could do was pick out whichever drunken fantasy most appealed to him.

More was known about the other great country, America, because that was where most of the first colonists to Alpha-Centauri came from. Its primitive capitalistic government provided limited legal protection of individual liberties and property rights. It was, of course, well-known to clansmen that the Apache side of their ancestry had originated in ancient North America, so Dawnboy was naturally anxious to learn about their early history. But his interest turned to skeptical disbelief when he was told that the American tribes had advanced from Stone Age savagery to atomic power and space travel in about three hundred and fifty years. His mind, conditioned by a society that had remained practically unchanged for over ten centuries, could not accept such a fantastic claim. Granting that the clan's arrested development was a matter of choice, still even the great city-states and nations of Apache Highlands were only a few decades into the industrial era. Obviously the historians were mistaken about America's early development, or else they were trying to pull off an elaborate hoax.

Skipping over that period, he hurried on to find out how the east-west Cold War (what a strange, contradictory phrase!) had turned out. For a while the threatened nuclear confrontation had been sidetracked by two less disastrous maneuvers: several small-scale brushfire wars in which the superpowers manipulated weaker nations to gain strategic advantages; and a nonviolent contest for aerospace superiority, resulting in the exploration of Earth's moon and neighboring planets.

But while all this was going on, many influential citizens of the capitalist and soviet nations alike began to question their governments' wisdom in waging small wars and probing space. Calling themselves environmentalists and consumerists, they argued persuasively that all the material and manpower being expended in war and space could be much better used to improve human living conditions on Earth. Their viewpoint steadily gained popular support until, near the end of the 1990's, they were able to pressure the American and Rus governments into abandoning their space programs entirely. That enabled vast amounts of national resources to be poured into "quality of life" projects, which produced the Golden Age of Humanitarian Social Service—or so it was named by its supporters. Critics called it Welfare Utopia.

But there was another, much smaller, class of Earth men and women who feared that the retreat from space might eventually cost humanity far more than the increasing benefits they were enjoying. They called themselves Astrophiles (star lovers) and believed that man's deepest instinct—the driving force behind all his material and spiritual progress—was an inherent yearning to reach out to other worlds in the universe. To them, conquering space meant more than just the satisfaction of flexing national egos or gathering important scientific data—it was the only thing that made belonging to an intelligent species worthwhile. With the sublime faith of saints, fools, and young lovers, they *knew Homo sapiens'* destiny was somehow to escape Earth and roam the distant starways. Besides that mystical conviction, they also put forth the practical argument that human colonies on other planets would increase their species' chances of survival if an atomic holocaust or some natural disaster should ever devastate Earth.

Unfortunately, their appeals had little impact on world leaders or on the vast majority of their people, who were pragmatically satisfied with life on Earth. So the Astrophiles decided to make their reach for the cosmos a private affair. Though most of them were Americans of moderate means, they were able to find helpful sympathizers in all walks of life from other nations. Combining their money, labor, and knowledge, they purchased all the surplus aerospace material that had not yet been scrapped, and went to work in a remote part of the Rocky Mountains, secretly assembling an advanced interstellar craft.

It wasn't easy.

For over fifty years, one generation after another of

star-loving fanatics labored on the project through heartbreaking failures and countless frustrations. But finally the ship was as spaceworthy as she would ever be, and the surviving Astrophiles drew lots to determine which three hundred among them would ride her out to find a new world—or the loneliest death ever known to mankind. Then, in the chill, bleak dawn of February 18, 2059, the *Mayflower II* blasted starward with a conscious crew of ten, plus two hundred and ninety men, women, boys, and girls blissfully unaware, in suspended-animation tanks.

They got away just in time, as things turned out, for the great welfare bubble that had promised paradise on Earth was about to burst. Both the American and Rus governments had agreed to a program of gradual disarmament and to donate their defense budgets to help feed and industrialize the underdeveloped nations. But only America, being an open, democratic society where keeping military secrets had become unfashionable, felt conscientiously compelled to fulfill her end of the bargain; her totalitarian opponents were easily able to conceal and maintain their war potential while waiting for the Americans to become defenseless. Then they revealed their strength and delivered an ultimatum.

Surprisingly, the pleasure-loving Americans found the backbone to refuse the demand for their unconditional surrender, and managed to put up a stubborn guerrilla resistance to the Rus invasion. Eventually America was beaten into submission, but only after suffering such great loss of life and property that her conquerors were left with a hollow victory. The entire western world's industry and economy were a shambles, and the soviets, who had never originated much technology of their own, found it impossible to force their newly acquired slaves to work at the high pitch of creativity that only freedom seems able to generate. Soon the leader of Rus-China or Sov-Nazi, or whatever the eastern powers were called, fell to fighting among themselves over the bones of western civilization. All systems of government decayed, and Earth slipped into centuries of Dark Ages—from which it had never fully recovered despite the many civilizations that had risen and fallen on the planet since then.

Those events meant little to the Astrophiles on the *Mayflower II*. Having irrevocably cut their psychic umbilical cord to Earth, they wandered like the ancient Hebrews for forty years through the wilderness of space before reaching the gravitational field of Alpha-Centauri. There, luckily, they found a rugged but humanly habitable planet and burned the last of their fuel setting down on it.

Many tough challenges faced the first settlers on New America—as they unanimously voted to name their adopted homeworld—but they were more than equal to them. Fired with the enthusiasm of pioneers and equipped with the best tools and knowledge that a million or more years of human advancement had produced, they were no less confident of their ability to tame their wild surroundings than their parents and grandparents had been sure of building the *Mayflower II*. Believing that totalitarian collectivism resulting from overgrown governments had been the major cause of Earth's downfall, they agreed that their new society should be a laissez-faire capitalist democracy in which the individual citizen would be free to do as he pleased so long as he did not harm others by force or fraud.

The system seemed to work very well indeed—for as long as it was allowed to function unchanged. For several generations, the New Americans prospered, multiplied, and spread over the planet at a fantastic pace. They even built up a space industry of their own and sent out colonists to discover and settle more distant worlds. But in time the inevitable differences of opinion that arise between individuals and groups flared into angry conflicts that tore the fabric of the one-world community. Unhappy dissidents broke away to establish settlements of their own, initiating the old familiar Earth pattern of nationalistic pride, trade restrictions that led to reduced freedoms, and border disputes that led to war. It took over nine hundred years to accomplish, but finally New America—which had become Old New America by then—went the way of Old Earth. The only consolation was that humanity was so widely dispersed among the stars by then that the species had a fair chance of even surviving its own apparent determination to destroy itself.

Dawnboy's cram-study of history left him more confused than ever about the human saga and the role money had played in it. Countless scholarly theories based on the premise that "Money is the root of all evil" had been put forth speculating on various ways that men could rise above materialism and enjoy a higher spiritual existence. Many of the theories had even been put into practice by human and nonhuman societies, whose spokesmen claimed impressive results. But the individual fredom offered by capitalism was nevertheless attractive, despite all of the system's shortcomings and the ways in which unscrupulous businessmen could abuse and exploit it. His father's claim that business was some sort of a game in which it was all right to try to become rich as long as you played according to the rules seemed the best course to follow.

But who made the rules? he wondered. And how was a player to know if they were fair or not?

So, with man's age-old problem of Money still unresolved in his bright, inquiring mind, the young space student eagerly looked forward to their arrival at the business planet of Capitalia, commercial center of the universe.

10

"WHAT'S THE MATTER?" Dawnboy yawned, as he stepped onto the bridge and saw his father lounging in the pilot's seat, casually nibbling a raw carrot.

"Nothing, I just thought you would like to see our

destination, as we make our orbiting approach to it,"
Ranger said. He nodded to the forward bulkhead-telescope without looking up. The strong rays of Croesus,
the M-class star they were bearing down on, had been
filtered out to make its single planet visible as a dimly
glowing blur.

"So that's Capitalia?" Dawnboy moved forward to
get a better view, curiosity sharpening his sleep-dulled
brain. "Doesna look like much."

"It isn't supposed to. When you're the richest planet
in the universe, you don't have to be ostentatious about
it." Ranger glanced at his son, then did a sharp double
take at his attire. Or rather his lack of it. "Mind telling
me why you're wearing nothing but your skin, Son?"

"Whose skin do ye think I should be wearing?"
Dawnboy asked with a straight face.

Ranger groaned and said: "Now see here, Lulu, you
know I'll put up with a lot of things, but having you
turn my kid into a third-rate comedian isn't one of
them."

"Don't blame me," Lulu protested. "He found that
tape of old jokes all by himself. You should hear some
of the really awful ones! Not even a machine should be
forced to take such abuse."

"Lulu sounded so urgent when she woke me that I
came running without bothering to grab my kilt,"
Dawnboy explained his nakedness. " 'Tis the Apache
way o' responding to an emergency. There's a famous
poem about how the great warrior Duncan Foxgrin had
to fight off a surprise attack by the Mongol-Sioux while
wearing nothing but his—"

"I think we can live without hearing about that just
now," Ranger said.

"There's no emergency, so go get dressed before you
cause Lulu to blow out a transistor."

"I was an art teacher, remember?" Lulu said. "By
the way, Dawnboy, you're looking rather peaked. Have
you been drinking enough soy-milk?"

"Aye, Grandma," Dawnboy said wearily. "And
eating all my vegetables, and spending time under the
sunlamps every day." He had quickly discovered that

Lulu's motherly instinct was even greater than his Aunt Eve's. The only way he had found to get back at Lulu was to call her Grandma, which he thought irritated her. Actually, it pleased her no end.

"Well, your pectoral muscles could use more development," Lulu said. "So try to work out with the barbells more often."

"Yes, ma'am." Dawnboy started to return to his cabin, then looked back at his father. "What was that word ye used? Osten—?"

"Ostentatious." Ranger crunched his carrot contentedly. "Look it up. You'll never get a proper education if I do everything for you."

"It means being a pretentious show-off," Lulu said.

"Thanks, Grandma!" Dawnboy threw a smug look at his father and hurried out of the room.

"You're spoiling him, Lulu," Ranger scolded.

"I know; that's what grandchildren are for," Lulu said fondly.

Ten minutes later Dawnboy rejoined them, now fully dressed in standard shipboard garb. He still hadn't gotten used to trousers, and would have been more comfortable in his kilt. But he knew he would have to make a lot of adjustments if he ever hoped to become a good spacehand.

He settled into the copilot's seat and sipped the mug of citroffee he had drawn in the galley. He had acquired an instant liking for the nourishing drink, brewed from beans native to Nueva Brasil, which combined the tangy sweetness of orange juice and the mild stimulant of coffee.

Glancing up at the telescope, he was surprised to see how much clearer the planet had become, now that they were closer to it and Lulu had increased the electronic lens magnification. "I did na ken it has rings," he murmured.

"Of course it has," Ranger said. "Didn't you do the research assignment on Capitalia that Lulu gave you?"

"I guess my other studies got in the way o' it," Dawnboy confessed. "I kept putting it off, figuring that I could learn all I needed to know when we got there."

"You're probably right," Lulu said. "It's a pretty dull place."

"Depends on your point of view," Ranger grunted. "Being free of all materialistic temptations, you naturally feel bored in a society where business is the predominant concern. But for those of us who still have to work for a living, even constant talk about 'dirty old money' can be fascinating." He turned to Dawnboy again. "Well, I guess you really didn't miss much by skipping that assignment. The planet's physical composition isn't very remarkable. It's sort of a combination of Sol's Jupiter and Saturn. The innermost ring is made up of gases and ice particles, and the outer two are belts of asteroids ranging from pebble-sized to several miles in diameter. About two hundred thousand miles beyond them are four small moons that are used as guard posts against any space pirates who might try to raid Capitalia's wealth. The planet itself, like Jupiter, has a dense rocky-metallic core, a frozen bare surface, and a deadly atmosphere of ammonia and methane gases. Not exactly what you'd call a pleasant vacation resort."

"Nay, I wouldna call it that," Dawnboy agreed. "But if 'tis such an unfit world, how do people live and do business on it?"

"They don't. The business offices are located in starscrapers built on the asteroids of Wall Street, the first belt. Easy Street, the second asteroid belt, is the residential area. Don't ask me to explain those names; it's just traditional for businessmen to say they work on Wall Street and live on Easy Street."

"They actually have homes on the asteroids?" Dawnboy asked incredulously. "Then the planet itself is o' no use to 'em at all?"

"On the contrary." His father smiled. "That's where the bank vaults and safe deposit boxes are located. Capitalia's unique value as a secure storage depot, and its convenient location at the juncture of the most important starlanes, are what made it the best choice for a universal trade center. Without those special qualifications, it would not have been feasible to—"

"Better let school out for now, Cap'n," Lulu interrupted. "Lunar Guard Station Number Three just contacted us for indentification."

"Then we'd better give them what they want. Those guys can develop nervous trigger fingers if they're kept waiting too long." Ranger pressed a stud to override the autopilot and activated his photophonic communicator.

The image of a handsome young black man appeared on Ranger's visiscreen. He wore a severely cut military tunic with the name tag "Vice-Ensign Tongo Jones" over his heart, and an equally severe expression. "You have just entered the spatial jurisdiction of the Conglomerate of Capitalia," the vice-ensign said flatly. "Please identify yourself and state your reason for wishing to orbit here. Also, if your vessel is not listed in *Heathcate's Universal Registry,* please give me references to authenticate your noncriminal and nonhostile origins. Be advised that this world's entire defensive system is tracking you; any suspicious action on your part will be regarded as aggression and treated accordingly."

Ranger touched his transmit switch. "Guard Station Three, this is the merchant ship *Gayheart;* Ranger Farstar commanding. Dawnboy MacCochise is serving as First Mate and sole crew member. Our registry number is Delta-183624097-Alpha. Corporation listing on the Capitalia Stock Exchange—Farstar and Company. Purpose of this visit: to conduct confidential business with Interstellar Investments, Incorporated. For personal and professional references, contact Rothfeller Hughes, Chairman of the Board of Interstellar Investments."

The young official punched the computer keyboard in front of him. His stern features relaxed a bit as he listened to the feedout of his earphone. "Yes, sir, that information checks out; and your voiceprint matches the sample in our files. Now, with your permission, we'd like to scan the interior of your ship and neutralize your armament."

"Permission granted," Ranger said. He cut off transmission and said to Dawnboy: "Actually they've been scanning us since they first made contact, but they like to observe the formalities."

"What are they doing, exactly?" Dawnboy asked.

"Searching the ship for possible contraband or unlisted passengers. When they've finished that, they'll put an electronic beam lock on our arsenal and heavy-gun controls, to make sure we don't attempt to use any of our weapons while we're here. The lock will automatically dissipate when we leave Capitalia's space limits again."

"What if we tried to remove the lock afore then?"

"Then all of our worldly problems would be over. The lock is tied in to our luxium pile in such a way as to cause destabilization at the first sign of tampering. The entire ship would be instantly vaporized."

Dawnboy shuddered. "They do na believe in giving a mon the benefit o' the doubt, do they?"

"They can't afford to. Capitalia is more than just a place where money and goods change hands. Everyday financial decisions are made here that affect the lives and prosperity—sometimes the very survival—of entire solar systems containing billions of people. If one of the major banks down there were robbed, or if anything else happened to seriously disrupt the flow of business, it could upset galaxywide trade agreements that have been centuries in the making. The Capitalians don't take their responsibilities lightly."

"Nay, I do na reckon they do," Dawnboy said solemnly.

"All right, Captain Farstar, you're cleared," Ensign TongoJones said. "May we have your destination, please?"

"The Hughes estate, *Tres Ojos*, on Easy Street."

"Very good, sir. The present coordinates of that residence will be fed into your computer banks, along with the latest compilation of this world's laws, customs, and moral standards. We trust you will do your best to respect and observe our prevailing mores, and we hope your stay on Capitalia will be a most enjoyable and profitable one." The officer's cold features suddenly melted into a broad, friendly smile. "Welcome aground, gentlemen!"

"And lady," Dawnboy added under his breath.

"Thanks," Lulu said. "But biocomputers are supposed to be sexless. Which is too bad, because I could really go for that good-looking spacecop—if I were a hundred years younger, and if he'd get the stuffing out of his shirt more often."

"He's just doing his job," Ranger said. "Which is what you'd better start doing and slow us down before we barge into a heavy-traffic area."

"Not to worry, Boss. Any day I can't fly this tub expertly, carry on a conversation, and beat you at 3-D chess—all at the same time—you can retire me to an agricultural planet."

"Where your cotton-picking mind would be right at home," Ranger jibed. "Just get us safely where we want to go, and I'll grant your conversational and chess-playing skills."

"You want to go directly to the Hughes's place, or shall we take the scenic route?"

Ranger looked at his chronometer. "You may as well make one complete orbit to give Dawnboy an overall view of the planet and its rings. That'll kill enough time to put us at *Tres Ojos* at the close of the business day. I don't think we need bother Mr. Hughes at his office, and his home's a nicer place to wait for him."

"If you like opulent decadence," Lulu said.

"Ye've never told me much about Mr. Hughes," Dawnboy said to his father. "Except that he's one o' the richest men in the universe, and yer major stockholder."

"I wanted you to be able to judge him for yourself, without any preconceived impressions," Ranger replied. "But I guess I should warn you that his physical appearance is somewhat . . . unusual."

"That's the understatement of the decade," Lulu said.

"He is no alien being, is he?" Dawnboy uneasily recalled the 3-D images of several nonhuman intelligent species that he had encountered in his studies.

"Not exactly," Ranger said. "He was a native of Denebali, which endured a severe nuclear war a century or two ago. It left the inhabitants with a strange genetic mutation that expresses itself in peculiar and unexpected ways. A family there may produce normal offspring, or far-out freaks, or both. Not that the results are all bad—some of the mutants are supergeniuses or have other outstanding qualities. Hughes has one of the most brilliant business minds in all time, but as for the rest of him . . . Well as I said, I want you to be able to judge him for yourself. Just try not to be overly influenced by first impressions."

"I'll try," Dawnboy promised. "But after the buildup ye've given the mon, I scarcely know what to look forward to."

"Star-drive deceleration beginning," Lulu said. "We should be close enough to the first moon to switch to antigrav in ten-point-eight minutes."

"Should we strap in?" Dawnboy asked, looking at the couches.

"Won't be necessary, since we're not going to planetside," Ranger said. "Just relax and enjoy the view."

The blurred features of the largest moon cleared with the abruptness of an eye blink as they sped forward and went smoothly into antigrav drive. Dawnboy stared curiously at the small, airless satellite's barren, rock-ridged, and meteor-scarred surface. The tallest mountain peaks were crowned with giant scanner disks that probed deep space and flashed back impulses to Guard Station Three's electronic nerve centers in deep sublunar chambers. But he could detect no sign of the combat-ready interceptor ships, robot missiles, and banks of powerful energy beams that the station could instantly deploy to defend Capitalia.

"Just hope you never see this watchdog's teeth," his father replied ominously to Dawnboy's remark about the moon's innocent appearance. "Because they'll be the *last* things you'll ever see."

Lulu slipped them inside the orbits of the four guardian moons and began a long, spiraling approach to the outermost ring. Dawnboy watched in growing wonderment as the ring changed from a misty, sunlit halo to individual bodies of matter of all sizes and shapes. Most were just naked hunks of rock, and it was difficult to judge their dimensions even in relation to one another, until the ship reached some developed asteroids and he could use the man-made structures for scale. He guessed the largest of them that he could see —which was roughly pear-shaped—to measure about one hundred miles by twenty by sixty. But the asteroids' natural attributes seemed almost insignificant compared to what their inhabitants had done to them.

Many of the occupied asteroids were partially or completely covered by transparent bubbles. Within these protective bubbles were elaborately constructed apartment dwellings and palatial mansions with artistically landscaped grounds and gardens colorfully abloom with exotic growths. Some of the grounds even sported fountains, pools, and game courts surrounded by graceful statuary and other works of art. But far more breathtaking were the occupied asteroids that seemed to have no shielding at all from the deadly vacuum of space. Yet they were obviously livable, as demonstrated by the tiny human figures that could be seen lounging about their indescribably beautiful and luxurious landscapes. None of the people, in these cases, seemed to be wearing protective clothing.

"Prefab jobs," Ranger described the bubble-dotted asteroids, with a wry smile. "Where the poor folks live. Anyone who can't afford a powerful antigrav unit to hold on to his atmosphere, and a luxium reactor to regulate temperature, ranks pretty low on the Capitalian social and economic ladder. But fortunately that's something we'll probably never have to worry about, since just a week's living expenses here amounts to more than a lowly starship captain earns in a year."

"I can well believe it," Dawnboy said in awed tones. "Why, just the expense o' bringing all this material here—" His jaw dropped and he stared pop-eyed at an even more incredible sight.

For some time he had been idly watching the busy traffic—all manner of vehicles from dashing sports-model antigrav cars to huge passenger and cargo trains—that flowed between the asteroids. Now he saw that there was also *pedestrian* traffic out there, as groups and individual figures drifted in lanes alongside the vehicles. "Now, how in the name o' Einstein—?"

"With enough money, anything is possible," his father assured him. "And actually, they're just doing the same thing we did on the training spacewalks I put you through, with vac-suits and antigrav packs. The only difference is, their equipment is more compact and more efficient than ours—and a lot more costly, too. But if you think that's something, wait till you see the latest people-moving device the Capitalians have started buying from Newtonia. It's a matter-transporter, which can actually separate a man's molecules, send them instantaneously through space, and reassemble him as good as new at his destination."

"Oh, sure, I know all about that." Dawnboy smiled, determined not to let his father think he was gullible enough to swallow every wild yarn he heard.

"Think I'm blowing comet dust at you?" Ranger asked. "We'll see how skeptical you are when you've seen some of the latest scientific gimmicks at *Tres Ojos*. Isn't that right, Lulu?"

"Don't ask me about these newfangled gadgets," Lulu said haughtily. "I never have believed the Machine Age is here to stay. People ought to rely entirely on us biocomputers, as the Good Lord intended they should."

"Well, at least I think I've figured out the meaning behind the name o' Mr. Hughes's estate," Dawnboy said. "*Tres Ojos* is Old Earth Spanish for 'Three Eyes.' It refers to the first letters of Interstellar Investments, Incorporated. Right?"

"Clever lad," Ranger said. "Now, aren't you glad I told you to study some of the dead languages from which basic Unilingo is derived? And you're about half right with your deductions."

"Oh? What's the ither half?"

"You wouldn't believe me if I told you. Besides, it's more fun to grav you with tall tales about the crass

Capitalian who decided to show off his wealth by building a house of solid gold. Which we should be coming up to in about— There it is."

Dawnboy's eyes became glassy at the sight of the glittering spectacle before them, and for a while he was too speechless to ask any more questions.

11

BY THE TIME Lulu announced that they were approaching the Hughes estate, Dawnboy had seen so many extravagantly elegant homes and haunts of the very rich that he didn't think he could be further impressed by another plutocratic display of gracious living. But that was the case when he first saw *Tres Ojos*.

The estate appeared to be just a large but simply designed mansion, with outer buildings of white pseudo-marble in a naturally beautiful woodland setting. Only when he realized that there was nothing natural about the setting—that a master landscaping artist must have painstakingly planned every last detail down to the smallest mound of soil and sprig of grass, to create a living masterpiece on naked, featureless rock—did the place's true beauty and majesty hit him with stunning force. Even the buildings matched the scenery so perfectly as to give the impression that they might have grown right out of the ground. That was additional proof, if more was needed, of the designer's genius at raising art above the level of mere technique to apparent artlessness.

"The basic design was taken from an ancient Earth mausoleum called the Taj Mahal," Ranger said, as the *Gayheart* drifted slowly to a halt above the asteroid. "But of course it was greatly modified to suit the needs of living people. Hughes had it built with the first fortune he made cornering the silicon trade to the Lithophages in the Trifid Nebula, and he's constantly having new improvements added to it. The estate is even equipped with a star-drive, so the whole thing can be sealed up and used as a spaceship. He claims that was an economy move, to spare him the expense of keeping several vacation homes around the universe, as many other businessmen do."

"I canna say I blame him," Dawnboy said, staring down at the mansion's still reflection in the rectangular pool. "I wouldna care to leave such a bonnie home either, were it mine."

"And you've only seen the exterior so far." Ranger flipped on his photophone. "Let's see if the family is home and receiving callers."

The screen revealed a large, muscular man wearing swimming briefs and seated at a table beside an indoor pool. Dawnboy tried not to be too shocked by his bright-blue skin and glowing orange eyes. After all, Ranger had warned him that Rothfeller Hughes was a mutant. The man smiled vacantly at them and flicked back a shock of platinum hair. "Ah, Captain Farstar. Good to see you again, sir. Welcome aground. That is, when you get aground. Have a good cruise here?"

"Very good, David, thank you. Is Mr. Hughes in?"

"No, sir, but he should be home from the office shortly. Please come in and let me serve you something while you wait for him. Oh, wait a moment—I think Miss Helen and her husband should be arriving about now. I'll switch you to the 'porter room."

The scene shifted to a room so jam-packed with electronic equipment that only a small area in the middle of the floor remained unoccupied. Dawnboy tried to study the machinery, but it was all so strange and confusing that he could make nothing of it.

"Then that mon wasn't Mr. Hughes?" he asked.

Ranger shook his head. "That's David Goliath, Hughes's major domo, chief bodyguard, closest friend, companion, and anything else Hughes wants him to be. They go back a long way, to when they were boys to-

gether on Denebali and the planet was conquered by—
Wait! Watch this closely now."

Dawnboy peered intently at the visiscreen. In the
empty center of the cluttered room two brilliant spots
of light had appeared. They rapidly grew in size and
brightness until he had to blink moisture out of his
eyes. When his vision cleared again, the outlines of two
human figures surrounded the dots. As the lights faded,
the outlines filled in with the shapes of a man and
woman.

"Is that the matter-transporter contraption ye told
me about?" he whispered to his father, keeping his eyes
glued to the screen for fear he might miss something.

"Yes. It's such a radically new invention—and so
fantastically expensive to build and operate—that there
are only about a hundred of them in existence. So far
their effective range is about a hundred thousand miles,
but someday they may be developed enough to replace
starships as a safe, cheap means of space travel. Can't
say I'd be happy to see that happen, though."

"Don't worry; it isn't likely to happen during our
lifetimes," Lulu said confidently. "I was on Newtonia
long enough to learn that the scientists there aren't
wizards—despite their boasts to the contrary."

Dawnboy was too entranced by the scene unfolding
before him to notice anything else. The two figures
were as motionless as statues, but they had become solidly three-dimensional enough for him to make out their
features. They both appeared to be about thirty and
were of average size and appearance. The woman was
a slightly plump, washed-out blonde wearing a gauzy
wraparound garment that left her shoulders, arms, and
midriff bare. Her plain face wouldn't have rated a second look, except that something about her violet eyes
and the tiny crinkles at the corners of her mouth gave
the impression that a gay smile was constantly waiting
to spring forth. The man beside her would have been
fairly handsome, but for a sardonic half-sneer that
seemed to be his permanent expression. He wore an
upper garment similar to the woman's, green-velvet
knee breeches, and high-topped boots. His round head

was shaved, leaving only a six-inch-long topknot caught up in a jeweled clasp.

For a few moments they remained frozen still, then suddenly came to life with sharp intakes of breath.

"Well, another trip safely made without our heads ending up on the wrong bodies," the man said, looking himself over. Then he glanced up—evidently at his visiscreen, because he broke into a wide grin and cried: "Ranger! You old son-of-a-spaceape! So you finally condescended to honor us with your presence? How the hell have you been?"

"Can't complain, Juan. I'm glad to see that you're looking so good. I always said a good wife was just what you needed to make a human being out of you." Ranger shifted his attention to the woman. "Helen, you're more beautiful than ever. When are you going to shoot his lazy bum and marry me?'"

The woman was wearing her promised smile now, and Dawnboy saw that his father was right. In a hard-to-explain sort of way, she was beautiful.

"Don't think I haven't been tempted, Ranger," she said, giving her companion a tender look. "But after a while, he kinda grows on you." Then she looked at Dawnboy, her eyes widening in disbelief. "Don't tell me this is . . . ?"

"You better believe it is," Ranger assured her. "Son, meet an old girlfriend of yours, Helen-of-Troy Hughes-Orfo. You were madly in love with her when you were about two or three years old."

"If that's true, then I'm sorry I canna remember it," Dawnboy said. "For I'm sure it must've been one o' the happiest times o' my life."

"I see you've inherited your father's charming way of telling women the lies they want to hear," Helen laughed. Then her eyes softened toward Dawnboy. "And I can see a lot of your mother in you, too. She and I were close friends."

"And this is her husband, Juan Orfo," Ranger completed the introductions. "Sorry Juan. I guess I should've introduced you first."

"That's all right." Juan shrugged. "I'm used to being

referred to as *Mister* Helen-of-Troy Hughes. Serves me right for marrying the boss's daughter."

His wife poked him in the ribs. "Worth it, isn't it?"

He put his arm around her shoulders and hugged her to him. "Well, the work's hard, the hours long, the pay's lousy—but I sure can't gripe about the fringe benefits." He looked up at Ranger again. "Say, where are you calling from? Your ship?"

"Right. We just arrived over *Tres Ojos*, and I wanted to call ahead to see if Mr. Hughes was at home before we dropped in."

"Since when do *you* need advance permission to come calling on us?" Juan demanded indignantly. "You two get your tails down here, before I come up there and drag them down. I'm dying for a drink, and you look too damned sober and healthy for your own good, so let's see how space-warped we can get before the old man comes home and makes us talk business."

"Yes, do hurry," Helen urged. "I have a special surprise for you. Daddy will be along shortly in his antigrav limousine." She glanced around the room and giggled. "After spending so much money on all of this equipment, he's too old-fashioned to use it. He's afraid his molecules might get scrambled or lost in transit."

"Okay, we'll be right down," Ranger promised. He ended transmission and rose from his seat. "Come on, Son, and get your first lesson in why people want to become rich. Mind the shop while we're gone, Lulu."

"Will do, Boss. But first, you might like to know that I've intercepted an interesting bit of news while you were gabbing with your friends below. An IFIB war vessel of starcruiser class has entered Capitalian space. Destination: *Tres Ojos*."

"Damn! I was afraid of something like that. Any indication of why they're coming here?"

"The captain said Rothfeller Hughes invited them, and the guard station had a message confirming it."

Ranger look startled, then laughed. "That's just what the old fox would do. 'When in doubt, twist the lion's tail for quick results,' as he often says. Only this time, it might be *our* heads in the lion's mouth."

"What does it mean?" Dawnboy asked.

"That's what we're here to find out. You've studied about the IFIB and the PHAP, haven't you?"

"Aye." Dawnboy quoted from his recent lessons in interworld social studies: "The Interstellar Family o' Intelligent Beings is a self-proclaimed democratic empire composed o' fifty-two or -three inhabited planets ranging from the old Carinan Confederacy to most of the worlds o' the Pentapeds in the Sadlady Galaxy. Present total population: ninety-one billion, six hundred million—give or take a few million. As a system o' government, it gradually evolved from a militant social-reform movement founded a hundred and sixty-seven years ago by a group o' Novaslavian university students and teachers calling themselves Otherniks, from the philosophy o' Otherism, which was computerized from the Golden Rule by the famous Surmarian mystiscientist, Sophronia Cleer. Both Otherism and IFIBism spread rapidly from world to world for about thirty years.

"Then a powerful reactionary resistance movement called the Protectors o' Human Advancement and Purity sprang up on Beta-Centauri, which was renamed Anthropocentauri and was made the capital world o' the new astro-empire. PHAPism, called a Monarchyship-o'-the-People by its supporters, was organized by Victor Hanoleon, an itinerant photophone stringer and self-taught master o' intuitive objectivity. While under the influence o' an experimental drug, he wrote the universally acclaimed book *Toward Equitocracy*— though some say he cribbed a lot from Sophronia Cleer's works in it. Mainly he disagreed with her premise that *Homo sapiens* could peacefully coexist and fraternize with other species; he said that absolute equality for all humans is possible only if we avoid contact with aliens and exterminate all freaks, mutants, and other genetic deviants in our race. Anyway, the book became the foundation of a strongly militaristic political doctrine with Hanoleon as its Prime Equal, as the PHAP leader is called. Since then the PHAPists have kept the IFIBists out of their territories, while extending their own dominion over thirty-nine planets with a combined population o'—"

"All right, we don't have to go too deeply into that now," Ranger cut in. "The important thing to realize is that both groups are ruthless, aggressive totalitarians with differing ideologies but identical goals: annexing every habitable planet in the universe and conquering or destroying every last member of all intelligent species. They stick fanatically to that plan whether they're fighting each other or working together under a temporary truce—as they are now—to subdue and carve up neutral worlds. They're especially keen on competing with us independent explorers in finding unoccupied planets that can be colonized by their expanding slave populations. Exiling discontented subjects has always been a good way for tyrants to reduce the chances of a revolt that might overthrow their oppressive governments."

"But why canna the other worlds—those wi' truly democratic governments—get together and force the IFIB and PHAP to be more peaceful?" Dawnboy asked. "It seems that a powerful organization like the Sentient Species Association could get enough warships and troops together to defeat both empires."

Ranger smiled ruefully. "I'm afraid you still have a lot to learn about interstellar politics. For all the SSA's pretense of being an effective universal regulatory agency, it's really little more than just a neutral meeting ground where the representatives of its member governments come to discuss their differences. Occasionally they even manage to work out peaceful settlements for disputes that might otherwise have led to war. But the numerous independent worlds and small confederations are rarely able to overcome their own petty jealousies enough to make a united stand against aggressions committed by the big powers. That isn't surprising, considering that the IFIB and PHAP were original Covenant Members of the SSA and they pretty well dominate most of the meetings of both the Select Conclave and Common Assemblage branches. About the only important thing they've ever agreed on was the establishment of the Protectorate Patrol, which does a fair job of fighting space pirates and keeping the natives of under-developed planets from being too badly corrupted by outsiders. But they're too few and far between to be a significant peacekeeping force when the big boys start playing rough."

"You haven't told him how all that relates to you and Rothfeller Hughes," Lulu reminded Ranger.

"Oh, yes. Sorry about that, Son. Sometimes I digress so far from the point that I can't find my way back. Well, you remember when we were on Apache High-lands and I told you that I'd received a message that others were interested in the unclaimed planet I hoped to locate? The message was from Hughes; he had dis-covered that one of his employees had leaked informa-tion about my planet hunt to either IFIB or PHAP agents. Evidently it was to the former; so Hughes has obviously invited their exploration ship's captain here to try to determine just how much the man knows about my plans. That can't be very much, or he would already be on his way to the planet's sector, instead of coming here to scrounge around for more data."

"Wish I could be there to see you, Hughes, and the IFIB captain trying to feel each other out," Lulu said cheerfully. "That should be quite an entertaining show."

"Your sense of humor should be arrested for violat-ing the SSA ban on hallucinogenic warfare," Ranger said sourly. "I'm sorry now that I even revealed so much of my plans to Hughes, when we met at the In-dustrialists' and Financiers' Convention on Puerto Mi-ami three months ago. But I needed his financial sup-port, and we've been friends for so many years that I thought he was the one man in the universe who could be trusted to keep a secret."

"Well, at least ye've no need to worry about *me* spill-ing anything," Dawnboy said. "Because ye haven't told me anything about the planet yet."

"You'll be told all you need to know when you need to know it," Ranger promised. "Right now, let's go aground and meet the poor little rich folks."

"Wait! You haven't heard *all* the good news," Lulu said. "While we were talking now, a PHAP battle frigate spaced in, also bound for *Tres Ojos*."

"You sure know how to make my day, don't you?" Ranger growled. "Come on, son. Let's grav out of here before she reports an outbreak of Nonithian spore pox in the hydroponics tanks."

12

THEY STEPPED OUT of the air lock and drifted in a free fall that steadily gained momentum as they drew closer to *Tres Ojos*'s artificial Earth-normal gravity field. Being above the asteroid's atmosphere, they had to wear vac-suits, so Dawnboy took advantage of the light-filtering properties of his transparent helmet to look over Capitalia. The view wasn't very inspiring.

The planet's permanent ammonia cloud covering was of a dull seasick-greenish hue and monotonously featureless. Even the two other rings, from this angle, appeared flattened and insignificant. He guessed it was just as well that the Capitalians were so rich, because money was about the only thing that could possibly make their world a desirable place to live.

"Grav on!" Ranger's voice snapped in his earphone, and Dawnboy's right hand leaped to the control buttons on his chest harness as he saw he had entered *Tres Ojos*'s atmosphere and was plunging groundward at an alarming speed. Daydreaming in free fall was a dangerous habit he would have to break, before it broke him. He came to a jerky midair halt that left him breathless.

Ranger floated down beside him and they opened their visors to the warm, sweet air before continuing to the mansion. They came in low over the reflecting pool, and only then did Dawnboy begin to appreciate fully the great beauty and tremendous size of the place.

The pool area alone could have parked a hundred *Gayhearts*, with room to spare. Graceful fountains sprayed out multicolored waters while ducks, otters, brown-haired fish from Apache Highlands, and other varieties of aquatic life-forms swam lazily about. Along the tiled sides of the pool stood not just impressive modern and antique still statues, but even group sets of cybersculpture whose figures moved and spoke to perform entertaining dramas.

Approaching the main building, Dawnboy felt like an insect about to land on a mountain. Unbuttressed walls soared upward over a hundred feet to support domes of synthesteel that could be made transparent or opaque by altering the energy charge flowing through them. Rising above the domes were slender minarets whose delicately decorative appearance concealed their practical usefulness as observation towers for armed guards. For although crime was rare in this society, Ranger explained, occasionally a Capitalian did try to steal business secrets from a rival, or even kidnap a member of his family. And, too, there was always the possibility that a cunning space marauder might find a way to slip past the lunar guard posts. All of the real wealth was kept safely in burglarproof vaults down on the planet's surface, but several fortunes could be picked up even out here on Easy Street, if a thief were clever and lucky enough to get away with it.

They alighted on the huge colonnaded front porch before a thirty-foot-wide doorway covered by synthesteel lamé curtains that were rigid and tough enough to resist any force short of a luxium-powered cutting torch.

"Open sesame!" Ranger called. "Or whatever this week's password is."

The curtains instantly became as pliable as silk, as their energy charge was changed. Then they parted to reveal the blue-skinned man standing just inside the doorway. Up close he was even more impressive, with his seven-foot-tall frame carrying some three hundred pounds of fat-free muscle and bone.

"Welcome to *Tres Ojos,* gentlemen," David Goliath said, smiling. "Please come in."

"Thanks, David," Ranger said, going forward to exchange warm handshakes with the blue giant.

Dawnboy was introduced and had his hand crushed nearly to a pulp. He couldn't help liking the big mutant, however, even if his manner was similar to that of the fawning teddysaurs of Cretacia, who had on occasion been know to gobble up their masters in overzealous displays of affection.

Besides his swimsuit, David was wearing antigrav jackboots. At the snap of his fingers, a robo-valet rolled up to offer similar footgear to Ranger and Dawnboy. They put on the boots and gave their vac-suits and antigrav packs to the machine, which scurried away to have them cleaned and serviced.

"The family is in the grotto room," David said. "Right this way." He turned and took a single stride that carried him fifty feet.

Dawnboy only knew about antigrav boots from his studies, so he needed a few moments to get accustomed to covering great distances by effortlessly flexing his toes. But he soon saw the necessity of such footgear in a house of this size. The foyer and visitors' gallery alone appeared spacious enough to contain the entire MacCochise castle. Furthermore, everything about the place—the lavish furnishings, ornaments, its architecture—were on a massive scale. Yet all was so tastefully done, that even as he felt put-off by the obviously shameless display of conspicuous consumption, he couldn't help admiring the grandiose *style* that just managed to carry it off. He understood now why clan law forbade under penalty of death the importation of modern conveniences and luxury items. Any brave exposed to surroundings like these for very long would become too soft ever to go on the warpath again. Lulu had been right when she called this a decadent, materialistic society whose arrogant vanity would surely cause the gods one day to destroy it. But in all fairness he had to add wistfully: what a way to go!

Following his father's lead, Dawnboy sprang through a doorway and found himself in the room where they had first seen David on the photophone. The swimming pool looked more like a small lake, complete with a few boats and a sandy island where lazy flamingos drowsed on one leg. The room was cavernous in every sense of the word, with rocky, uneven walls and limestone stalagmites and stalactites that, along with the underwater lighting and deep, shadowy recesses, gave the place an eerie but restful charm. The man and woman they had seen materialize were at poolside, relaxing with drinks around a table and robo-bar.

At Ranger's arrival, they sprang to their feet and greeted him with happy embraces. When Dawnboy came up, Juan Orfo gave him a firm handclasp and appeared to be not such a bad fellow after all—now that he'd had time to unwind with a couple of drinks. Helen insisted on kissing Dawnboy and making the usual female inane observations about he had grown up since she last saw him. When that was over, Juan thrust a starjuice cocktail into Ranger's hand and asked what Dawnboy was drinking.

When Dawnboy requested only a cup of citroffee, he snorted: "Hell, kid, you'll never blast off on that low-grade booster fuel. Let me get you a Capitalist's Ambition—two swallows and you'll think you own the universe."

"Make it an extra-weak one," Ranger said, overriding Juan's order to the robo-tender. Dawnboy was grateful for that when he sipped the creamy-smooth liquid: it made his stomach feel like a sun going nova when it hit bottom.

"Well, what have you two been doing with yourselves?" Ranger asked when they were all seated around the table.

Helen giggled. "Look behind you, and you'll see. This is the surprise I mentioned."

Ranger turned his head as a robo-baby carriage rolled up to him and opened its covering to reveal two sleeping infants. "Well, I'll be . . . When did this happen? And why wasn't I told? I didn't even know you were expecting."

"It happened about six weeks ago, and how could I tell you with you gallivanting around the universe and not keeping in touch?" Helen replied, coming around the table to tenderly tuck in the babies' blankets. "It was only blind luck that Daddy ran into you at the convention, and you know he never thinks to talk of anything but business."

"This one's Rothy and that one's Ricky, after my grandfather," Juan said, pointing at each baby in turn. "I can always tell because he has the same cranky expression Grandpa had. We thought about naming one after you, but we couldn't bring ourselves to call the poor kid Rangy."

"Just as well; he'd probably never have forgiven you for it," Ranger said. "Next time we come, I'll bring them presents, if I can think of what you give to the baby who has everything. Are they . . . all right?"

"Yes, they're perfectly normal," Helen smiled. "We were worried about that, too, but the doctors say there's a good chance that the wild genes have finally been bred out of the family. At least as far as my children are concerned, thanks to my mother's normality."

"Is yer mother still living?" Dawnboy asked.

"Yes . . . but not here. She was one of the most beautiful women on New Scandinavia—a prize catch for even a man as rich as Daddy. He offered her a fortune if she would stay with him for five years and give him at least one child. At the end of that time she could either leave or renew her contract, if she had come to care enough for him by then. Well, evidently she took a long, hard look at me and decided to quit while she was ahead."

"Oh," Dawnboy said, slightly embarrassed. He hadn't meant to pry into private family matters; he'd just wanted to keep the conversation from becoming boringly centered around the babies.

He looked up to see a vac-suited figure on an antigrav scooter come zooming at them. The rider came on at full speed. Helen gasped and protectively pushed the baby carriage out of the way.

At the last possible instant, the driver cut power and twisted the handlebars sharply to bring his mount to an abrupt halt just inches from the table. He stepped down, chuckling at their relieved expressions, his dark-tinted visor obscuring his features.

"Better watch those crazy shenanigans, Daddy," Helen scolded. "What happened—did the limousine break down again?"

"No, I felt restless, so I scooted in the last few miles," the man said, stripping off his vac-suit.

He was medium-sized, robust, and appeared to be in his late fifties or early sixties. His swarthy complexion, kinky red hair, aquiline nose, and three bright-blue eyes indicated a mixed ancestry that hadn't turned out too badly. In fact, his overall appearance was so ordinary that it took a moment for the full impact of the extra sight organ in the center of his forehead to sink into Dawnboy's consciousness.

Probably even the third eye wouldn't have been very disturbing, if it had matched the other two. But it was larger and seemed to protrude slightly as the small iris moved independently, constantly roving back and forth, up and down—as if never quite satisfied with what it saw.

And just what did it see? Dawnboy wondered uneasily about that, recalling old Apache Highlands legends about demon-touched sorcerers, and witches who possessed strange terrifying powers. Of course that was just superstitious nonsense, as his new scientific knowledge made laughably clear. But still . . .

Hughes kissed his daughter, nodded to his son-in-law, and leaned down to exchange baby talk with his grandsons. Then, family obligations taken care of, he turned his brisk businessman's gaze to Ranger and accepted a drink from the robo-tender.

"So you finally got here? Good; we can't afford to waste any more time." He looked Dawnboy over. "This your son? Fine-looking specimen. Not surprising, considering the good stock he comes from. I'll give you a hundred thousand stellars for him."

"No sale," Ranger smiled, before Dawnboy could decide if he should feel insulted or flattered by the offer.

"Just as well," Hughes grunted. He then gave his vac-suit and scooter to David, who left the room with them, and turned back to Ranger. "Nothing new to report on the situation since my last message to you. I still haven't determined who the traitor in my organization is, though I have strong suspicions. Evidently he informed both the IFIB and PHAP about your plans, so I've invited the commanders of their two exploration ships to dinner here tonight."

"Yes, we just heard that they've entered Capitalian space," Ranger said. "Do you think we'll be able to learn anything useful from them?"

"Worth a try. Come into the den now; I want to have a few words with you in private. Helen, see that our young guest is properly entertained. Show him around the house, and if he sees anything that takes his fancy, it's his. With the exception of my favorites, which you know about."

"Yes, Daddy," Helen said as her father donned antigrav boots and bounded out of the room with Ranger.

13

RANGER FOLLOWED HIS host down a huge corridor until they reached a semicircular door that dilated in response to their body heat. They entered a room that, compared to the rest of the house, seemed claustrophobically small. Hughes gestured Ranger to an old-fashioned upholstered chair and seated himself behind an antique desk that appeared to be made of genuine oak wood. In fact, most of the room's furnishings were archaically nonmechanical, although there was a photophone wallscreen.

The room's cozy, cluttered, and nonfunctional atmosphere always put Ranger nostalgically at ease. It provided Hughes with one of his few means of escaping the pressures of work, and his stern features instantly relaxed as he sat behind the desk. More significantly, the room expressed a friendly, informal side of the business tycoon's personality that few men were privileged to observe. Ranger considered himself lucky to be among that select group.

Hughes finished the drink he had brought with him, put down the glass, and reached out to a row of buttons on the desktop. The photophone screen brightened with the image of a balding, stockily built Eurasian male of about Ranger's age.

"Yes, sir?" the man said, looking respectfully at Hughes.

"Do you have those reports ready for me yet?" Hughes asked. Then he said to Ranger: "You know Major Yomata, my Security Chief, don't you?"

"Of course," Ranger said. "How have you been, Nikki?"

"Fine, thanks, Ranger," the major smiled. "You're looking good." He shifted his gaze back to Hughes. "Yes, sir. I have the data all arranged . . ." He touched a button on his desk and his image was replaced by that of an older man with gray-streaked hair. "Homer Arklas, a vice-president of your Intergal Shipping Company," said the major. "Has a weakness for gambling and other expensive habits. We couldn't find any hard evidence against him, but he has been living conspicuously beyond his means lately. And then there are . . ."

The pictures of six men and women, all of them employed by Hughes, flashed on the screen in succession, as Major Yomata gave brief accounts of their backgrounds and recent activities.

Hughes listened carefully, but when the report was completed shook his head decisively. "No, I'm confident the leak didn't come from any of them. They all have had personal and money problems in the past and they know they can depend on me for a loan if they really need help. They wouldn't feel desperate enough to sell information to our enemies, when they know how I would react to that."

Yomata looked relieved. "I'm glad to hear that, sir. I had cleared most of them in my own mind, but I thought I should bring them to your attention."

"You're doing well, Major. Keep digging, and let me know the moment you find anything even slightly suspicious." Hughes blanked the screen and looked at Ranger. "Any suggestions?"

Ranger shrugged. "It's your organization. The only thing I can think of is, maybe you should hire a Brainsponge to run a telepathic check on any of your people whom you think may have betrayed you to IFIB and PHAP."

"I considered that, but decided against it. Brainsponges are too ethical to probe anyone's mind without obtaining his permission, and a lot of people just don't like to have their mental privacy invaded. The same goes for lie detectors and truth serums. I can't fire otherwise loyal workers just because they refuse to submit to such tests."

"It's a tough problem," Ranger agreed. "Do you suspect anyone in particular?"

Hughes hesitated, scowling down at his hands, then said: "Frankly, I at first hoped that Juan could be proven the guilty party. But I'm afraid that's just wicked wishful thinking on my part. I have always hated him and would welcome an opportunity to see him disgraced in Helen's eyes. He is obviously just a fortune hunter, and I resent him trying to use her to get my money."

"Well, that's hardly reason to call him a traitor," Ranger said. Because he sincerely liked Juan, he added: "I think you're being very unfair to him. After all, he was a great success in his own profession once, and he just might turn out to be a good businessman after all. Even if he did marry Helen for your money, she is definitely in love with him. So the best you can hope for is that he'll learn how to help her manage the fortune when you retire."

"You're right, much as I hate to admit it," Hughes grumbled. "And he does seem to be getting the hang of business at last. Just recently he managed to put over a very tricky and profitable speculation in Upper Pleiaden touch-spice futures. If he keeps that up, I may have to give in to Helen's request that I make him a full partner." He grimaced distastefully at the prospect. "But my family problems aren't your concern. Nor is it your responsibility to find out who betrayed us. You'll have your hands full just coping with the IFIB and PHAP military agents who have been sent to grab your planet. I understand their ships are equipped with the latest electronic tracking devices."

"I've had some experience with them before," Ranger said. "Have you learned anything else about them?"

"Just a few details about the vessels and their commanders." Hughes activated the screen again. "I'll give you a tape of the ships' technical descriptions, so that you can study it later. That stuff is just gibberish to me. But here's a picture of Commodore Second Class Hildegriff val Murphy, who commands the PHAP battle frigate *Littlegart*. I wasn't sure at first that she actually is a woman. She certainly looks tough enough to put any man in his place."

Ranger saw what he meant. The PHAP officer was about forty and her body appeared solidly well muscled in a drab unisex uniform. Her squarish face was topped by a rigid crew cut of black hair and small brown eyes stared coldly out at them. "Yes, I would say she is a lady who can take care of herself. PHAP will be getting plenty more like her, both male and female, now that they have annexed Reichworld." He peered at her rows of campaign ribbons. "I think one of those is for the Hanoleon Star, PHAP's highest combat medal. The Prime Equal himself awards it to outstanding warriors."

"Annexation isn't the right word for the way those

two militant powers joined forces," Hughes pointed out. "Although the Reichworld empire consisted of only eight planets in three systems, their arrogance and the total militarization of their people made them feel equal to PHAP's superior numbers. So the PHAP government had to agree to give the Reichworlders full citizenship before the latter agreed to the merger. In fact, Prime Equal Charlkan was even persuaded to accept the Reichworld Dolfman, Sigfritz the Third, as his regent and successor. Now, with Charlkan getting on in years, it seems certain that an ambitious Reichworlder will be the next Prime Equal of the combined empires."

"What a development for the peaceful planets to look forward to," Ranger sighed. "I almost wish PHAP and IFIB would have a total war and wipe each other out, but that would also cause much death and misery for innocent beings around them. Anyway, thanks for telling me that. I've been so busy and so far out of touch with civilization lately that I haven't kept up with current events."

"Sometimes I think ignorance is the best policy, as hopes for a lasting interstellar peace grow dimmer every day," Hughes said gloomily. He changed the picture on the screen. "Here's Ship-Controller Autry Lopezov, of the IFIB starcruiser *Dzuntoy*. He doesn't appear to be as imposing as Commodore val Murphy, but he must be competent or he wouldn't have been given this mission."

Ranger stared transfixed at the blandly good-humored expression of a man who appeared to be a few years older than Hughes. His plump face, soft hands, and twinkling blue eyes made him look like the ideal grandfather-figure who loves everyone and wouldn't dream of harming an insect. On Apache Highlands he would have been taken for a garrulous shopkeeper or freehold farmer with an equally fat and jolly wife.

Ranger chuckled softly to himself. "Well, Autry, I guess it was inevitable that we should meet again someday."

"You know him?" Hughes asked in surprise.

"Well enough not to underestimate him," Ranger answered soberly. "He's the kind of man who enjoys playing the fool, until he can catch his enemies off-guard. Then he strikes with deadly accuracy."

"I know the type. When did you first meet him?"

"About seven years ago, during the short war between IFIB and PHAP over possession of the Pentaped worlds. As you know, IFIB managed to retain control of all of those planets except Trusky, but PHAP gave them a tough fight. Late in the war, space hostilities around Trusky became so intense that all trade with the planet was cut off and its inhabitants faced starvation. So the SSA's Department of Welfare and Compassion chartered several civilian cargo ships to take emergency relief supplies to the Pentapeds there. It was a dangerous run, but the hazardous duty pay was so tempting that I signed on. I got through safely on my first two trips, but on my third time out Autry Lopezov got on my tail. He was commanding a heavily armed sub-ether destroyer, and I didn't feel like committing suicide by trying to resist that much firepower, so I surrendered."

"I don't blame you," Hughes said understandingly.

"That's what Autry said, when he and his officers entertained me in their wardroom. They were most anxious to cheer me up, since they knew what would happen to me when they turned me over to their political superiors. But I guess I don't have to tell *you* about that." Ranger glanced at his friend's impassive features. Sometimes if was difficult to remember that Hughes had not always been so rich and powerful that even important leaders hesitated to act against him. "Well, they took my ship in tow and it looked as if my life as a free man was finished. Then suddenly two PHAP ships jumped us, and everybody around me scrambled to their battle stations. In the confusion, I managed to get back aboard my ship and slip away from them."

"A lucky break for you," Hughes said. "Have you encountered Lopezov again since then?"

"Yes, we've run across each other now and again, under more peaceful circumstances. He has always been very friendly and considerate. Like most military professionals, he prefers to do his job and not pay much attention to his government's propaganda. But deep down I suppose he is as dedicated to the ideals of Otherism as any member of his society. Nonetheless, I rather like and respect Autry. I don't relish being pitted against him again, but at least he is a familiar opponent. I don't quite know what to make of the other one, Commodore val Murphy."

14

"I HOPE MR. Hughes didna mean what he said about giving me anything I want here," Dawnboy said, fighting down the urge to take the old man at his word. "I wouldna ken what to choose—everything is so tempting."

"It was more or less a formality," Juan said. "Capitalians are notorious for their generosity. But the receiver of an expensive gift is expected to outdo the giver by refusing it, or donating it to charity."

They had just entered a large room containing the Hughes Currency Museum, the most extensive and expensive private collection of its kind in the known universe.

Shortly after Rothfeller Hughes and Ranger had left them in the grotto room, the twins had awakened hungrily. So Helen had excused herself to feed them and Juan had taken on the duty of showing Dawnboy around the house. It was an exhausting tour, even in antigrav boots, and the young Apache was so dazzled by the rich variety of things he saw that he wondered if he could ever again be impressed by displays of great wealth.

Juan leaned against the robo-tender, which followed

at their heels like a well-trained domestic animal, and gestured carelessly with the glass that seemed to be a permanent fixture in his left hand. "Behold the evidence of intelligent beings' search for the perfect medium of exchange." He half grinned. "I doubt that any other activity has had so much loving attention lavished on it, or has caused so much joy and misery. Before you is a twelve-foot stone tablet once used as money by the Yap Islanders of ancient Earth. Over there is a facsimile of a human slave with his monetary value branded on his forehead. Such unfortunates were once traded like cattle in the ZuJu Empire of the Magellanic Clouds, and some say the practice still persists in remote backward areas. Over here, in this case, we have an authentic letter of credit tape issued by the High Intender of Fabrica. His creditors thought the tapes were as good as gold, until they discovered that the tapes erased themselves when presented for payment."

"Speaking o' gold," Dawnboy said, taking something from his pocket. "Could ye explain Capitalian money to me? I listened to a lesson tape on it, but the whole subject is still somewhat a mystery to me."

Juan looked at the thin plastic disk in Dawnboy's hand and smiled. "Oh, yes, that's our basic monetary unit: the stellar. The only reason it is difficult to understand is because the principle behind it is so simple that economists have deliberately tried to make it seem complicated. Economists, like all pseudoscientific charlatans, know that they can hold on to their high-paying jobs only as long as they keep the common people convinced that money matters are so mysterious that only economists can understand them. You see how the stellar is stamped with the design of a ten-point star? Each point can be detached and reattached independently to make up a unit of any desired denomination."

"I ken that much. The idea comes from the ancient American dollar, which could be broken into eight pieces, or bits. They were referred to as two bits, four bits, and so on."

"That's right," Juan agreed. "But unlike the dollar in

its later years of paper-and-ink degradation, the stellar has more than just symbolic value. Each point of the star contains one one-hundredth of an ounce of gold, clearly visible in the transparent plastic. It is the simplest and most easily circulated currency so far evolved and its use is rapidly spreading throughout the universe."

Dawnboy nodded. "Aye, we've even heard o' stellars on Apache Highlands, although I never saw one there. Clansmen prefer the solid feel o' metal coins, when they bother wi' money at all."

Juan ordered another drink and continued speaking without seeming to notice Dawnboy's remarks. "To add to the stellar's convenience by safeguarding it against counterfeiting, the Newtonian scientists have produced an inexpensive and compact energycell-powered device that gives a spectroscopic analysis of any gold-bearing object pressed against it. The gadget is called a touchstone, after the ancient practice of rubbing gold or silver against a piece of jasper or basalt to judge its quality by the streak left on the stone. So the stellar has a good chance of remaining a solidly reliable form of money as long as ambitious politicians don't meddle with it."

Juan paused only long enough to gulp down a large swallow of his fresh drink. "Many times throughout history, government power-seekers and their idealistic advisers have tried to do away with gold as a form of money. Some high-handed leaders with no respect for civil rights have even passed laws prohibiting the private possession and exchange of gold. They gave various reasons for doing so: gold was a barbarous relic of no practical use to anyone but jewelers and dentists; its possession encouraged people to hoard their wealth instead of putting it into circulation, where the government could collect taxes on it; and a citizen's preference for gold expressed a lack of faith in fiat money, which meant he lacked faith in his government's promise to guarantee the value of its paper money. The perfect economic system, the anti-gold theorists argued, would be one in which citizens gave up their dirty old gold and believed their government's claim that its paper money was worth what the government said it was worth.

"As persuasive as those arguments were," Juan continued, "they failed to outweigh the fact that gold has been repeatedly proved to be more reliable than any government's ability to keep its promises, or sometimes even to survive. When a man saw his well-ordered society collapsing into chaos, his property and security lost to invading armies or domestic looters, his own and his family's lives endangered—then it was mighty comforting to have a bag of the precious yellow metal on hand to snatch up as he ran for hiding. Even during the conquest of the original America, the crafty Yankees who had put some of their assets into gold had an advantage over their less-prudent fellow-citizens. The Rus-China or Sov-Nazi occupation forces turned out to be easily corruptible by bribe offers and black-market deals, despite their avowed intention to establish a new world order of perfect communism in which money would be nonexistent. That is a strangely inexplicable weakness that seems to crop up in every idealistic, anti-materialistic reform movement, including those of the IFIB and PHAP."

Dawnboy was intrigued by Juan's long-winded discourse, although the man's sarcastic tone was irritating. When Juan was too busy drinking to talk for a moment, Dawnboy said: " 'Tis indeed a puzzle why gold has been the most popular form o' money o'er the centuries." He stared spellbound at the shining specks sealed in plastic. "Just the sight o' it fascinates a mon's imagination."

"That's no mystery," Juan replied, holding out his glass to be refilled. "Gold has natural advantages over all other media of exchange. Being the most corrosion-resistant, malleable, and ductile metal, gold can be easily divided into smaller portions or merged with larger ones without losing its value. Because gold is a relatively scarce element, it has always been regarded as a luxury item. That guarantees its continuing demand, since desires for luxuries are eternal and unlimited.

Also, gold's classification as a luxury item gives it a high unit value, making it conveniently portable. It can be easily carried in small amounts that can be exchanged for much larger amounts of other materials and services.

"All of these innate advantages of a gold-based monetary system have been discovered by men through thousands of years of trial-and-error experience in the business of exchanging goods and services, even if they aren't fully understood by those who consider themselves above such vulgar activities. The incomparable value and convenience of gold has been established scientifically where it really matters—in the great laboratory of life. That is basically why gold has always incurred the wrath of economists and political scientists, who traditionally hate the unyielding objectivity of science almost as much as they dislike the rational restrictions that politics imposes on their desires to ram their untested theories down the public's throat."

"I never thought o' science in that way," Dawnboy said, turning the new idea over in his mind.

"That's a dangerous mistake people often make," Juan said. "They fall into the habit of thinking that scientists are priests or magicians with supernatural powers for understanding the mysteries of life. When scientists are treated with such fearful reverence, they are tempted to exploit the people. Some worlds have even been ruled by governments of scientists who have used their people as experimental animals. And many pseudoscientific gold-haters greeted the advent of star travel as a possible fulfillment of their long-promised liberation of mankind from the gilded yoke. 'Just you wait,' they gleefully predicted, 'until space explorers encounter highly advanced civilizations that have learned the secrets of perpetual peace and productivity without knowing what gold is, or until gold is found in such vast quantities that it will become the most common and debased element in the universe.'

"In a way those prognostications did come true. Rich unexploited gold deposits were discovered in distant star systems. But high development and transportation costs, along with the increasing demands of growing populations, served to keep the price of gold fairly stable over the centuries. Even more ironic is the fact that most alien civilizations that managed to get along without gold until they encountered humans have considered their lack of the yellow stuff as more of a handicap than a blessing; instead of teaching us how to live without gold, they have accepted it as a handy commercial medium. So, whether we like it or not, the theoretically unscientific, obsolete, and impractical gold standard and capitalism have gone hand-in-hand with human expansion in the universe. In spite of the efforts of powerful forces like IFIB and PHAP, Capitalia and the other business communities have managed so far to keep most of the universal economy 'as sound as a stellar'—as the popular saying has it."

15

"I DON'T QUITE know what to make of Commodore val Murphy," Autry Lopezov said, tugging at the high, tight collar of his dress-uniform tunic. His neck seemed to have gotten fatter even while he'd been dieting a few pounds off his ample paunch, and he longed to get back to the comfort of less formal attire.

"She's simple enough to understand," Lieutenant Primary Grade Alexia Ustich remarked in a bored tone. "She is just a typical Reichworlder: brave, intelligent, strong-willed, hardworking—and totally unimaginative. If we had to face her in battle I would be worried, but I don't think she will be a threat to us on a mission that requires more guile and creative thinking than raw courage and swift reflexes."

"You're probably right, but I don't want to risk underestimating her. Oh, damn this hangman's noose!" The plump ship-controller angrily tore open his tunic and rubbed his chafed neck. "I'm not going to strangle myself just to obey Fleet Regulations."

He walked across his cabin to the wardrobe locker and selected a semi-formal tunic with a V-neck. He sighed happily as he slipped into the garment.

"You should always wear this sort of uniform," Alexia smiled, helping him fasten the tunic's catches. "It shows off your physique."

"I can dress myself," Lopezov said stiffly. "And save your flattery for the younger men."

A shrewd, experienced commanding officer, he had never permitted himself to become intimate with a female crew member, not even one who viewed him affectionately as a father-figure. Still, he had to admit he enjoyed being fussed over by a beautiful young woman, especially one who always knew the right thing to say. But then that was part of Alexia's job as *Dzuntoy*'s communications and conditioning officer. She was a qualified cyberpsychologist with an extraordinary understanding of human nature for a girl of twenty-six.

"Well then, dress yourself and let's get back to our guests," Alexia urged. "Frankly I don't care much for their company. But we might as well try to learn all we can about them, since that's what you invited them aboard for."

"What, you aren't anxious to rejoin the handsome Sub-Captain Alrik Bell-the-Cat?" Lopezov asked with a sly grin.

"Oh, please spare me," Alexia begged. "I don't mind a little conceit in a man, but he thinks he invented male sex appeal." Then, relenting a little, she said: "All right, I'll admit that I find him attractive and charming, even for a Paraterran. But he's too superficial to be my type. Even if we were both on the same side, I don't think I could ever become interested in him."

"I'm glad to hear that, since you and he are not on the same side," Lopezov said. "But don't let him know how you feel about him just yet. He might let something important slip, if you keep him relaxed and hopeful."

"Yes, sir. I know my job," Alexia said dutifully.

"Good. Then let's return to the wardroom before our PHAP friends become restless at our absence. Oh, just a moment."

Lopezov used his earphone and throat mike to contact his ship's bridge. The duty officer there reported that they were proceeding according to schedule. The PHAP battle frigate drifted alongside them, and *Tres Ojos* was still half an orbit away.

Lopezov and Alexia left his cabin and walked back to the wardroom. The past hour with Commodore val Murphy and Captain Bell-the-Cat had produced so few positive results that Lopezov almost regretted having invited them aboard. But the two ships had entered Capitalian space almost simultaneously, so he couldn't just ignore the battle frigate's existence. And when the PHAP commander had established photophone contact to wish him the best regards of her government, he had been required by common military courtesy to ask her over for a brief visit.

To his unspoken relief, she had brought along only one of her officers and the enlisted operator of her shuttlegig. Although IFIB was presently at peace with the universe, he didn't care to have several members of a potentially belligerent power looking over his ship. Besides, one never knew when hotheaded crewmen might remember old battles and try to settle personal scores with their fists. After all, now that the PHAP empire included the Reichworlders, he couldn't expect those savages to behave as politely as his own well-disciplined men and women.

When they reached the wardroom door, Alexia said: "By the way, Commodore val Murphy planted a spy-bug in the female officers' lounge when I went in there with her. The poor dear thought she was being so clever that I didn't have the heart to let on I'd seen her do it."

"And I saw Bell-the-Cat place one under the cyber-domino table," Lopezov said. "They probably have half of the ship bugged by now. It will be good practice for the crew to search them out, after our guests have left."

"It's such a futile waste of time," Alexia said sadly. "Do you think their people will miss any of the bugs we put on her shuttlegig?"

"Probably not, but we can hope for the best." The door slid open and Lopezov put on a broad smile. "Here we are back at last. Please forgive us for leaving you for so long, but duty calls. I hope you weren't bored without us."

Commodore val Murphy smiled back at him, looking up from the low sofa she shared with an IFIB officer. "Not at all, Controller. Your Executive Officer has had me enthralled with descriptions of his visit to Old Earth. I hope I will be able to go there someday and rediscover my cultural heritage. Even if the poor planet has degenerated to a primitive backwater of civilization, at least one can observe our species in its purest form there."

She lowered her voice and cast a meaningful glance at Lancet Habbth, the Pentaped Medical Officer of the *Dzuntoy*. Habbth continued his game of cyberdominoes with Alrik Bell-the-Cat, seemingly unaware of the woman's reference to him.

Lopezov nodded understandingly. and ignored Alexia's angry flush at the Commodore's disgusting bigotry. Obviously, he thought, she was an old-line follower of Victor Hanoleon's rabid preachings against nonhumans. Unlike her young sub-captain, she had not adapted to the recent revisions in PHAP ideology that encouraged toleration of alien sentients. It was ironic how often new converts to PHAPism, such as the Reichworlders, became more zealous advocates of the movement's fundamental principles than those who had belonged to it for generations. But Lopezov supposed that the Reichworlders had to have somebody to hate in order to keep their warlike spirit constantly at a high pitch. He was glad he had never gotten involved with IFIB's political and propaganda confusions. Of course, he had learned the popular slogans and quotations from

Sophronia Cleer, so that no one could ever question his loyalty. But for the most part he had been pleased just to do his duty as a soldier and leave the intellectual intriguing to those whose minds were better suited for it. Now, with his retirement nearing, he looked forward to a long rest in a quiet country cottage on his homeworld of Surmar, where his wife had waited patiently for him all these years. This would probably be his last mission, and he was almost sorry that he could only make it successful at the expense of his old friendly adversary Ranger Farstar. Well, at least it would give him the satisfaction of paying Ranger back for the embarrassing way Ranger had gotten away from him during the Trusky campaign.

Commander Bushkow, the Executive Officer, rose from the sofa and bowed to val Murphy. "Please excuse me. I go on duty soon and I haven't had my lunch yet. It's been a pleasure chatting with you, Commodore."

Val Murphy smiled after Bushkow as he left the room. "What a delightful man! I must compliment you, Controller, on the superior quality of your crew members."

"Thank you. Most of them have been with me for years." Lopezov took a seat facing her. "I like to think of them as members of my own family." He glanced at the cybersculpture bust of Chief Cleerhead Dabosalski in its shrinelike wall niche and quickly added: "Which is of course the way I feel toward all members of the, shall we say, Family."

The bust served ostensibly as a symbol of IFIB's spiritual and political unity. Its tapes were programmed to speak quotations from Sophronia Cleer's thoughts and other inspiring words at unpredictable intervals. But the statue also contained snooper-recording devices that only Alexia was allowed to monitor for her secret reports to the fleet's Psyche Police Division. No IFIB citizen ever knew when a few careless words might cause him to be summoned before a Loyalty Enforcement Review Board. Therefore, most IFIBists were careful not to utter any careless words.

"I can see why you are so proud of them," Commodore val Murphy said. "I wonder if I might have another cup of your excellent citroffee?"

"Certainly." Lopezov signaled to one of the Pentaped serving stewards.

The nonviolent creatures were useless in a fight, but they made fine servants and physicians. Lancet Habbth was one of the best surgeons in the fleet, and several of the *Dzuntoy*'s crew members owed their lives to the delicate skill of the eight slender fingers at the end of his multijointed feeding limb. Actually a Pentaped has only four locomotive limbs, and the uppermost pair can be used as arms as well as legs. The first human explorers of Pentaped worlds presumed that the intelligent natives were five-footed because they were observed at a distance while eating. To feed itself in its natural habitat, a Pentaped places all four feet solidly on the ground and uses the highly flexible fingers of its feeding limb to pluck the tiny grass seeds that are its staple diet. The humans soon learned they had been mistaken in thinking the feeding limb was a fifth leg, but by then it had become an established habit to call the natives Pentapeds. The natives themselves didn't care what they were called; they could tolerate almost anything, except hostility.

The steward brought them two cups of citroffee and val Murphy politely refused Lopezov's offer to lace it with something stronger. Lopezov reflected gloomily on the futility of trying to loosen a Reichworlder's tongue with alcohol, or anything else.

Val Murphy talked amiably about shipboard activities and other unimportant subjects, but she coolly evaded his efforts to probe her knowledge of Ranger Farstar's planet-hunting expedition. He thought she probably knew even less about the venture than he did. Lopezov was annoyed to have her meddling in what he considered to be a personal contest between himself and Ranger, but he doubted that she would be a serious threat to his success. What he most needed was more information about Ranger's plans and how Rothfeller Hughes figured in them. The IFIB undercover agent on Capitalia had not been able to learn much about that, even with the help of the informer in the Hughes organization. Lopezov didn't know who the informer was and didn't care: espionage and treason had always been distasteful to him.

Lopezov thought wistfully of how much easier his work would be if only the Capitalian news media were free to compete commercially, as had been the case on many of the worlds that IFIB had conquered. In such societies newsmen had so little sense of responsibility that they eagerly published any important secrets people leaked to them. A good military intelligence organization did not even need to use spies to learn the weak points of a government that feared to muzzle its journalistic watchdogs. But unfortunately the Capitalians had logically concluded that, because communication is the most vital link in holding a civilization together, the news media were too important to be left under the control of newsmen. News-reporting on Capitalia was handled by a public-service company staffed by civil servants and supervised by democratically elected officials. The practice drew criticism from those who argued that news should be sold commercially like any other commodity, since Capitalia was dedicated to free trade. But even they had to admit that most Capitalian news, because it concerned only business, would probably be too dull to sell on the open market.

At any rate, Lopezov told himself, he might be able to learn something worthwhile at the Hughes dinner party tonight. It was daringly dangerous for the financier to invite his enemies into his home, but the move displayed a coolly sophisticated style that Lopezov could not resist admiring.

Alexia left the two ship commanders to their conversation and went over to Sub-Captain Alrik Bell-the-Cat, who had just finished winning his cyberdomino game against Lancet Habbth. Pentapeds are too gentle to excel at competitive sports, even nonviolent ones. If Alrik was aware of that fact, it didn't seem to diminish the pleasure of his victory. He turned his triumphant grin from Habbth to Alexia.

"Ah, my proud beauty returns. I feared that perhaps my criticism of your beloved Sophronia Cleer's pseudophilosophy had driven you to your cabin for a good, long cry."

Alexia gave him a brittle smile. "Don't flatter yourself. I haven't cried since I was eight and my brother gave me a bloody nose with his toy blaster."

"Excuse me, I must be getting back to Sick Bay," Lancet Habbth warbled musically through his glottal slits. He rose and tottered away on his hind limbs.

Alrik lolled back on a sofa and patted the seat beside him. "Shall we make up? Or do you want to argue some more?"

Alexia despised his arrogant personality and everything he stood for. His homeworld of Paraterra had been settled by Old Earth Mediterraneans and his Latin-Semitic blood was evident in his lean, handsome features, tumbling black curls, dancing eyes, and quick smile.

But then she wasn't hard to look at either, Alexia reminded herself. She had been born in Transylgrad on Novaslavia, where the Other movement had gotten its true start and where the Interstellar Family of Intelligent Beings had established its Capital Headquarters on the blasted bones of the Student Martyrs. Her middle-European ancestry had given her ample physical beauty to go with her sharp mind.

"I'm too particular and too compassionate to carry on an intellectual battle with one who has no intellect," Alexia replied to Alrik's questions. "You gunnery officers should never attempt to discuss anything more abstract than a laser beam's angle of fire."

"A laser beam doesn't have an angle of fire," Alrik laughed.

"That's what I mean," she said. "If you stick to your own specialty, you can make me appear as foolish as I make you appear in a philosophical discussion." Alexia sat down at the cyberdomino table. "I'll even do you the favor of letting you beat me at a game or two. That is, if you don't think it is beneath your dignity to play against a woman."

"Not at all." Alrik came grinning to the table. "Women are my favorite kind of competition, in any game."

Alexia switched on the table as Alrik sat opposite her and nudged her knee with his. She scowled at him and pulled her knees back. But she didn't move again when his leg came probing gently after her. Instead, she decided to discourage him by making it clear that his caress gave her no pleasure, and she almost succeeded in believing that herself.

As Alrik made the first move with the dominoes, Alexia caught a glimpse of Commodore val Murphy glaring across the room at her. Alexia wondered if Alrik and the Commodore were lovers. The thought filled her with revulsion. She was always disgusted by women who felt they had to act like men to get ahead in the rugged man's world of the armed forces. Not that toughness wasn't often required in military women. A female officer, especially, had to know how to control lower-ranking men who might resent her authority over them. But a wise, ambitious woman knew that there were better ways of handling men than in a head-on confrontation, and Alexia had never denied that she was ambitious. She prided herself on being able to know when to be man-tough or woman-soft with people, and on having the self-control to use either method at will.

Then why did she suddenly feel so meltingly female at Alrik's touch? She angrily willed herself to be strong and ignore the tingle that shot up her leg and caused her breath to catch in her throat. But even as she was struggling to throw off the sensation, she knew that resistance was useless. She had felt this way too often before: it was simply the irrational animal mating urge. She did not love Alrik and was sure she could never care for him in that way even if she wanted to make herself do so. She hated him—both as an individual and as a member of a ruthless power structure that threatened everything she believed in.

Somehow she would have to be calm and cure herself of this madness before it led to disaster. Alrik would be leaving for his own ship soon, but even that wouldn't solve the problem. She might be tempted to desert her post or find some other wildly irresponsible way to be with him again. She needed something that she could interpose between Alrik and herself. Something that would cool her blood toward him or at least prevent her from thinking so much about him. She needed another man.

But who? She quickly reviewed all the men on the *Dzuntoy*, but none had the special qualifications to serve her needs. She had already had brief affairs with the only two officers aboard who really appealed to her. A few of the enlisted men might do, but it was bad for morale to fraternize with them. It might cause all of the enlisted men and women to lose respect for her, and that could be fatal for someone in her sensitive position.

So who else was there? Surely not Controller Lopezov. The idea was as impossible as it was absurd, and she dismissed it immediately. The ideal candidate, she thought dispassionately, would be a man who was as attractive as Alrik and as intelligent as herself, but too inexperienced to outmaneuver her. That would probably mean he would have to be younger. But she wouldn't mind that. In fact, it wasn't necessary that she should feel any physical desire for him as long as she could keep the upper hand and not let him know that he was being used to shield her from her feelings about Alrik. Yes, a man like that would be the perfect solution for her. But where could she find him?

"It looks like I've got you cornered," Alrik said, looking up from the dominoes with a suggestive smirk.

"Don't be too sure about that," Alexia said flatly.

16

JUAN AND DAWNBOY had come to an attractive sun porch in their tour of the house and had decided to rest there for a while. Several of the sweet-scented exotic plants in the room were carnivorous, and Dawnboy was curiously watching one of them as it slowly dissolved bits of raw meat in digestive acids at the bottom of its cup-shaped white blossoms. The plant, called a nolily, was a native of Vampiria.

Juan sprawled in a pneumatic chair, seemingly determined to consume drinks faster than the robo-tender could mix them. It was a close contest. Dawnboy marveled at the man's capacity for alcohol, which would have put even a hard-drinking Highlander to shame.

"What ye said about gold was very interesting," Dawnboy said thoughtfully. "I wish I could discuss it further with ye, but I do na very well understand money and business."

"Neither did I, when I first came here," Juan said.

"Then yer na native o' Capitalia?"

"Very few people are."

Juan sipped his drink and reached down to scratch the antennae of a small half-insect, half-kittenlike creature that rubbed coyly against his leg. Dawnboy learned later that it was a muskmantis from Arachne, in the Betelgeuse System. They made good pets and household vermin hunters, once their toxic scent glands were removed. "The big money to be made here attracts business talents from all over the universe," Juan continued, "while the tough competition weeds out those who were born here but aren't suited for commercial success in the first rank."

"That hardly seems fair."

"Life is unfair. The system here is Social Darwinism in its purest form. Government is minimal and exists only to protect the lives, freedom, and property of all sentient beings within planetary jurisdiction. No activity here is declared against the law unless it can be clearly proved to be harmful to others. You can probably imagine what loopholes that creates for greedy, unscrupulous wheeler-dealers. But 'that's just something that goes with the territory,' to use an archaic business expression that no one seems to know the meaning of anymore. If that offends your delicate ethics, just compare it with the situations on other worlds, including your own. What's so fair about a culture that acclaims violent warfare as man's noblest endeavor and condemns defeated and peaceful individuals to be the victors' inferiors?"

Dawnboy reluctantly admitted that he had a good point, although he still wasn't convinced of the morality of unregulated business competition. "Ye seem to ken a good deal about Apache Highlands," he remarked to Juan.

"I should. Epic poetry was my specialty, and that's one thing the barbaric war worlds produce in abundance. I was born on HeyRube, an agricultural planet on the outer limits of the Milky Way. In all probability I would have had a happy, uneventful farmer's life there—if I hadn't made the mistake of revealing a talent for literature in school, which won me a scholarship to Musendowment, the artists' planet."

"Oh, I've heard o' that place," Dawnboy said eagerly.

"Everybody has, thanks to the inhabitants' insatiable appetite for recognition and praise." Juan's habitual half-sneer went all the way to both corners of his mouth.

"Well, they canna be blamed for boasting when they have so much to boast about," Dawnboy said defensively. "After all, Musendowment is the creative heart o' the whole universe; the source o' all our artistic standards and inspiration."

Juan laughed, emptied his glass, and ordered another refill. "Oh, they're experts at convincing others of their indispensability; you have to give them credit for that. I'm only glad I was able to escape that artsy-pretentious life by marrying Helen, when she was a student in my creative-recording class. Otherwise I'd probably be a starving starbard, going from planet to planet reciting dull verses for handouts. I would certainly never have gotten here, since the Capitalians wisely forbid entry to anyone associated with the arts."

"They let *ye* come here," Dawnboy pointed out.

"Only because I was the son-in-law of a rich and influential Capitalian who agreed to sponsor my bid for citizenship—something he did most reluctantly and only at Helen's insistence. Even so, I had to swear an oath that I would never engage in any kind of artistic work during my stay here. That seemed no great sacrifice at the time. But since then, I've often regretted the decision because the spectacle of big business has a compelling fascination that cries out for dramatization. It could hardly be otherwise, since competition is a natural condition of life. In fact, you could say that competition *is* life, since survival itself requires struggles against great odds. Even those with the safest and most boring lives have to overcome at least a few obstacles now and then. The greatest fraud of all time is the continuing effort of well-intentioned fanatics—including some artists, I'm sorry to say—to convince their fellows that they can obtain the security of non-competition if they will just surrender their individual freedoms. You are sure to hear the latest dogma in that old swindle from the IFIB and PHAP preacher-martinets who are coming to dinner here tonight. Incidentally, that's an ordeal I hope to avoid by drinking myself into oblivion before the first guest arrives."

Juan drove the point home by reaching out an unsteady hand for a fresh drink. Nevertheless, his voice was still clear and mockingly sardonic as he continued. "With conflict being necessary to life, artists couldn't help making it the primary subject matter of their work. But they tend to swing back and forth from exaltig the primitive competition of war and conquest to creating fantasies of impossible states of existence that are free of all competition. Artists fail to recognize that businessmen have hacked out a practical middle ground between those two extremes: the peaceful exchange of labor and property at prices freely agreed upon by voluntary bargaining. There is still plenty of conflict in that system, but as long as the government serves as a neutral referee between the bargaining parties, nobody gets fatally hurt by it. You can lose everything you own in the rough-and-tumble trading of Capitalia. But at least you'll still have your life and freedom left to start over with. You have to admit that's a big improvement over the results of war, even as it is waged by the most civilized races."

"Ye make a good argument, Mr. Orfo," Dawnboy said. "But I do na see why business should rule out war. For instance, what's to prevent a business mon, if he has enough money, from hiring an army to conquer a weak nation or planet and make it his private property?"

"That's a good point, which the collectivist security-sellers constantly bring up by calling capitalists warmongers who value profits above the lives and rights of sentient beings. Unfortunately, there's some truth in that charge. Commercial profit-making evolved from war-plundering, so not surprisingly some businessmen still have that atavistic smash-and-grab morality. But experience has taught most of them that war is too risky a venture to be good business. In business everything is done for money. But wars are fought for many complex reasons: patriotism, political ideology, religious beliefs, fear of foreigners, distrust of neighbors, love of pageantry and excitement, and so forth. A businessman can't control so many variables, so he may easily end up on the losing side. About the only businessmen I know of in modern times who have made war pay off are mercenaries like the Space Rangers, and they have such a strong sense of adventure that they are more closely allied to military than to commercial tradition. The major drawback to war is that a man could get killed at it. Preventing that is the whole purpose of substituting business for war. That's why collectivists are much more likely to resort to war: the loss of a few billion lives isn't important to them when they are on a fanatical crusade to extend the wonderful benefits of their life-style to other people. An enlightened businessman wouldn't do something like that, because he knows he can't sell anything to corpses or slaves."

It seemed to Dawnboy that Juan's rambling commentary left a lot of loose ends. But the entire subject of economics had turned out to be so much more complicated than he had imagined that he could only shake his head in bewilderment. "If all ye say is true, then 'tis a great pity that artists are barred from Capitalia. For it seems to me that artists could describe the virtues o' business in their artworks and show everyone the superiority o' capitalism."

"Yes, I have often said that to the authorities here, but they remain unconvinced. Now that businessmen have a world of their own, they've been delighted to learn how well they can get along without artists. Which in a way is poetic justice, because artists have always hated and insulted businessmen for being crass and insensitive. In fact, it was a group of artists who thought up the idea of planetary specialization that set aside Musendowment for artists, Capitalia for businessmen, Newtonia for scientists, and so on. Now, ironically, the artists are learning that they need businessmen much more than businessmen need them. That's why I left Musendowment. I got tired of the practice of feeding from the common trough."

"I do na understand that expression," Dawnboy said.

"It refers to the way artists are paid on Musendowment," Juan explained. "You see, it is every artist's dream to have a guaranteed lifetime income, whether he ever does anything to earn it or not, so that he will be free of the demeaning distractions of working for a living and can devote his full attention to creating. Musendowment has no nonartists to provide such handouts, so they have to sponge on each other. It has always been gospel to artists that true art is beyond com-

146

mercial evaluation and that any artwork that achieves widespread popularity and earns a lot of money must be artistically worthless. Therefore, it was declared the duty of the Musendowment government to correct that miscarriage of economic justice with a heavy progressive income tax that takes money away from artists whose work is profitable—which is, ipso facto, proof that it lacks merit—and gives it to those whose stuff doesn't sell, obviously because it's too good for uncultured art-buyers. Now, you'd think a perfect system like that would be sure to generate all kinds of creative energy and produce masterpieces by the thousands, wouldn't you? But strangely enough, each year less and less work gets done on Musendowment while more and more artists sit around in citroffee shops waiting for their negative income tax checks to arrive and talking about the great works they plan to do someday. It's such a puzzling mystery that the government has created several committees and agencies to investigate it. So far their most important discovery is that many artists seem to be unemployed because they aren't working."

Dawnboy was deeply impressed by what Juan said, but the sneering self-pitying tone of the man's drink-slurred voice irritated him beyond endurance. "Judging from yer present condition, sir, I presume ye were one o' those citroffee shop loafers yerself," he said sharply. "But ye might feel differently if ye had ever done a first-rate piece o' work like, say, 'The Star-going Heart.'" He instantly regretted the cutting remark and added in a gentler tone: "But I reckon 'tis na fair to compare ye wi' a poet o' Johnny Orpheus's genius."

Juan made a mocking bow that nearly toppled him out of his chair. "Thanks for the compliment. But I was never really a genius; just a hard worker."

Dawnboy started to make an angry retort, then laughed. "Ye almost got me wi' that one. I'd surely have thought ye were serious if I didn't know that Johnny Orpheus is a teen-age—" He was halted by a sudden startling thought, and stared blankly at Juan.

"See, it doesn't take much imagination to make

Johnny Orpheus out of Juan Orfo," Juan smiled. "My agent thought it would be a more impressive professional name. Actually, I was twenty-one when the song was published. But since it had taken me four years to write it, I figured I was entitled to fib a little about my age."

"Ye really mean it, don't ye? Ye really are Johnny Orpheus!" Dawnboy's voice was a dry whisper, and his spine prickled as he gazed at the man whose name and work had influenced his childhood so strongly. In those days he would have given his soul for the privilege of meeting the young demigod he was sure Johnny Orpheus must be. Now his heart sank as he looked at the bleary-eyed, drink-guzzling wreck seated before him.

"But why?" Dawnboy almost wept. Words failed him and he gestured emptily. "Why *this?*"

Juan shrugged helplessly. "As I said, on Musendowment the haves are legally robbed for the benefit of the have-nots. When I saw my fabulous earnings go to support lazy, pretentious frauds who never intended to do an honest day's work, my talent dried up. I looked around for a way out, and Helen happened to be there."

"But why stay here, living like yer wife's gigolo?" Dawnboy blundered on tactlessly. "I've seen how yer father-in-law scorns ye. Ye do na suffer such abuse just for the love o' riches, do ye? Why, a mon with yer reputation would be welcomed with honor on a thousand worlds!"

"I've often thought about moving on," Juan admitted. "But a funny thing happened a few months after I came here. I made the astonishing discovery that I had fallen in love with my wife. That's an occupational hazard of marrying for money. Oh, I'm sure Helen would chuck all this and go with me if I asked her to. But I had promised to give her father's business a try, and then the twins came along and tied us down. After all, the Hughes fortune is part of their birthright, so I feel obliged to stick around and help hold it together until they are old enough to manage it themselves. Besides, I have to admit that the world of big business really fascinates me. I know I'm not cut out for it, but I keep hoping that if I work hard enough I'll finally become competent at it."

Dawnboy searched for something encouraging to say. "Well, I reckon it's yer decision," was all he could think of.

"Yes, I've made my bed," Juan said with his twisted smile. "And an extremely comfortable one it is." He straightened up and a hard, clear glint came into his bloodshot eyes. Then the glint slowly misted over and his shoulders slumped. "But Great Space, how I miss my old life! Sometimes I would give anything to be on Musendowment again for just an hour. What a pleasure it would be to sit with those lazy, crazy, artsy fakes and have an intelligent conversation about something besides business."

"Then why don't ye . . . ?" Dawnboy began.

But Juan had sunk back in his chair. His chin fell heavily on his chest. For a few moments he seemed to struggle to stay awake, then he slipped slowly into unconsciousness. The affectionate muskmantis rubbed against Dawnboy's leg and he reached down absently to pet it. He thought, unhappily, that he seemed to be losing his boyhood illusions pretty rapidly. First, he had had to abandon his ambition of becoming a warchief. Then his father had turned out to be little more than a merchant with a starship, instead of the swashbuckling adventurer he'd always imagined him to be. Nor was his own career in space promising to be all he had hoped for. Now, here was the great idol of his youth, Johnny Orpheus . . .

If this is what it meant to grow up and become a man, he reflected sourly, it hardly seemed worth the effort.

17

"*More* MEN SHOULD wear skirts," Lulu said to Dawnboy as he was dressing in his cabin. "It looks so cute."

"It's a kilt," Dawnboy sternly corrected her. "Skirts are for girls." He peered into the mirror to adjust his tam at a rakish angle. Because the Hughes dinner party was a formal affair, his father had said that he could wear his clan regalia to it. Ordinarily Dawnboy hated to get dressed up, but he looked forward to the opportunity of showing these effete Capitalians what a man from a real man's world looked like.

"Well, whatever it's called, you look devilishly handsome in it," Lulu commented. "The ladies at the party will swoon when they see you coming. I almost wish I could go with you."

"You probably wouldn't look any stranger there than most of the other guests," Ranger's voice said.

Dawnboy turned his head, and stared in amazement at his father, who was standing in the doorway. "Where did ye get the fancy costume, Dad?"

"It's my old Ranger uniform. I thought it would be appropriate, since there will be so many military people at the party." Ranger flexed his shoulders self-consciously in the snug-fitting blue tunic. "I was surprised to find it still fits."

"Just barely," Lulu commented. "Don't eat too much tonight, unless those trousers are elastic."

"Aye, the suit is appropriate for the occasion," Dawnboy said with a faint smile. "In case Mr. Hughes needs another butler."

"If you two are finished poking fun at my noble appearance," Ranger said with strained patience, "we can get on with more serious matters. Major Yomata just photophoned to signal that two of his best men are on their way up in an antigrav car. They should be at our air lock anytime now."

"All right, I'm ready to leave if you are," Dawnboy said. He gave his tam a final adjustment, then followed his father to the bridge. "I wish I could stay aboard, though. I do na like to leave strangers alone in the ship."

"I know what you mean," Ranger said. "But you and I have to be at the party to make our little trick work. Don't worry; Nikki assures me that these two men are reliable and trustworthy. If things go according to plan, they should be able to handle it smoothly."

"That seems a mighty big 'if' to me," Dawnboy complained. "How can ye even be sure the IFIB or PHAP commander will take yer bait and send a spy over to search the *Gayheart*?"

"We can't be sure of anything, but it was the best tactic I could come up with. So unless you can think of something better . . ."

Ranger looked inquiringly at his son, who scowled and shook his head.

"Visitors at the air lock," Lulu announced.

"Send them in," Ranger ordered.

Dawnboy still wasn't satisfied with the arrangement even after he met the two well-built, efficient-looking members of Hughes's private security force. At first he had been impressed when Ranger had told him about the plan he'd worked out with Hughes. Ranger had said that at the party he would try to learn just how much the IFIB and PHAP commanders knew about his planet-hunting plans. Then he would pretend to become drunk and carelessly reveal that he had maps showing the planet's location aboard the *Gayheart*, although actually that information was locked safely in his memory. Hopefully, Lopezov or val Murphy would pick up the false clue and send someone to look for the maps. It would not be difficult for a skilled spaceman to enter the *Gayheart*, even with Lulu instructed not to open the air lock for anyone but Ranger or Dawnboy.

The intruder would know that their biocomputer was constitutionally incapable of taking action against humans and he would walk unsuspectingly into the waiting arms of the two security men. With the intruder in custody, they could file charges with the Capitalian authorities against him and his ship commander. The case probably would not win a conviction in court, but at least it would tie up one of the military vessels long enough for the *Gayheart* to get underway. That would reduce the odds against Ranger and Dawnboy considerably.

As Dawnboy had mentioned, the plan hinged on a mighty big "if"; and the more he thought about it, the more he doubted it would produce any positive results. But he was willing to go along with the maneuver if it made his father happy. There didn't seem to be anything else they could do to cope with the problems of the IFIB and PHAP forces.

Ranger finished his instructions to the security men and told them to make themselves comfortable, but to stay alert.

"All right, let's go, Son," he said, leading the way to the air lock.

"I still do na feel right about leaving Lulu alone like this," Dawnboy said uneasily.

"Thanks for your concern, but I'll be all right," Lulu assured him. "In fact, it's rather flattering to have so many men fussing over me."

"Don't let it spoil you," Ranger said as he and Dawnboy entered the antigrav car and cast off.

Dawnboy looked out at the sleek battle lines of the two warships that were space-parked a few miles away. "Is there any chance they might notice that there are only two people in this car and guess two more are still in the ship?"

"I don't think so," Ranger said. "This car is shielded against probe beams, so it would have appeared to be just an unoccupied robot sent to pick us up for the party. Don't worry about it. Mr. Hughes is very careful when dealing with IFIB and PHAP."

Dawnboy could well believe that. Ranger had filled

him in on Hughes's and David Goliath's backgrounds, when they had left *Tres Ojos* to dress for dinner. The two mutants had once been university students together on Denebali, the fourth planet in the Denebola System.

The third planet in the system, Squish, is a steamy water world of shallow seas and swamps occupied by the highly intelligent Brainsponges, to whom the Earth-tropical climate of Denebali is too dry and cold for habitation. The Brainsponges welcomed the arrival of human settlers in their system, and enjoyed more than five centuries of unbroken friendly relations with them. In the rich cultural exchange between the two species, the brilliantly adaptable Brainsponges learned the techniques of space travel and taught their new neighbors some of their amazing mental practices. The Brainsponges even rendered valuable service as go-betweens in the peace negotiations to end the nuclear civil war that, later, caused the Denebalians' genetic mutations and had nearly sterilized their entire planet.

Conditions on Denebali had been getting somewhat back to normal when, during Hughes's and David's second year at the university, an IFIB invasion force conquered the planet. The two students were sent to a slave-labor camp on the system's outermost planet and forced to work in a low-grade luxium mine. Hundreds of thousands died there of overwork, starvation, and radiation sickness; and Hughes would surely have been one of these without the protection of David's great strength. When they were both nearly at the end of their endurance, the sporadic war between the IFIB and the PHAP forces flared up again and Denebali was captured by the latter power.

At that time, the PHAP movement was still dominated by Victor Hanoleon's obsession for human purity and supremacy throughout the universe. So Denebali's new masters systematically set about cleansing the population of its abnormal members. Hughes was among the first mutant scheduled to be "salvaged"—a PHAP euphemism for having the usuable parts of one's body removed and stored in organ banks for the benefit of more favored PHAP subjects. But the guards who came for Hughes hadn't counted on David's protective fury, and five of them ended up with broken heads before the angry giant was overpowered. The salvage-camp authorities forgot about Hughes while they took David's brain apart to see what made it tick and left him a barely-living vegetable.

Meanwhile, help for the Denebalian mutants came from an unexpected quarter. The Brainsponges' strict policy of nonintervention in the struggles between otherbeings had made it impossible for them to offer anything but sympathy to the suffering Denebalians. But then the PHAP High Command made the mistake of declaring that the inhabitants of Squish—being nonhuman and, therefore, an abomination to intelligent sensitivity—must be exterminated. That gave the Brainsponges no choice but to use their full mental powers against their attackers. By the time a million or so PHAP troops had gone mad and slaughtered each other, their leaders got the message and beat a hasty retreat from the entire Denebola System.

Denebali had been so badly devastated that many of its people lost all hope of rebuilding their lives there, and immigrated to other worlds. Hughes used his blossoming business genius to get to Capitalia, bringing David along in a biostasis tank. Over the years David underwent dozens of brain operations and educational-conditioning courses that gradually brought his mentality up to its present level. And if medical science should devise any means of helping him further during his lifetime, Hughes was determined that David would get it—at any price.

Dawnboy had been soberly impressed by the horror of the story. He wondered how Hughes, after having suffered so much at the hands of IFIB and PHAP, could even bear to live in the same universe with them, much less accept their representatives as guests in his home. Ranger told him that a businessman could not afford to carry grudges. Furthermore, Hughes was well aware, he said, that military members of a totalitarian power had no choice but to obey their orders, no matter how bloody and repulsive those orders might be. So

Hughes respected and tolerated the individual citizens of IFIB and PHAP while hating the systems they served. But that didn't prevent him from enjoying the vengeful pleasure of occasionally pulling off a sharp business deal at the expense of those systems.

The situation reminded Dawnboy of his grandfather and Chief Chatto, who had changed from mortal enemies to close friends. Life was indeed strange, and the strangest things about it seemed to be the workings of the human mind. He hoped those mysteries would eventually become clear to him.

But just then he was curiously looking forward to finding out exactly what the reputedly monstrous IFIB and PHAP space ravagers were really like.

18

WHEN ROTHFELLER HUGHES gave a formal affair, he didn't stint. That fact was obvious to Dawnboy as he looked around at the other three-hundred-plus dinner guests in the huge dining room. The assorted beings were seated, or in some cases reclining, on couches or benches at several small tables around the room. The arrangement enabled the diners to enjoy the more intimate company of their tablemates; or, if they chose, they could use their implanted earphones to tune in on any of the conversations going on around them.

"Is everything all right here?" Helen inquired of Dawnboy.

Dawnboy looked up from where he sat to see the smiling hostess standing over his table. Garbed in anti-grav boots and a glowing electro-psychedelic gown, she roved about the room supervising the cyber-servers and seeing to her father's guests' needs. Her solicitous performance smoothly glossed over the conspicuous absence of her husband, whom Dawnboy had helped undress and put to bed a few hours before.

"I ha' no complaints." Dawnboy smiled back at Helen.

"Nor I," Alexia Ustich said, looking up from her plate. "The food is superb!"

"The only thing missing is your own beautiful and charming company," Alrik Bell-the-Cat added gallantly.

Helen laughed. "Careful, Captain. Flattery might get you someplace."

"I certainly hope so."

The hostess rumpled his hair and moved away, her swirling costume seeming to change shape and color at every step. Even when an observer knew the effect was entirely illusionary, it was still an intriguing display, especially during the split-second intervals when she appeared to be wearing nothing at all.

Her visit had interrupted a lively conversation around Dawnboy's table. During the pause that followed, Dawnboy studied his tablemates with new interest. All of them were older than he, but still young enough to stimulate their conversation with much laughter and teasing. Alexia and Alrik especially fascinated Dawnboy, because they were surprisingly different from his grim preconception of IFIB and PHAP militarists. Alrick's obvious wit and courage marked him as an outstanding warrior, and Dawnboy was enthralled by the gunnery officer's tales of daring space battles.

But that was nothing compared to the charming way Alexia had captivated the young Apache's attention. From the moment they met, the Novaslavian beauty had dazzled Dawnboy with flirting glances and ego-boosting compliments. In fact, she seemed so determined to make a lasting impression on him that it almost appeared that she'd been hoping to meet someone exactly like him. But Dawnboy was too overwhelmed by her flattering interest to care about that. Behind his assumed indifference to women, he gloried in his new-found power to attract them. His conquest of Alexia was made even sweeter by Alrick's obvious jealousy.

Alrik was too stubborn, however, to let himself be entirely cut out of the competition. Both he and Alexia were zealous believers in their causes and were eager to make new converts. Since Alrik could not compete with Alexia's irresistible sex appeal, he tried to win Dawnboy's favor by arguing the superiority of PHAP-ism over the IFIB philosophy of Otherism. Their conflicting claims made Dawnboy's mind reel, and they were at it again as soon as Helen left their table.

"Dammit, I'm not a specieist!" Alrik snapped in reply to a cutting remark from Alexia. "Some of my best friends are otherbeings. And if you'll just listen to them, they'll tell you they want the same thing we want—to stay with their own kind and be allowed to develop in their own way, without interference from outsiders who think they have a right to tell everyone in the universe how to live."

"Oh? And I suppose it was the tolerant PHAP policy of 'live and let live' that exterminated the Pentaped population of Trusky," Alexia asked sarcastically, "when your pirate fleet stole that world from us?"

"And how did IFIB come to be in control of Trusky in the first place?" Alrik countered. "Let's not go into ancient history. We admit we made mistakes in the formative years of the Monarchyship-of-the-People, unlike some stubborn fanatics who try to sweep all of their sins out the air lock. Many of Victor Hanoleon's early followers were overeager and wrongheaded in putting his teachings into practice. But *they* were flushed long ago. If you'll read the latest annotated edition of *Toward Equitocracy*, you'll see that we now understand and are determined to live according to the true intent of Hanoleon's inspired instructions. For example, his First Directive: 'Tolerate not the Unhuman to live.' That caused a lot of early genocide, but it really means only that we shouldn't allow them to live *with us*."

"I'm familiar with your Equality-Through-Apartness

and with all the other Hanoleon hokum," Alexia said in a bored tone. "It's incredible that supposedly intelligent minds can still believe such uncomputerized nonsense, especially since the great Sophronia Cleer explained *everything* by scientifically proving her Principles of the Otherhood of Allkind."

"Oh, please spare us such dull gibberish," Alrik groaned. "Hanoleon disproved her theories ages ago, after incorporating her few sensible observations in his own work."

"Nay, I want to hear more about Otherism," Dawnboy said. "I've looked into it, but 'tis still somewhat a puzzle to me, especially the part that says 'I am my Other's Keeper.'"

"That's easy to understand," Alrik grinned. "It means the IFIB imperialists have a moral-sounding excuse to conquer other races and keep them in slave-labor camps."

"Stop trying to poison his mind with PHAPist propaganda," Alexia ordered. She turned a melting smile to Dawnboy. "Our keepnests are merely incubation and educational centers for new members of the Interstellar Family of Intelligent Beings, where they are cured of old hostilities and taught to practice the loving behavior of Otherism. The basic principle of our system is summed up in the ancient Christian Golden Rule, but it took Sister Cleer's brilliant insight to explain it properly. Up till then, most people thought it had a negative meaning—that we shouldn't do anything to others that we wouldn't want them to do to us. But she explained the rule's positive meaning: that we are commanded to do for others everything that we would want them to do for us. If you want love from others, then you must love them; if you want others to give you their money and property, you must give your money and property to them; if you want others to obey and serve you, you must do that for them. What it all amounts to, simply, is that we all live our entire lives for the benefit of others, even to the point of dying for them, if necessary. Of course, others are doing the same things for you, so there's really no sacrifice involved. Which makes it quite obvious that Otherism is the only absolutely fair and moral way for any intelligent species to live."

The girl's eyes were glowing with such passionate conviction that Dawnboy was forced to concede: "Ye do make it sound like a good thing. But would it na be just as fair and moral—and much easier for simple minds like mine to grasp—if everybody just lived for his own self, and let others do the same for their selves? After all, it seems that a mon would know better what *he* wants to get out o' life, than what others want from it."

Alrik laughed deeply and clapped Dawnboy on the shoulder. "A remark like that could earn you a long stay in an IFIB keepnest, from which you'd be unlikely to emerge with your sanity intact. You've hit the main weakness of Otherism dead-center, just as Hanoleon did. We level-headed PHAPists have no such sentimental illusions about others being unselfish enough to repay acts of kindness and sacrifice. That's why we have our Hierarchy of Equals to safeguard the individual's right to take anything he wants—as long as he doesn't get caught at it."

Alexia regarded Alrik with contempt and pity. She could afford to be charitable, now that she had Dawnboy's unwitting help in resisting Alrik. "I guess your muddled thinking is unavoidable," she countered, "considering the senseless words you have to think with. Hanoleon was a genius at twisting language to fit his own ends, as even the name he chose for himself reveals. He wasn't content to be plain Bevin Shulrick. He wanted to be as victorious as Hannibal and Napoleon, so he borrowed syllables from each of their names. That's as childish as the Reichworld leader calling himself the Dolfman, after the ancient German dictator-king Adolf Kaiser."

"Yes, it's nearly as childish as an old-maid schoolteacher named Sylvia Mudd calling herself Sophronia Cleer," Alrik retorted.

Their argument degenerated into petty bickering, and Dawnboy's attention wandered as he thought about the custom of people choosing descriptive names for themselves. He had once thought that was a unique tradition of the clan, but it appeared to be a universal practice. Even Rothfeller Hughes and David Goliath had done it, according to Ranger, although he was not sure which historical names they had resorted to.

That reminded Dawnboy that he would soon have to choose an adult name for himself—which brought up the question of exactly when did an apprentice starrover come into full adulthood. The profession didn't offer a clear-cut test of manhood, such as killing an enemy in honorable combat, as was clan custom. But there must be some space-age equivalent to that. He would have to remember to ask Lulu about it.

His gaze moved restlessly around the room, halting at the main table, where Hughes entertained Ranger, Ship-Controller Lopezov, Commodore val Murphy, and a few other favored guests. Ranger was doing a lot of loud talking and laughing with the two officers. Dawnboy supposed he was carrying out his plan of pretending to be drunk and give away secret information. Dawnboy didn't think his father was putting on a very convincing act, but they had nothing to lose by trying to fool their opponents in this way.

Dawnboy stirred uneasily as he stared at Hughes's third eye. The extra organ was a beguiling feature even in this somewhat unusual company, and Dawnboy speculated anew on what useful function the eye might actually perform. Ranger had said he thought the eye was merely a freakish mutation that was blind and totally useless as a sensory organ. In Ranger's opinion, Hughes could have easily obtained a normal physical appearance by having the eye surgically removed, but he chose to keep it for the unsettling psychological impact it had on superstitious minds. Since not even the most level-headed and sophisticated modern beings were entirely free of age-old subconscious fears of the supernatural, it was to Hughes's advantage to have people think that he could see more about them than they wished to reveal.

Most scientists agreed with Ranger's probable conclusion. But even they—because the businessman was so secretive about his abnormality—were often tempted to theorize on the possible *physiological* values of a third eye. For thousands of years occultists had believed that the seemingly functionless pineal gland in the frontal-central area of the human brain was the seat of latent psychic powers. The more practical men of science admitted there might be something to that, if the gland could be connected to an external sensory receptor, or even to a transmitter such as an antenna. Some reptiles—most notably the pit vipers—do actually have a vestigial third eye, which functions to detect low-energy radiation in the heat spectrum. And the Triclops, a recently discovered humanoid race in the Praesepe Cluster, seemed to be similarly endowed. But so far, Rothfeller Hughes was the only known *Homo sapien* with such a characteristic; and he—knowing when he had a good thing—kept his mouth shut about it.

Although Hughes's abnormality was impossible to overlook, Dawnboy was surprised at how quickly he came to take it for granted. It was not that easy, however, to get accustomed to others of the aliens in the room. Some of them were so contrary to human concepts of beauty that Dawnboy could almost sympathize with the murderous xenophobia of the early PHAP fanatics. Fortunately, the separate table arrangement helped spare the digestions of those whose gastronomic pleasures might be disturbed by the eating habits of some of the otherworldly guests.

Of those, Dawnboy was especially fascinated by the Lithophage ambassador from the Trifid Nebula. As a member of the only known intelligent silicon-based life-form in the universe, the ambassador would have attracted attention even if he hadn't been the first rock-eater the young Apache had ever seen. As it was, Dawnboy could not help staring, even though it set his teeth on edge to watch the hulking, diamond-toothed creature shove chunks of granite and basalt between his massive jaws, crush them to gravel, wash them down with gulps of scalding lava, then almost delicately nibble a silica-jel pastry. It was rather like watching a self-loading cement mixer at work.

In direct contrast was the extreme daintiness with which the Vampirian business representative sipped his pseudoplasma through a straw. That dapper humanoid and his stunningly beautiful wife made such an attractive and aristocratic-looking couple that it was hard to put much credence in the hair-raising stories about the fate of many of the early human visitors to Vampiria. That was before the natives had learned to synthesize the liquid nutriment that their peculiar metabolism required from vegetables, and they had to obtain it directly from animal sources.

But by far the oddest—and to some the most unappetizing—method of ingestion Dawnboy saw was that practiced by Fido Amicus, the Brainsponge who was an old friend and business associate of the host. This unusual being sat at the main table with Hughes. Through "sat" was hardly the word to describe what the Brainsponge was doing. Actually he was half submerged in a transparent tank of saline solution from his native watery environment—somewhat like Lulu's container, but without the maze of wiring that connected her thought centers to the *Gayheart*'s computer and flight controls. Fido himself was a black, deeply-convoluted organism roughly resembling a human brain but about six times as large. He fed by osmosis, absorbing liquid nutriment through his semi-permeable skin-covering. That in itself would not have been too disturbing, except for the way the nutriment was rendered liquid and placed in the tank. Each Brainsponge is attended by his Altergänger, a twelve-tentacled, concave-topped slave creature of low intelligence that is controlled telepathically by its master. To locomote, the Brainsponge is lifted atop the amphibious Altergänger and held securely aboard by two pairs of the latter's tentacles while it uses the other four for walking, running, or swimming. In order to eat, the Brainsponge has to order his servant to consume solid food and liquify it in its own digestive system, then squirt it into the tank through a long, prehensile, snoutlike tube.

There had been a lot of scientific speculation about the origin of the Brainsponges and their relationship with Altergängers. The most popular theory held that, eons ago, the two creatures had been a single being—the Brainsponge the "head" and the Altergänger the "body"—with an autonomic nervous system much more highly developed than man's. The "head's" lack of an exoskeleton enabled it to develop its tremendous size and powers, but the added weight made it difficult for the "body" to avoid the many dangerous predators on Squish. So, through many generations of natural selection, the Brainsponge evolved the ability to detach itself at will from its carrier. When danger threatened, the Altergänger was commanded to hide its master in a safe place and run away, hopefully leading their enemy on a fruitless chase. If the Altergänger survived, it returned to pick up its Brainsponge. If not, the Brainsponge waited and hoped for an opportunity to commandeer another Altergänger.

A similar theory postulated that Brainsponge and Altergänger were the two sexes of their species. This was still mere speculation, however, because no otherbeing had ever been permitted to study Brainsponge or Altergänger anatomy or to learn any of the highly secretive details of their reproductive functions. When questioned about these, the Brainsponges answered primly that they considered such things to be private matters that shouldn't be discussed or performed in public, despite the practices of some other intelligent species they could mention. Most human scientists wondered what they meant by that.

Since Brainsponges communicated with each other directly, mind-to-mind, and identified each individual by his unique brain-wave pattern, they had no need for names. Many of them had, nevertheless, adopted the human practice of individual appellation for convenience in dealing with otherbeings. Fido Amicus had been so named by a New American traveling salesman, and he had considered it a high honor to be thus designated as one's faithful friend. Even after learning of the long-standing canine affiliation of the word "Fido," had continued to regard it as a compliment, saying that the dog must indeed be the noblest of all creatures to have remained man's best friend for so long. No Brainsponge had ever been accused of lacking wit.

19

"THAT TUNE!" ALEXIA, cried cutting off Alrik's attempt to resume their political discussion.

Dawnboy, startled out of his study of the Brainsponge, followed her gaze to the end of the room, where a twenty-one-piece cybercombo provided musical background for the guests' dining pleasure. The lifelike figures were so well tuned and programed that he almost believed they were human, especially the attractive throaty-voiced vocalist who threw winks and kisses to admiring male diners.

"What about it?" Alrik asked.

"Don't you recognize it? It's 'The Stare'—the new dance that's become so popular." Alexia was on her feet and tugging at Dawnboy's hand. "Come on, dance with me. I don't want any dessert, anyway."

"But I do na ken this dance," Dawnboy protested, but not very strongly, as she pulled him to his feet and started to lead him toward the cleared dance area of the floor. "I'm na too graceful at new steps."

"That's the beauty of this dance—there are no steps to learn. It's easy; I'll show you."

Confused, but not unwilling, Dawnboy allowed her to clasp his arm to her side and steer him around the tables to the dance floor. He was learning, to his surprise, that being ordered about by a woman wasn't so bad, after all—as long as she looked, felt, and smelled as good as Alexia did. He didn't even protest when she pressed a small round object into his hand and closed his fingers around it. He recognized it by feel as a recorder button—a more advanced and miniaturized version of the audiovideo tapes he had used on the *Gayheart*.

"It's a condensation of Sister Cleer's most important computerizations on Otherism," she explained. "You can play it on your ship's computer when you have the leisure time to give it your full attention. We in the Family like to attract new members, but we try not to bore them with long-winded speeches." She flashed him a winning smile. "Unlike our thickheaded PHAP counterparts."

"I'll gi' it a fair study," Dawnboy promised, slipping the button into his sporran.

They had reached the dance floor, where a few other couples already stood with their hands on each other's shoulders. Their feet did not move, but their bodies swayed slightly with the music as they stared soulfully into each other's eyes.

"See, I told you it was easy," Alexia said, facing him and placing his hands on her shoulders. "We just gaze into each other's eyes and let our minds go with the music."

"It doesna seem to make much sense," Dawnboy commented.

"It's not supposed to. Dancing is for fun, not for intellectualizing. Don't they have dancing from where you come from?"

" 'Course we do, but nothing like this. Though I admit 'tis an improvement on some o' the shameless frolics I've heard of, with men and women holding each other's bodies chest to bosom in plain view o' others. Why, at a clan fling-festival, such goings-on would cause no end of scandal."

"How marvelously quaint!" Alexia laughed. "You must take me to visit your world someday. Now, no more talking. Just concentrate on my eyes and let yourself drift. You'll be surprised at the sensations you can experience this way."

Dawnboy followed her instructions, and was not surprised at all by the first sensation he experienced at having his hands on such a lovely and vivacious woman. But since Alexia's blank expression showed no sign that she shared his reaction, the feeling soon passed and was replaced by mild boredom as he wondered why he had let himself be persuaded to give up his dessert for something as pointless as this. Then, gradually, the soothing rhythms of the music and the hypnotic caress of Alexia's unblinking gray eyes, aided by her fresh-scrubbed scent of open fields and wild flowers, began to cast a subtle spell over him.

Awareness of the room, the music, the people around them—all faded away. He even seemed to become detached from the physical sensations of his own body. Only the mystic enchantment of Alexia's gaze remained, as their souls drifted together through time and space ... back to Apache Highlands ... back to that world's dim, lost beginnings ... He was the original Dawnboy, the mythical first man of the clan. And she was Evening Girl, first woman. Adam and Eve, they were mistakenly called by some ignorant city folk. (Of course, every member of the clan knew the history of the colonization of the planet, but there was no law against romanticizing it.)

Actually, in the beginning, it was told that Dawnboy and Evening Girl had been a single creature made up of all the opposing elements of male and female forces. But the gods had feared that so powerful a mortal might challenge their own supremacy. So Father Sun and Mother Dark had cut them apart with the Sword of Day and let them ease their wounds with the Balm of Night. Since then, the strongest urge of men and women has been to join together and again make themselves one in their children, in the hope of someday creating a perfect being of male-female balance, whose wisdom and power would surpass even that of the gods.

But before Dawnboy could make Evening Girl his bride, she had been stolen from him by the treacherous

Trauma Trolls and taken far beyond Skull Mountain to Fulfillment Valley, where they sold her to the misshapen Orgy Ogres for the Cup of Everfull. The ogres intended to sacrifice her to their satyrgod Dino, but instead gambled her away to Sod, chief of the Scatotalky tribe, who cruelly left her dangling from Hang-up Rock over Heckfire Pit and guarded by a lonely monster. At last Dawnboy had learned of her whereabouts from Blindsight, the talking pegasus who befriended him. He set out to rescue her with his magic blade, Swiftstab, with the Eye of Eternal Vigilance to guide him and watch over him when he slept. After experiencing several wondrous adventures and exciting battles against the forces of evil, Dawnboy reclaimed his mate and brought her back to the MacCochise stronghold, where they established the clan, with many strong sons and beautiful daughters . . .

"I said, the dance is over." Alexia's voice dimly filtered through his enchanted musings. "You can let go of me now."

"Oh, sorry." He dropped his hands from her shoulders and blinked away the last of his daydreams, observing that the other dancers had left the floor and the cybermusicians were preparing to play another number. "Let's sit the next one out, if ye do na mind. One dance like that is all a mon can take, for a while."

"Gets to you, doesn't it?" Alexia grinned, allowing him to lead her from the floor. "I told you it would be fun."

Returning to the table, Dawnboy was pleased to discover he had not missed his dessert, after all. Helen, after learning Dawnboy's favorite homeworld delicacy from Ranger, had ordered the cyberchef to prepare him a jellied cactus sherbet—this one flavored with Upper Pleiaden touch-spices. The youth dipped his fingertips in the spice bowl and savored the tingling stimulation that rushed to his taste buds, enhancing and prolonging the sherbet's taste. The spices were very rare and expensive condiments, but he could easily see how even a thrifty Highlander might become addicted to them. So it was just as well that these had not yet reached the Apache Highlands markets.

The only thing that spoiled his enjoyment of the sherbet was a drunken old man who had wandered up to their table and was talking to no one in particular about organizing a starship expedition to search for the legendary lost planet of Free Lunch.

Dawnboy recognized him as Benedict Stanley, who had been—a dozen or so years before—Chief Cleerhead of Otherism. As such, he had been in effect the absolute dictator of the Interstellar Family of Intelligent Beings. It was a position few people had held for very long, thanks to Sophronia Cleer's fear that too much leadership might sap the reformatory vigor of her movement. Since she believed in the revolutionary overthrow of all governments—even her own—she had instituted a peculiar form of political succession called revolectionary selection. Every year, fifty IFIB citizens, selected by lot, were each given a gun containing one bullet-ballot with which they voted against the reigning Chief Cleerhead as he ran across an open courtyard in front of them. If he survived, he was re-elected.

Most Chief Cleerheads had been sporting enough to play the game fairly, if fatally, until Stanley's successor had gotten smart enough to have the guns loaded with blank cartridges. Stanley himself, neither very sporting nor smart, had decided just before his first revolection day that Otherism really wasn't for him and had hastily departed IFIB jurisdiction. Such un-Otherly behavior had earned him the contemptuous IFIB classification of ULO (Unrecognized Living Object), which was why no IFIB officer in the room would speak to him or even acknowledge his existence, and the PHAPists followed suit out of professional courtesy. Alrik and Alexia blandly ignored Stanley, as they chatted with each other and with Dawnboy.

Like many ex-collectivists, Stanley had come to depend on capitalist charity for his survival, mooching cast-off clothes and dinner invitations from tolerant Capitalians who thought him amusing enough to have around, or boring enough to be paid to stay away. Like most beggars, he hated his benefactors for making him feel inferior. The Capitalians' generosity—far from convincing him of the advantages of capitalist individualism—only strengthened his determination to find the perfect collectivist society, as epitomized by Free Lunch.

The name, Dawnboy learned later, was taken from the Old Earth saying "There's no such thing as a free lunch." Which was the cynic's way of saying that no service performed by a government could actually be "free," however noble and altruistic the motivation behind it might be, because it would eventually have to be paid for by the people through taxation, inflation, or some other form of political chicanery. But as often as the validity of that truism had been proved, the diehard adherents of collectivism continued to believe that somewhere in the universe there actually was a Free Lunch, where all the inhabitants' needs and desires would be satisfied by government edict and no one would ever have to work or pay taxes if he didn't want to. Several search parties of eager-eyed dreamers had ventured out into space to look for Free Lunch, with no reported success so far; but that only made people like Benedict Stanley more certain than ever that greedy capitalists were keeping the planet's location a secret.

Somehow Stanley's maudlin tirade had turned into an off-key song about the utopian joys of Free Lunch. Tears salted his drink as he described how every guy and lass had his or her own glass at the Champagne Fountain, and love was as free as the breeze that blew narco smoke through the Welfare Trees—

"Please forgive me for overriding your comm-controls," Rothfeller Hughes's voice spoke abruptly from every guest's earphone. "But a serious emergency has just been reported from the PHAP battle frigate *Littlegart*. Commodore val Murphy wishes to have witnesses to any defensive actions her crew might have to take, so she has asked me to put her communication with the ship's Duty Officer on the wallscreen. Please give it your full attention."

Everyone looked up as the image of the frigate's bridge appeared on the screen. A young, tense-faced Commander Third Grade was standing behind an enlisted gunner-tech who peered into the sightscreen of his computerized weapons bank. ". . . still no response after repeated demands for identification and three warning laser blasts fired in front of him," the commander was saying. "We are now flashing the interstellar battle signals with all the ship's lights. If he doesn't react to that, he's either blind or ignoring us."

"And he's still coming straight at you?" val Murphy asked.

"Affirmative, Skipper."

"All right, prepare to fire a one-quark depth charge. But first let us have a good look at him. Or it, if it's some sort of robot."

"Yes, ma'am."

The scene shifted to an overview of *Tres Ojos*, as seen from the frigate. Far above the asteroid, but still a thousand or more yards from the ship, was a dimly visible figure in a vac-suit and antigrav pack. It was difficult to make out any details about the figure, except that it seemed humanoid in shape and was craddling something under its left arm. Something that could have been a weapon, which explained why the duty officer was so tense.

Even the most combat-prepared military starship was almost totally helpless against a suicidal one-man attack with a magnetic nuclear mine. In deep space such an intruder was hard to detect with sensory scanners, and most computerized weaponry—designed for pinpoint long-range accuracy—was useless on a small and nearby slow-moving target. Even a powerful force-screen was no barrier to a man in a polarized vac-suit, since its main function was to shield the ship from high-velocity meteors, missiles, and energy beams. All of which explained why the dining room buzzed with excited observations and comments on the situation, as all eyes were glued to the wallscreen.

"Wonder how they got the authorities to remove

their weapons lock?" inquired one voice, whose professional detachment indicated a military background.

"We're pretty understanding about that," someone answered him, "when we can't get a patrol craft on the scene to handle an emergency. But you can bet the frigate's being closely watched to make sure this isn't a cover for some offensive action."

"Such a treacherous suggestion is an unwarranted assault on the honor of PHAP officers," another man huffily protested. "Obviously this is an underhanded IFIBist attempt to provoke hostilities between us and our Capitalian friends."

"Please, no arguments," Hughes's voice cut in. "Everyone be quiet and let the Commodore talk to her crew."

"She should send out a scout ship with a good sonic blaster gunner," Alexia remarked casually.

"No; too much danger the attacker might vaporize the scouter and himself, if he panics," Alrik said, with the confidence of a specialist. "A quark charge is safer, as long as they don't let him get too close."

Evidently that was val Murphy's opinion, too, for she said calmly: "Very well, Commander. He's had ample time to declare his intentions or turn away. We must conclude his purpose is hostile. Fire the charge."

The duty officer relayed her order to the gunner-tech. A port in the *Littlegart*'s hull winked open and a shiny oblong object came tumbling out end-over-end.

"Charge away," the officer reported.

Dawnboy stared spellbound as the telescopic zoom lens followed the depth charge's lazy journey toward the vac-suited figure, who made a sudden frantic effort to change course. But it was too late. The lens magnification sharply detailed the man's features through his helmet visor, and for a split second Dawnboy gazed at the fear-twisted face of Juan Orfo, before it disappeared in a brilliant flash.

Dawnboy blinked rapidly to clear his vision. No trace of the depth charge or the man remained in view. The scene shifted back to the frigate's bridge.

"Mission accomplished, Skipper." The duty officer

smiled. "I don't think there was anyone else with him, but we'll scout the area to make sure."

"Well done, Commander. Carry on."

"Well, as I was saying about the Cleer method of infant indoctrination," Alexia resumed, snitching a spoonful of Dawnboy's sherbet.

"More silly nonsense," Alrik scoffed.

"Oh, give me a home where doctors never send a bill to cloud your sky," Benedict Stanley sang drunkenly. "On Free Lunch it costs you nothing to get ill or maybe even die."

20

DAWNBOY STARED AROUND in shocked amazement. What was the matter with these people? Helen had fainted and was being carried out of the room by two cyberservers, and Hughes was hurrying after them. But nearly all the guests were cheerfully carrying on with their dinners and conversations, acting as if seeing a man die violently meant nothing to them.

No, that wasn't quite true. They were not acting.

Dawnboy looked from Alrik's handsome, charming face to Alexia's captivating beauty, and was suddenly afraid he might become physically ill. How could they, of all people, treat a war death so contemptuously? He realized that they were themselves warriors and probably were accustomed to seeing men killed in combat, but that was all the more reason for them to take it seriously. An Apache brave was expected to slaughter his enemies without mercy. It was even permitted to torment and torture a captive, to tear the scalp from his living skull and wave it tauntingly in his face, if that was your caprice. But when he was dead, you had to treat him with the respect due a valiant foe. You gave him a decent burial and chanted the Death Song over him to ensure his soul's admission to the Happy Battlegrounds. You didn't dare offend the gods by committing the unforgivable insult of ignoring him—as if his death mattered no more than the crushing of a pebblebug's egg.

Even an ordinary man's death deserved more consideration than this. But Juan had been a great poet once; probably most of the people present had heard and enjoyed "The Star-going Heart" at least once. The passing of such an artist merited the highest honors, even if he had deteriorated into the alcoholic wreck Dawnboy remembered with pity and disgust. But maybe none of the other guests were aware of Juan's real identity.

He stood up to call for their attention, intending to demand that they at least drink a toast to Juan's memory. When he was on his feet, a wave of sickening dizziness swept over him and he had to grip the edge of the table to keep from falling.

"What's the matter?" Alexia asked. "You look ill."

"S'all right. Just need some fresh air," he muttered, turning and lurching away from them.

"You have to learn to be careful about mixing too much touch-spices with booze," Alrik called good-humoredly after him. "It's no fun getting drunk if you just get rid of it right away."

Dawnboy stumbled blindly toward the nearest exit. Yes, he did have a great sickness, but not in his stomach. In the past two weeks—especially today—so many new ideas and impressions had been stuffed into his mind that he hadn't had time to digest all of them. Now they boiled inside him like the gassy bubbles of unchewed food, making it impossible for him to think straight. He heard Juan saying, "It's every artist's dream to have a guaranteed lifetime income," just as his first breath taking view of *Tres Ojos* flashed across his inner visual screen. Somehow Rothfeller Hughes's third eye and David's blue skin got mixed up with Alexia's persuasive explanation of Otherism. Then that gave way to a sudden xenophobic revulsion toward the alien creatures present, and he yearned to be safely back in the clan, where a man knew what was expected of him. But superimposed over everything else was the haunting image of Juan's expression the instant he knew he was going to die, with a loving wife and family and untold riches in view.

Why had he done it? What could make any man throw away all of this on such a pointless venture? Had he been too drunk to know what he was doing? Or did he have some secret plan that failed to work out?

Suddenly Dawnboy was aware that something had happened to his right arm. He turned his head and saw his father holding the arm, supporting him and guiding him between the tables. "Father, did ye see . . . ? Why would he . . . ?"

"Get hold of yourself," Ranger said sternly. "We'll talk about this later. Right now we have an emergency of our own to take care of. The security men aboard the *Gayheart* have just captured an intruder."

Dawnboy was so stunned that he was hardly aware of his father leading him out to an antigrav car and lifting off from *Tres Ojos*. He didn't fully recover from his daze until they entered the *Gayheart*'s bridge and saw the two security men guarding a third man with synapse disrupters.

The intruder was a nondescript individual of about thirty-five. He was stripped to the waist and stood casually at ease with his features set in a blank stare.

"Good work," Ranger complimented the security men. "Have you tried questioning him yet?"

"Yes, sir," one of the security men replied. "But he won't say a word. He has probably been narcohypnotically conditioned for this job. We won't be able to get anything out of him until a medical team has worked him over."

"Let me have a crack at him," Lulu requested. "I have some computer tricks that might break down his mental defenses."

"We don't have time for that," Ranger told her. He asked the security men: "Was he carrying any identification? Anything to indicate if he is from IFIB or PHAP?"

"No, sir. We searched him thoroughly, but couldn't find anything on him except the vocal simulator that he used to imitate your voice to open the air lock. That's unusual. These people ordinarily have some sort of weapon to fight their way out of a trap, or kill themselves to avoid capture."

"I guess he just wasn't expecting any opposition here," Ranger surmised. He frowned thoughtfully as the spy's abdomen suddenly twitched involuntarily. That stirred some dim memory at the back of Ranger's mind, but he couldn't recall if it was important enough to mention. "All right, take him down to your security headquarters," he decided. "Your antigrav car is waiting at the air lock. I'll be sure to tell Major Yomata what a good job you did here."

The security men were starting to escort their prisoner out of the bridge. The spy's abdomen twitched again, and abruptly the old memory burst fully into Ranger's consciousness.

"Gangway!" Ranger shouted warningly, rushing forward and grabbing the prisoner in an armlock. "Lulu, prepare the emergency air lock to jettison dangerous cargo. Everybody hit the deck!"

"What are ye . . . ?" Dawnboy began in surprise. But already the security men had thrown themselves flat on the deck and Ranger was swiftly dragging the spy toward the air lock.

"Don't ask questions!" Lulu snapped. "Take cover!"

Dawnboy crouched behind the copilot's seat and waited. A few moments later he heard the air lock open and close rapidly. Then there was a muffled sound from outside and the ship quivered slightly.

"All right, the danger's over now," Ranger announced.

Dawnboy and the security men stood up as Ranger re-entered the bridge. He was pale and trembling, but looked relieved.

"Are you all right?" Lulu anxiously asked Dawnboy.

"Of course I am," Dawnboy replied. "What was the matter, Dad?"

"It was something I remembered seeing once before, a long time ago in combat," Ranger explained. "The man had swallowed a mini-grenade sealed in a time-release capsule. His stomach twitch indicated that his digestive acids had dissolved the capsule enough to release the grenade's safety catches. If he had completed his mission successfully and returned to his own base in time, he could have had his stomach pumped and been none the worse for wear. But as things worked out, he was prepared to self-destruct before we could learn anything from him."

"And he would have taken us with him," one of the security men said admiringly, "if you hadn't been so sharp-eyed and keen witted."

"It was just a lucky guess," Ranger smiled. "His twitching stomach could have just been a sign of indigestion, but I didn't want to gamble on it. Sorry I have to send you fellows back to Yomata empty-handed."

"At least we still have our hands," the security man laughed, starting out with his companion. "Good luck on your cruise, sir. I hope we have the honor of meeting you again someday."

When the men were gone, Dawnboy thought soberly about the spy who had chosen death to captivity. The act would have been worthy of respect even on Apache Highlands, if it had not been accomplished with the aid of narcotics and hypnosis. Even so, the episode demonstrated that IFIB and PHAP members were certainly dedicated to their principles. He wondered if the principles were worth it.

"Prepare the ship for liftoff, Lulu," Ranger ordered, going to the pilot's seat and switching on his photophone.

It took him a few minutes to contact Rothfeller Hughes. The financier looked very old and tired. Ranger asked him how Helen was taking Juan's death.

"She has been given a sedative and put to bed," Hughes answered. "How did your plan work out?"

Ranger told him briefly what had happened to the spy.

Hughes nodded. "We should have expected something like that. Just as I should have expected Juan's act of madness, if I had paid closer attention to him. He was the one who leaked information about your planet hunt to IFIB and PHAP. He left us a message tape explaining everything, in case he failed in his efforts to place explosives on the *Dzuntoy* and *Littlegart*, which he did."

"I canna believe Juan would be so treacherous," Dawnboy said sadly. "Why did he do it?"

"He wanted to impress me with his business skill," Hughes answered. "The IFIB agents in the Upper Pleiades learned that the touch-spice growers co-op there had secretly voted to reduce next season's plantings, to make the spices scarce and drive up prices. They offered the information to Juan, who used it to buy up all of the available touch-spice supplies before the price started to climb. What IFIB asked in return didn't seem very important to Juan—until he saw you again today and realized how much he had betrayed a friend. He could think of only one way to make up for that."

"Poor Juan," Ranger sighed. "The situation really wasn't serious enough for him to risk his life on it. Since neither IFIB nor PHAP consider my project important enough to assign more than one ship to it, I should be able to lose both of them easily in deep space."

"I suppose it was mostly my fault," Hughes said. "I belittled and insulted him so badly in front of Helen that he felt he had to do something to prove he was still a man." He touched a button on his desk. "Part of his tape was addressed to you, so you should see it."

The old man's face disappeared from the screen and was replaced by Juan's. The poet was speaking with his usual mocking half-sneer: "... *so I'm going to try to destroy the two warships and be back safely in my room before anyone learns that I'm not really as drunk as I pretended to be. Ranger, I'm sorry I caused you so much trouble. You have always been a good friend to*

*me, and I hope you'll continue to be one to my wife
and children, if I don't survive this undertaking. By the
way, you have a pretty good son of your own. Take
good care of him. But if he ever shows any promise of
becoming a poet, do him a favor and beat hell out of
him before he gets serious about it . . . . And as for
you, my filthy-rich father-in-law, I don't have time to
tell you fully what I think of you, but you can take all
of your goddam money and . . ."*

Juan's image faded away as Hughes's came back on
the screen. "You can imagine what he was going to say
next," Hughes said. "I don't know how I'm going to
face Helen after this, but there are worse things on my
conscience that I've had to live with. However, Juan
was mistaken in thinking I didn't respect him. I hated
him, but he had one special virtue that made up for all
of his shortcomings. He was a good husband to Helen.
It is no small thing for a man to be able to make a
woman happy, as I well know."

Ranger cleared his throat. "If there is anything I can
do . . ."

"No, but thanks. This is something that Helen and I
will have to take care of. It's unfortunate that it often
takes something like this to make one realize how important his family really is to him, and just what his
family duties are."

"Well, then, we'll say good-bye," Ranger said. "This
side-trip has already used up a lot of valuable time and
it hasn't done us much good. Thanks for your hospitality and help."

Dawnboy stared at the old man's expressionless face.
His two "normal" eyes were empty of emotion, but just
before Ranger blanked the screen Dawnboy saw a single tear brim at the corner of Hughes's third eye and
start to trickle slowly down the curved bridge of his
nose.

"Are we all ready to get under way?" Ranger asked.

"Yes, sir," Lulu answered.

Ranger reactivated the photophone and turned to
Dawnboy. "Here's a little surprise I was hoping to give
you under more cheerful circumstances, but you may

as well see it now." A long series of words and numbers flashed across the screen. "These are the corporations listed on the Capitalia Stock Exchange, the prices of their stocks, and the numbers of shares traded today. I ordered a change made in— Here it is now."

The flowing stream of data halted on: *Farstar & Co., Inc.* As Dawnboy watched, the name changed to: *Farstar & Son, Inc.*

"Welcome to the family business, Son," Ranger smiled. "You are now part-owner of a half-million-stellar mortgage on this ship, and a few other outstanding debts."

Dawnboy stared from the screen to his father's face. He sensed that this was an important moment in his life, but he had undergone so many other emotional strains recently that he hardly knew how to react to it. Just as he was afraid he might go mushy-soft and choke up with girlish sentimentality, the practical-minded side of his nature took over.

"Well, then, I reckon we better get to work and pay off some o' those debts," he said. "Come on, Lulu, let's burn ether out o' here!"

"Aye, aye, sir," Lulu said, with as much pride as humor in her voice.

PART III

TO DAWNWORLD

21

DURING THEIR FIRST twenty-four hours out of Capitalia, Dawnboy closely watched the sub-ether madar screen for any signs of pursuit. After the monotonously sweeping arm of the Microwave Amplified Detecting and Ranging set turned up only a few blips within its thousand light-year range—all easily identified as meteoric particles or other space junk—he began to relax.

"Doesna look as if we're being followed," he reported to Ranger. "I reckon we got away before the IFIB and PHAP captains could get their crews together and start tracking us."

"No, they're back there," Ranger said confidently. "Keeping safely out of our range and sniffing along like patient wolves."

"But how could they be? Is their scanning equipment better than ours?"

"Probably not. But it doesn't have to be. They had plenty of time over *Tres Ojos* to sprinkle our hull with microwave transmitting devices. How about that, Lulu?"

"Right, Boss. I've already found at least two electronic fleas on number three and four tubes. You'd better go out and delouse me before I start scratching."

"Just what I was planning to do." Ranger rose from the pilot's seat. "Take the helm, son. You can watch me on the snooper monitor, and learn how to clear a ship of these pests."

Dawnboy watched with interest as his vac-suited father graved around *Gayheart*'s outer skin, searching every square inch with electronic detection gear. Whenever he found an IFIB or PHAP "beepbug," as he called them, he would hold it up for Dawnboy's inspection, explaining how it worked and the easiest way it could be deactivated. In four hours Ranger found nine of the devices—some of them so ingeniously miniaturized that they were no bigger than a man's thumbnail and were nearly transparent to the naked eye.

It was a tedious task, but Ranger insisted on doing it again the following day—wisely so, it turned out, for he found a "bug" he had missed the first time around. Then, as a training exercise, he sent Dawnboy out to repeat the entire job on his own. By the time he was at last satisfied that the ship was clean of spy devices, they had been under way for nearly five days, and a faint shadow had appeared at the rearmost limits of the madar screen.

"So now she pokes her nose out of her shell," Ranger mused. "Looks too small for a cruiser; must be the *Littlegart*. But you can bet your warpaint that our fat little Autry Lopezov is right behind her."

"What do we do now?" Dawnboy asked. "Fight them?"

Ranger grinned at him. "Just like a Highland Apache to think of that first. I'm beginning to wonder if there's any of my peace-loving cowardice in you at all. No, they're both so superior to us in speed, maneuverability, and weapons that they could easily vap us if they wanted to. But they would just play with us until we got tired and went back to leading them to our planet."

"Then what are we going to do?"

"The thing your father does best in a fight," Lulu said. "Run away."

"You better believe it," Ranger affirmed. "Go strap down on your couch, and I'll show you how I beat more retreats than any other pilot in the Rangers."

Dawnboy did as he was told. Ranger braced himself in the pilot's seat and slapped the light-speed accelerator forward to maximum. A sharp, blood-stagnating jolt left Dawnboy gasping breathlessly for several moments. After that passed, they resumed so smooth a course that he was about to say he couldn't see why he had to strap down for such a minor maneuver—when Ranger fired up a rocket burner that thrust them violently off to port, then several more in rapid succession to whip the vessel into wildly gyrating zigzags. Every time they seemed to be coming out of the eyeball-rattling dips and turns and geting back to a fairly steady ride, Ranger would repeat the process with just enough variations to keep his son's stomach from adjusting to the weird motions.

After ten minutes of the torturous ordeal, Dawnboy thought he knew only three things for sure: (1) he didn't want to be a spaceman, after all; (2) his father was a sadistic brute; and (3) he was going to vomit. On second thought, he decided not to open his mouth, for fear that he might lose all of his internal organs, which felt as if they had been crushed up into his head.

"My, how time flies when you're having fun," Ranger said cheerfully. "But even the best of times must eventually come to an end." He brought them back on an even keel and eased back the accelerator. "Looks like we managed to shake off our unwelcome guests. But I can't tell for sure yet, so you better stay strapped in a little longer."

"I wasna going anyplace," Dawnboy weakly assured him.

"You could have at least given him a dose of dimenhydrinate before putting him through all that," Lulu scolded Ranger. "Just because you took spaceflight training under a hard-boiled Ranger instructor is no reason to make him suffer the same way."

"Oh? Did that little tail-shaking exercise bother you, Son?" Ranger asked kindly.

"O' course na!" Dawnboy forced every ounce of his indignant warrior's pride into his trembling voice. "Matter o' fact, I'm a wee bit sorry we lost our trackers so easily, when I was just getting to enjoy the ride."

Ranger looked at the madar screen and frowned, then smiled. "Well then, this is your lucky day, because at least one of them has found us again. Hang on now, while I show you some *real* evasive action."

185

"Ye should na gi' me so much good news at once," Dawnboy said through clenched teeth.

But, surprisingly, he did become adjusted to the rigors of evasive maneuvering in a fairly short time—at the cost of missing a few meals. In the next two days Ranger repeatedly strained the *Gayheart* to the very limits of her endurance as the telltale blip clung stubbornly to the madar screen. He was even able to stay in the copilot seat and help with the last complicated series of jerks and twists that finally left them apparently alone in space. After several hours of searching the cosmos without result, Ranger declared them safe from pursuit and sent his exhausted business partner to bed.

Then, ironically, Dawnboy *did* miss the gut-flipping excitement of their escape, as they settled back into the dull routine of hyperspace cruising. Even the study of new subjects seemed to have lost its fascination to him, and he found his thoughts constantly wandering back to the unsettling events at *Tres Ojos*. Juan's death haunted him; a deep nagging in his conscience told him he was somehow partially responsible for it, because he too was involved in this strange world of business that made men gamble their lives for the mystery of money that he still couldn't fully understand. He told himself it was stupid for him to feel that way: an Apache brave accepted death as a normal part of existence, and forgot about it when the period of mourning was over. But still the guilty feeling persisted, until he was forced to conclude regrettably that he was no longer just a simple-hearted Highland Apache. Too many changes had taken place within him during the past several weeks. He was becoming, in spite of himself, distressingly civilized.

He tried to remember everything Juan had said to him in those last few hours of his life. But the confused impressions that the poet's jumbled words had made on him did not help clarify his thinking very much. Nor could he find much enlightenment in what he had learned from Alexia and Alrik, although there did seem to be a certain appeal in the various social systems that did not base survival on the mad scramble for money. His father and Lulu didn't seem able to give satisfactory answers to his questions, either.

"Look, I know Juan's death upset you," Ranger said one morning, losing patience with Dawnboy's persistent demand that he explain what life is all about. "I feel the same way. I can't help thinking I might have been able to help him, if I'd taken the trouble to get to know him better and tried to understand his problems. But it's over now. We can't change the past, and it won't help anybody to worry and blame yourself for it."

"I ken that," Dawnboy said. "And 'tis na just Juan I'm thinking of, but all the unfortunate ones like him who've played and lost and suffered in this business 'game,' as ye call it. It must be a terribly cruel game to cause so much misery. It seems to me that intelligent beings could ha' found a better way to do things, in all the thousands of years they've been trying to become civilized."

"Well, let me know if you ever find that better way," Ranger grunted, turning back to the cosmography charts he was trying to study. "I haven't come across one yet—especially not among the IFIB and PHAP, for all their bragging about having achieved social perfection."

"Aye, there are serious flaws in their theories," Dawnboy agreed. "But at least they're trying to find a reasonable and fair system to replace the old, selfish, dog-eat-dog immorality of capitalism. They might make better progress at that if the capitalists would stop fighting 'em every step o' the way. There must be some good things in their systems, after all, for them to have extended them to so many people."

Ranger looked at him and sighed. "Now look, Son. I know you're full of new discoveries and new ideas just now, and you have the young idealist's desire to make over the entire universe in a way you think will help everybody. That's part of your education and I approve of it. But I've been around a lot longer than you have. Even if that hasn't made me any smarter than you, at least it's enabled me to see many worlds where people experiment with vastly different ways of dealing with life's problems. I haven't always liked what I saw—in some cases I was strongly opposed to it. But I knew there wasn't much I could do to change the situations, so I learned to keep my opinions to myself. You might say I had to force myself to tolerate the intolerable, because that's the only way I could stay in business. At any rate, I've come to respect the rights of others to do things their own way, and I expect them to give me the same courtesy. But I've grown sick and tired of hearing people who've made messes of their own lives and societies blame me and other businessmen for all the problems in the universe, just because we try to turn over an honest profit. I'm certainly not going to take such abuse from my own son, in my own ship."

If Dawnboy had experienced a more normal upbringing with his parents, he would have known it was time to bring the discussion to a close. But instead he retorted bluntly: "Well, sir, maybe 'tis time ye did listen to somebody who sees things a wee differently than ye do, if ye think—"

"Ten-hut!"

The command cracked like a whiplash across Dawnboy's unprepared mind, leaving it stunned and smarting. He had never heard that sharp authoritative tone of voice—or seen that harsh, glaring expression—from his father before. But even while he was wondering about it, his reflexes—conditioned by years of playing war games with boyhood companions and older braves—automatically snapped his body rigidly upright.

Ranger rose to his feet, his eyes narrowed and his jaw set grimly.

"You seem to have trouble remembering who's in command of this vessel," Ranger said, his voice edged with ice. "I guess that's my fault, for trying to make your apprenticeship easy and enjoyable. If you had had to go into space the way most of us did—as a midship-cadet in military service, or a sub-assistant spacehand on a merchantman—you would soon have learned that not even a little insubordination can be allowed to interfere with the operation of a starship. But it's not too late to teach you that. So, from now on you will obey my orders without question. You will not speak unless spoken to first. You will stand your duty watches in strict accordance with established procedure, with no idle stargazing or slipping off to the galley for snacks. And to set these rules firmly in your mind, you will spend the rest of today in your cabin studying the *Spaceman's Manual*—the chapters on 'Shipboard Discipline' and 'Chain of Command.' Is that understood?"

"Yes, sir!" Dawnboy snapped, his surprise replaced by angry resentment.

"Very good. Dismissed."

"Thank you, sir!" Dawnboy tried to put a strong dose of sarcasm into his voice, as he stiffly about-faced and marched out of the bridge.

"Boss—" Lulu began when the boy was gone.

"Don't interfere," Ranger said. "I hate this routine as much as you do, but he's got to learn the value of discipline somehow. And it's better that he get it from me than from the average iron-tailed skipper who would clap him in the brig for a little back talk."

"You're right, of course," she sighed. "But I wish . . ."

"We all wish for things we can't have. Leave it alone for now." He turned moodily back to his charts.

In his cabin, Dawnboy angrily flung himself down on his bunk and glared at the overhead. To think that he had given up the chance to become a great war-chief—maybe even Grand Laird of the Clan—for this! What the hell was so great about being a starman anyway? Any fool could easily learn to fly this ship, with the help of a biocomputer. And as for discipline, what talent did it take to say "Yes, sir!" and obey orders like a brainless robot?

"Sulking won't help," Lulu chided him gently.

"Tell that to our high and mighty captain," he snorted.

"Don't be too hard on the old man. He's had some pretty raw deals from the IFIB and PHAP, which makes it hard for him to listen to anyone speak favorably of them. Maybe you'll feel the same way when you've lived that long."

"I doubt it. The members o' those organizations I've met so far have been a lot nicer and friendlier than some o' Dad's Capitalian friends."

"Naturally. If all monsters looked and acted like monsters, there would be no problem. Everybody could easily recognize them for what they really are and kill them on sight. But unfortunately they've learned to wear very attractive and charming masks to put prospective victims off-guard. Totalitarianism has come a long way since Tamerlane and Stalin and the other heirs of Genghis Khan who built pyramids of human skulls to terrify their captives into submission. Today's dictators use all sorts of scientific mind-bending techniques to make their suffering subjects think they never had it so good. And they have the willing help of large select classes called 'party members,' or some such innocent-sounding name, who gladly truckle to their masters' whims in exchange for the power to dish out the same treatment to those poor slobs who rank below *them*. Your beautiful Alexia, for example, is a 'conditioning officer' on her ship. That means she oversees the constant political indoctrination of the crew, and anyone of them that she suspects might be less than eager to die for dear old IFIB gets her recommendation for a slave-labor-camp vacation."

"Ye have an advantage on me there," Dawnboy conceded. "I havena studied accounts o' actual conditions on IFIB worlds yet. But wait—"

He went to his locker and dug out the sporran he had worn at Rothfeller Hughes's dinner party. In it he found the recorder button containing Sophronia Cleer's explanation of Otherism, which Alexia had given him. He had forgotten all about it, but now he hoped—with the rebellious anger of adolescence—that it might give him some good intellectual excuses for disagreeing with his father.

Against Lulu's objections, he tuned her out and put the button on his audiovisual player-recorder.

At first he thought he understood and agreed with the major philosophical points of Otherism. But soon the heavy, repetitious propaganda of the work became obtuse and boring. His attention wandered. He thought again of Juan, and snatches of "The Star-going Heart" drifted through his mind, especially the final stanza:

And when my godfire is gone

Let just a spark burn on

To light some other starfool's dawn.

Well, at least Juan had put a light to *this* starfool, Dawnboy thought wryly. But the dawn was still cloudy; he couldn't tell what kind of a day it was going to be.

22

THE ANIMOSITY OF family quarrels seldom lasts very long, especially when produced by nothing more serious than a temperamental clash between headstrong youth and stubborn maturity. During the next ten days of their journey, father and son gradually slipped back into their original and more comfortable roles as friendly shipmates. Lulu was pleased to think that her efforts at peacemaking were mainly responsible for the reconciliation, overlooking the fact that Ranger had little desire to enforce his new rules of military-school discipline when Dawnboy performed his duties so well without them.

Still, relations between the two men remained somewhat strained until one evening when Dawnboy entered the bridge to relieve his father at the helm. The first thing he noticed was that they had decelerated to sub–light speed, and the forward bulkhead-telescope lens was a swirling maze of misty lights.

Ranger was intently watching the madar screen, but Dawnboy saw nothing unusual about it when he peered over his shoulder.

"Well, I guess we weren't so smart about losing our devoted following as I'd thought we were," Ranger said.

"Why?" Dawnboy squinted at the screen. "I do na see anything."

"That's the trouble—we see nothing where there should be something." Ranger pointed to a tiny dark spot where the sweeping arm left a faintly glowing wake. "Remember the comet with the long drawn-out tail you spotted on your last watch? It occurred to me that might give us a good opportunity to check our backtrail. So I told Lulu to match our speed with the comet's and steer us into its tail. As you can see, we get microwave reflections on all the gases and particles that make up the tail, except in this dark area that remains a constant distance behind us."

"Indicating that space is filled by a solid object that displaces the gases and particles, but is na microwave reflective," Dawnboy concluded. "But how is that possible? I didna ken that a microwave-deflecting screen for starships had even been invented."

"It hasn't unless the IFIB or PHAP have some supergeniuses working for them. Besides, the thing's too small for a full-sized starship. What do you make of it, Lulu?"

"I'd say a compact high-powered job about the size of a two-man scouter," the biocomputer answered. "But I can detect no vital signs in it."

"Probably a robot-tracker. Without the necessity of installing a life-support system, they could build enough of it out of microwave-deflecting materials for the rest to show up on the screen as just cosmic dust. Damned clever."

"Which ship do ye think it's from? Not that it really matters."

"It's probably from the *Littlegart*," Lulu supplied. "PHAP scientists have done a lot of work in microwave research."

"Well, it's been back there long enough, wherever it's from," Ranger decided. "It's time we got rid of it."

"Ye aim to destroy it?"

"Not unless we have to. That would just tell them that we've caught on to their trick, and they'd move up to locate us on their madar before we could get away. The best solution is to send their electronic bloodhound off on a wild-meteor chase after something they'll think is us."

"And how do we do that?"

"Easily, if that robot has the sort of tracking gear I think it has. Most likely it uses laser scanners to pick up the faint traces of heat caused by our luxium reactor. So it will follow any heat trail, even one made by one of the sub-ether torpedoes we use to send emergency messages, or to avoid eavesdropping on our regular comm systems."

"Think that'll work?" Lulu asked.

"Worth a try. We'll program a torpedo for the Great Spiral Nebula in Andromeda, then cut our power the instant you launch it. Of course it won't have enough fuel to travel even a fraction of that distance, but it should give them a good, long run before they realize what's happened. Let's put a governor on it to make sure it doesn't go any faster than the *Gayheart* would." Ranger explained to Dawnboy: "A sub-ether torp can make several times our top speed, because it doesn't have to worry about the meteoric bits that can poke holes in a ship and let her air escape before the crew is aware of it."

"I know; I studied about the problems pioneering starship builders had in devising force shields to prevent such accidents. Many o' the early ships outran their own shields and collided wi' all sorts o' space junk."

"That's right. And while Lulu's programing the torp,

you want to bring me the cosmography map tapes you'll find in the top drawer of the chart locker? I guess it's about time I told you exactly where we're going to be doing our planet-hunting."

Dawnboy fetched the maps and watched eagerly as his father put them on the course-plotting viewscreen. Ranger pointed to a constellation shaped like a crooked finger, about three days' journey from their present location. "It's called 'The Beckon' by the few spacemen and astronomers who are even aware of its existence. To my knowledge, none of the stars in that area have ever been explored—mainly because nobody before me was crazy enough to think there could be anything of value out there."

"And how did ye get that crazy idea?" Dawnboy asked.

"About three years ago I passed through here as Second Officer on a panthropological expedition ship. It was owned and captained by a rich eccentric who had dreams of finding a lost civilization that had been left somewhere out here thousands of years ago by a now extinct race of superintelligent beings. There are several legends about that sort of thing floating around, but no one has ever found any hard evidence to support them. Nothing came of our expedition, either, but it did give me a chance to do some cosmographical observing on my own." Ranger's index finger touched the screen. "I discovered that a few of the stars in The Beckon—particularly this one—appear to be just right for producing Earth-style planets. I tried to convince my employer to go take a look at them, but he wasn't interested. So I memorized the coordinates and hoped that someday I'd be able to come back with my own ship."

"So we be that close to it already?" Dawnboy whistled between his teeth. "No wonder ye wanted to be double sure we are na being followed, before we made the final run for it."

"Uh-huh. How are you coming along with that torp, Lulu?"

"I'm just about— There, all set to launch."

"Okay, then let 'er rip."

"Ay, aye, sir. Power off, and torpedo away."

Ranger and Dawnboy watched the madar screen, where a small blip moved rapidly away from them. The dark spot behind them moved unhesitatingly after it. By the time the dark spot was out of the comet's tail, the blip had gone off the screen.

"Go get 'im, Rover," Lulu cheered. "Nothing I enjoy more than outsmarting a stupid machine. Unless it's outsmarting an even stupider human."

"Let's just hope Rover takes his master with him," Ranger said. "We'll play dead here for an hour and sweep the area around us—just in case."

The hour passed with dull, foot-dragging monotony for Dawnboy. The *Gayheart* drifted like a leaf on the comet's steady current, with no other object registering on the madar screen. But even when they were finally under way again, Ranger took no chances. For another hour he put the ship through rigorous evasive maneuvers, before he felt secure enough to set their course for The Beckon. Then at last he relaxed with a tired sigh, and Dawnboy grinned at him from the copilot's seat.

"Thanks, Dad."

Ranger looked up in surprise. "What for?"

"For telling me where ye think the planet is. That's been yer most private secret all this time, so I'm glad ye finally trust me enough to share it wi' me."

"Don't be silly; partners shouldn't have secrets from each other. It probably wouldn't have done any harm if I'd told you before this, but I just didn't think about it."

"If that's how you really feel," Lulu said meaningfully, "then maybe it's about time you told him *everything.*"

"What do ye mean?" Dawnboy asked, puzzled.

Ranger stared thoughtfully at the control panel before him for a long time, then turned back to his son with a strange softness in his eyes. "She's right. It is time I told you about your mother. You've proved you're man enough to take it."

"My mother? But she's dead. Be she not?"

"Well, yes . . . and no."

"What?" the youth cried. "What kind o' answer is that? Either she's dead or she's alive. Tell me which!"

Ranger ignored his mounting excitement. "I don't suppose you remember much about the old *Yankee Doodle*, the ship you were born on," he said musingly. "It was an ancient, falling-apart tub that should have been scrapped long before I bought it. We knew the light-energy converter was badly in need of repairs before we set out on that last cruise, with a load of citroffee beans from Nueva Brazil. There was good money to be made on that run in those days, much as I disliked the routine of cargo-hauling. But we let the repairs go because we were trying to economize and save up for a trip to Apache Highlands to see you. Then, when we were half-way to Aldebaran . . ."

Ranger closed his eyes, grimacing at the memory. But his voice was steady when he spoke again. "If the luxium pile had completely destabilized, then at least it would have been quickly and painlessly finished for us. But the radiation leak was just enough to give us severe burns before we discovered it and put on protective lead-lined suits. My tissue damage wasn't too bad to be regenerated, but Gay . . ." He grimaced again. "Well, I put her in biostasis and got her to Newtonia, but even the scientific wizards there couldn't save her body. Only her brain was left alive, undamaged, alert. When she found out what had happened, she begged me to let that part of her die, too. But I couldn't do it. So I accepted the director of the Darwin Institute's offer to keep her there and employ her for simple calculator operations."

"Ye mean she's part o' a biocomputer set-up, like Lulu?"

"Not exactly," Lulu said. "I'm content with this position because my physical body was nearing the natural end of a long, full life, anyway. But your mother was still young, beautiful, vibrantly in love with life. An existence like mine would have been mental agony for her."

"That's right," Ranger said. "So the scientists promised to use only her subconscious mind for their work. Her higher intelligence centers are maintained just below the level of awareness, although she is frequently given mental exercises with new data, in order to prevent tissue atrophy. They say she can survive indefinitely that way. Not very happily, I suppose, but then she isn't aware of being unhappy, either."

"So my mother is alive and well and working as an adding machine on Newtonia?" Dawnboy said with a bitter smile. "I hardly know what to make o' it. Perhaps I would've done the same thing in yer place, but I canna help thinking that she might be better off if ye'd done as she asked and let her die."

"You think I haven't felt that way, too—everytime I think of her?" Ranger demanded. "But as long as her mind and personality remain intact, there's always hope that science may one day find a way to do something for her. Someday the organ-transplant techniques may become so highly perfected that her brain can be placed in another body, and she'll have a second chance for a normal life. I owed her at least that much. It probably won't happen in our lifetimes; and even if it did, the new person she would become might not feel any attachment to us. So for your own peace of mind, you'd better learn to do as I've done—tell yourself that the old Gay we knew and loved is dead and gone forever."

"But ye do na really believe that, do ye?"

Ranger seemed about to give a ready answer, then hesitated and looked away from his son's piercing gaze. "No, if I really believed it, I would never have gone back to Apache Highlands for you. Instead, I would've found myself another wife and started life over again. But as long as just a small part of your mother remains alive, I can't stop being married to her. That's why I said I could never have anything to do with your Aunt Eve—or with any other woman."

"Aye, I can understand that now." Looking at his father's slumped shoulders, Dawnboy began to appreciate the great loneliness and guilt he must have been living with all these years. He wished he could think of some comforting words to ease his mind. But what could he say? That he forgave him? For what? Every man coped with life's problems the best he could in his own way, and it wasn't his place to judge Ranger's actions. This situation was just one of the countless unexplainable and unchangeable acts of fate that, in the Apache tradition, had to be fatalistically accepted and endured.

"Well, now you know," Ranger said. "I don't suppose you're pleased to share *this* secret with me, but it's a relief to have it off of my mind at last." He rose and stretched wearily. "I think I'll turn in now. You two keep your eyes open. I hope we've seen the last of our followers, but we can never be too sure about that."

"Don't worry. We'll hold the fort," Lulu assured him.

"Aye. Good night, sir," Dawnboy said absently.

After Ranger had gone, Dawnboy ignored Lulu's attempts at light conversation. Finally she took the hint and left him alone with his thoughts.

They were pretty confusing thoughts. At first he hardly knew what to make of the strange news about a woman he scarcely remembered. Aunt Eve had been so much a mother—and an intensely alive human being—to him that he found it hard to relate to an unfortunate semi-conscious brain floating in a tank of cerebrospinal fluid on a far-off world. So he tried to imagine how he would feel if it were Aunt Eve's brain—and that brought everything into clearer perspective.

Actually it was very simple: a kinswoman of his was in trouble, so he was honor-bound to do all he could to help her. His father may not have seen the situation in quite those terms, but then his father wasn't a Highland Apache. So, how would an Apache warrior deal with this problem? When Aunt Eve had been carried off by the Mongol-Sioux, Ravenslayer Lochnagar had hunted down her abductor and slain him in single combat. That method had great appeal to Dawnboy's romantic lust for action, but it was not very practical in this case.

No, this particular challenge required more intelligent analysis and careful planning than the brute strength and courage of a warrior. Ranger had said that his mother's only hope lay in the possibility that some-day medical science would find a way to put her brain into another body. Very well, then, he would just have to find a way to get the Newtonian scientists to speed up their efforts to perfect that sort of operation. He had no idea how many seemingly insurmountable obstacles still confronted scientists working on organ-transplant research; but he would not have been discouraged even if he had known about them. Because, for all of civilization's depressing and unmanly shortcomings, his study and experience with it had taught him one valuable lesson: money can make almost any activity go faster and easier.

So all he had to do was become fabulously rich and then use his fortune to set up a crash program in brain-transplant research. The seemingly insurmountable obstacles to that goal didn't faze him, either. It might take him years, or even his entire life to learn to be a sharp-dealing businessman and to accumulate enough money to do the job, but what of it? His future had looked aimless before; now he had a purpose, a focal point on which to concentrate his energies. The thought of it fired his imagination as nothing had ever done before. He would make his mother's resurrection his life's work, his—what was the old-fashioned word for it—oh, yes, his quest.

Like the warrior-knights of old, he would go quest-ing through the universe for the honor of his lady. It wouldn't be as much fun as becoming a warchief and killing the clan's enemies, but it still might someday make a good subject for a ballad or epic poem. Perhaps even Juan Orfo would have found his exploits inspir-ing, in his mocking way.

Dawnboy stared out at the beckoning finger of stars before them, and felt his blood surge with an eagerness to get there. Boundless self-confidence is one of the miracles of being sixteen and still a virgin in many ways.

23

"WELL, THERE IT IS," Ranger said simply.

"It sure is," Lulu concurred. "Congratulations, Boss."

Dawnboy peered intently at the planet they were slowly approaching. Second in a system of six, it appeared as featureless as a slightly flattened billiard ball. Not overly promising so far—but maybe it would improve as they got closer.

At least the "sun" looked inviting, after so many days of near-darkness in deep space. It was an F-class yellowish-white star, smaller and hotter than Sol, but made similar by a crown of dancing solar prominences. Dawnboy thought longingly of how good the heat would feel on his bare flesh—if there was any safe place for sunbathing in the system.

Ranger, evidently thinking along the same lines, asked: "Do you have a spectroscopic analysis of the sun yet, Lulu?"

"Affirmative, and everything seems to check out okay. Radiation, heat, light wavelengths are all well within the limits of human tolerance. Providing that your planet has a suitable atmosphere to filter them properly, of course. I'm still working on that."

"Okay, let me know when you have that data. And see if you can improve the telescope's lens magnification. Either it's getting weaker or my eyes are."

"Probably a little of each . . . There—how's that?"

"Much better, thank you." Ranger stopped squinting as the seemingly transparent bulkhead became clearer.

"What's that? A moon?" Dawnboy asked.

"Yes, it looks about the size of Old Earth's Luna,

using the planet's size for scale. How about that, Lulu?"

"That's right, proportionately speaking, although this planet is somewhat smaller than Earth. There seems to be another, smaller satellite on the opposite side of the planet. But I can't tell you much about it until we go into orbit and see it up close."

"How d'ye even know 'tis there?" Dawnboy asked.

"Clairvoyance. I used to be a gypsy fortune-teller."

"Sure, and the fact that you could bounce a madar beam off the sun and get a reading of the planet's opposite side," Ranger said.

"Spoilsport," Lulu pouted. "How can I ever teach the boy respect for his elders, when you are constantly telling him the dull old truth?"

"You just do your job," Ranger instructed her.

"I wish we could see through the cloud cover," Dawnboy said. "It seems to cover the entire surface o' the planet."

"With good reason," Lulu commented. "So far my scanners have detected nothing but liquid on the planet's surface."

"Oh, no!" Ranger groaned. "Don't tell me we came all this way just to find a giant-sized swimming pool."

"Is a water world o' no use to humans at all?" Dawnboy asked.

"Well, a few have been colonized. But it's usually more trouble than it's worth, and they can never be made to accommodate large populations. I doubt if many people would want to travel the great distance to this one. If we don't spot any land after a couple of orbits, we'll move on to the next star. None of the other planets in this system are of any use, except perhaps as scientific observation posts. And there're no profits to be made in that."

The two men watched gloomily as Lulu brought them up to the planet's gravitational field and slipped into orbit. Her computer analysis of the water world's atmosphere revealed it to be extremely humid, but otherwise perfectly suited for human life support. Even that news failed to cheer Ranger very much, but he soon forgot his disappointment as he became absorbed in studying the second satellite.

It was a miniature of the other moon—about five miles in diameter and roughly meteor-pitted and -dusted. He scowled at the dull sphere and muttered under his breath until Dawnboy inquired what was wrong.

"According to my calculations, that ridiculous little satellite shouldn't be there," Ranger answered. "Or at least it shouldn't have such a stable orbit, this close to the planet's surface. By the simplest laws of physics, the planet's gravity should have dragged it down for a collision by now. I can't even see how it got out here in the first place, without becoming subject to the other moon's orbit and gravitation—in which case it couldn't remain exactly opposite that one."

"Maybe it was originally a wandering asteroid that the planet's gravity captured," Lulu suggested. "If that happened a relatively short time ago, it could be gradually spiraling in for a collision and we're just too close to observe its orbital aberrations."

"I suppose that could have happened." Ranger was reading a computer printout of a preliminary survey of the satellite's elemental composition. Suddenly his attention perked up. "Hey, what's this? Trace of luxium? Now that's good news. Even a low-grade deposit there might yield enough to pay the operating expenses of this trip. And if there's more of it on the planet, or on the other moon—"

"Look there!" Dawnboy cried, pointing.

A break in the clouds exposed a wide stretch of gray water that was pleasantly interrupted by the jagged outline of a landmass.

"Land ho!" The happy excitement in Ranger's voice matched his son's. He rose from the pilot's seat and headed for his deceleration couch, as Dawnboy followed suit. "Get us down there, Lulu, and don't spare the G's. It looks like we might not have picked a loser after all!"

Lulu dropped the *Gayheart* into the planet's atmosphere with hull-scorching haste. But even at that swift rate of descent, they overshot the landmass by several thousand miles by the time they broke through the cloud cover. Rather than go to the trouble of braking and turning to reverse course, Ranger decided to go ahead and make a full orbit of their newfound world. They both were curious to look the place over, anyway.

As it turned out, there was not much for them to see except water, clouds, and more water. Apparently, almost the entire surface of the planet was covered by a vast ocean, in which they detected swimming creatures of many varieties and sizes. None of these displayed signs of intelligent behavior—which Ranger said was a mixed blessing. It was always a thrilling experience when a man encountered another sentient species; but if this world was already occupied by such a race, they would not be able to claim it by right of discovery. And just now Ranger was more anxious to find something he could sell.

"The land's coming up again," Dawnboy said, pointing to a vague shape on the horizon. "Do ye think 'tis big enough to be a continent? Or just an island?"

"We'll soon find out. Give us more altitude, Lulu. I want to get an overall view of it this time."

"Sorry, Boss. We're scraping the cloud bottoms as it is. This low ceiling is a mess to work with."

"Yeah, and I suppose there'll be plenty of fog over the land, too," Ranger surmised. "That won't bother our surveying instruments, but I always like to see what sort of claim I'm staking out."

"Do we have to drive stakes into it?" Dawnboy asked.

"That's just an obsolete figure of speech. Slow down, Lulu; I want to see that small islet just off the coast."

"Ever see an islet trailing a wake?" Lulu asked, reducing speed. "That thing's alive, Skipper, and big enough to make a Jonah of the *Gayheart.*"

They looked down at the broad leather back of a creature that plowed slowly through the water with rhythmical tail-sweeps. At the end of a long reptilian neck, a massive head that seemed to be entirely composed of row upon row of needle-pointed teeth reared up and peered from side to side. Much of the animal was submerged, but what they could see of it was over a hundred yards long.

"*Whooee!* What a whopper to catch for the frying pan!" Ranger sighed.

Dawnboy tried to remember his biohistory lessons. "What would ye call it—an ichthyosaur?"

"I'd call it anything it wanted me to call it," his father answered, "if I had to live in the same ocean with it."

As they watched, the monster plunged its head underwater. The body smoothly undulated after it, as the two liquid walls created by the dive closed like smacking lips over it. Immediately the water in front of the creature boiled with foamy eruptions as a school of multifinned fish the size of small cows fled in terrified, half-flying bounds.

"So much for the invigorating water sports on this lovely vacation world," Lulu said. "Shall we see what the land has to offer?"

"By all means," Ranger said. "Compared to this, it has to be an improvement."

They passed over reef-studded shoals that led to sandy beaches backed up by towering cliffs swarming with flying reptiles. Dawnboy was interested to note that a few of the larger soaring saurians strongly resembled the pegasuses of Apache Highlands, but he wasn't much tempted to try to ride them. Once they were over the cliffs, the land broke into rolling hills, broad valleys, and deep canyons. Rocks and boulders were colorfully blotched with moss and lichens, but no other vegetation appeared to have yet evolved beyond the level of simple sedges, grasses, and ferns that ranged from ankle-high to tree-sized.

About two hundred miles inland, a steep mountain range shot up abruptly to over ten thousand feet above sea level. They could see little of it, however, because the entire area was obscured by a furious thunderstorm, with only a few naked, rocky peaks rising above the lightning-laced black curtains of rainclouds. They took instrument measurements of the mountains and soared on to a high plateau of verdant plains, lush tree-fern forests, and more stream-carved canyons and narrow fissures like angry knife slashes in the land's tough hide. Clouds of steam gusted out of some of the fissures, indicating hot springs deep in their recesses, but there was no other visible evidence of volcanic activity. The plateau gradually sloped down to a wide river valley that seemed to be the central dividing line of the landmass; but here, too, their view was obstructed by large patches of rain and fog. Beyond the river rose another mountain range, with several snow-capped peaks registering nearly eighteen thousand feet in elevation. And then came another plateau, another range of smaller mountains, and a smaller river that tumbled down to a well-sheltered bay of the sea.

Taking a quick look up and down the coastline, they came about and retraced their course over the land, crisscrossing for a better overall view this time.

After several hours of careful scrutiny, Lulu summed up their findings: "It's an island continent of roughly rectangular shape lying along the planet's equator, measuring about four thousand miles longitudinally by two thousand latitudinally. The coastline is a sea lover's delight, with countless natural harbors and good beaches. Geology probes reveal rich deposits of iron, copper, uranium, gold, and other useful minerals, plus ample coal and petroleum. I can't say for sure about the soil until I've analyzed some samples, but it appears fertile enough to grow any sort of crop in abundance. Water is certainly no problem, with the mountains' superb watersheds to provide year-round irrigation and plenty of hydroelectric power. So I'd say the place offers excellent prospects for human occupation and industrial advancement, beginning with a population of a hundred million or so. You might not have much livable land space here, relative to the planet's size, but what you do have is first-rate."

"So ye think this is all there is above sea level?" Dawnboy asked.

"Yes, I'm afraid she's right there," Ranger said. "But we'll let her make a more thorough world survey just to make sure, while we get some rest." He yawned sleepily. "This planet's sun may say it's only noon, but it's way past my bedtime."

"That's right, go off and leave me alone to do all the work," Lulu pouted. "You men have no consideration for a poor girl's feelings. Just for that, I've a good mind not to remind you to register your claim with the SSA."

"Oh, yes, how could I have forgotten that?" Ranger exclaimed. "Prepare a message torpedo for me. I don't want to risk one of our followers' picking up a microwave beam and tracing it back to us, if any of them are still in the neighborhood. And program the torp for an erratic zigzag course, so they won't be able to backplot the course even if they are lucky enough to glimpse it shooting past them."

When Lulu had the torpedo ready, Ranger started verbally listing the planet's location, size, description, and other pertinent details on the missile's coded recorder banks.

Dawnboy, still peering down at the planet's misty surface, listened half-interestedly, until something his father said caught his attention abruptly. "What's that ye said?" he demanded.

"Well, I have to give the planet some name for registration purposes, so what's wrong with 'Dawnworld'?"

"Nothing's wrong wi' it, I reckon. 'Tis just that . . ." For the first time that he could recall, Dawnboy could think of nothing to say.

Ranger smiled at him. "It will probably be renamed by the people who buy and settle it, but for a little while you can have a world all of your own. So don't say I never gave you anything."

Dawnboy wondered how you thanked someone for a gift like that. Since there didn't seem to be any adequate way of doing it, he just gave his dad a lopsided grin and turned to look back at his planet.

It seemed to Ranger that he had hardly dosed off, when Lulu's voice roused him. A glance at his chronometer told him he had slept six hours, but he was still heavy-headed and gritty-eyed with fatigue. "What's the matter?" he growled irritably.

"Sorry to disturb your beauty sleep, Skipper," Lulu said. "But I thought you'd like to know that the madar screen has picked up a blip heading toward this system at plus-eight lightspeed."

Ranger snapped bolt upright, scrambling for his clothes. "What is it? How many of them are there? Why didn't you—?"

"Take it easy. I didn't know about it myself until just now. I can't tell for sure, but it's just about the right size for an IFIB starcruiser."

24

"So, CAPTAIN FARSTAR, we meet again." Ship-Controller Autry Lopezov laughed genially from Ranger's photophone. "Isn't that what the villain used to say on those old video melodramas?"

"I wouldn't know; that was never my favorite form of entertainment," Ranger drawled. "I must say it's an unexpected surprise to see you here, Autry, but you're looking extremely well."

"You, too, my dear friend. How about coming over for lunch? I'm dying for some shoptalk with a real space dodger. Some of the evasive maneuvers you gave us were absolutely brilliant. I'll bet Hildegriff in the *Littlegart* is still chasing your sub-ether torpedo!"

"Thanks. I'm just as impressed by your skill at finding us here. I don't suppose you would care to tell me how you did it?"

"Come to lunch. You never know what I might reveal over a few glasses of wine," Lopezov said teasingly.

"Sorry, we've just eaten. How about dinner instead?"

"Done. And do bring your handsome son along, too.

A certain young female officer on my ship hasn't stopped talking about him since Capitalia."

"I'm afraid one of us will have to stay here to mind the ship, much as I hate to cramp the boy's social life." Ranger glanced up to see Dawnboy blushing at the reference to Alexia. "By the way, welcome to our little world. What do you think of it?"

"Very nice, what there is of it. We of the Family could certainly use it for our burgeoning population. Pity we didn't get here first, but naturally you've already registered it with the SSA?"

"Naturally." Ranger gave the word a note of uncertainty to keep Lopezov guessing, while he tried to deduce from the other man's tone if he had spotted their message torpedo, or was just fishing for clues. It was an intriguing, but highly inconclusive, game. "Well, Autry, it's a pleasure communicating with you, as always, but we really must get back to work now. We have a lot to do before we can put this piece of real estate on the market."

"I understand. But I'm sure you won't mind if we do a bit of looking around on our own. The Family might be interested in making a bid, when you offer this planet for sale."

"Not at all. Be our guests!"

"Thank you." Lopezov reached for his photophone cutoff switch. "Until dinner tonight. I'm looking forward to it."

Ranger watched the screen go blank, then called the IFIB commander a few well-picked dirty names. But there was as much amused admiration as anger in his voice. "Someday, Autry, you and I are gonna have a real showdown." He smiled grimly.

"Now *that* I'd like to see," Lulu said. "From a safe distance."

"Ye're na really going over there tonight, are ye, Dad?" Dawnboy demanded. "Ye'd be riding into an enemy ambush!"

"No, it's not Autry's style to abuse an invited guest," Ranger said. "For all of his screw-loose ideology, he still has a soldier's professional pride. When he makes his move against us, it'll be according to military ethics—even if it does seem sneaky and treacherous. So I may as well have dinner with him and try to learn what he already knows about us, while he's trying to learn more about us from me. At least I'll get a free meal out of it."

"Well, you'd better make it clear to him that you've already registered your claim here," Lulu advised. "He wouldn't hesitate to vap us, if he thought he had a chance to stake it out for his own people."

"I don't think we have to worry about that, and I'd like to keep him guessing as long as possible. Besides, there's the remote possibility that someone else has already claimed this planet—and his government would be highly displeased if he got them mixed up in an interstellar dispute that might even lead to war, over a world of such minor importance. It will take at least a week for our message to reach SSA Headquarters and for them to search the records and send back a reply. So I think we can depend on our IFIB friends to remain cordial for that long." Ranger rose briskly from his seat. "Right now we have something more pressing to take care of."

"What's that?" Dawnboy asked.

"I want to find out how they traced us here. They must have some sort of directional beaming device planted on the ship, but I'm double-damned if I know how we missed it on our searches. Even if they made it liquid and painted it on the hull, I'm sure I would have found it."

"Which means—" Lulu began.

"That whatever it is has to be *inside* someplace," he finished for her. "I don't know how they could have managed that, but I want a thorough search made of this tub's interior—even if it means taking her apart rivet by rivet."

It didn't take nearly that much trouble to find their electronic spy. Two hours later Lulu, checking over her computer's memory banks, found something unusual and called it to Ranger's attention.

After puzzling over it a while, he suddenly swore an

oath as the realization hit him. "It's an electromagnetic field carried right on your circuits," he explained. "The reason our instruments couldn't detect its power source is because it used *our* power source. As long as your computer was functioning, it sent out a continuous beam to the IFIB receiver."

"No wonder I couldn't tell it was there," Lulu said. "It would have been like a light bulb trying to see its own shadow. Ugh! Get the nasty little thing off me. It's like having a parasite under my skin."

"It would be simple enough to yank those circuits and replace them with new ones. But first I want to find out how it got there. It had to be programed into your banks somehow. Did you receive any unscreened messages while we were over Capitalia?"

"Of course not. What kind of a loose woman do you take me for?" Lulu demanded indignantly.

"Wait—I think I may be the one responsible for this," Dawnboy said guiltily. "I would na ha' thought she would . . . I mean, how could she . . . ? Well, I'll go get it and we'll see . . ."

He left his father staring curiously after him and hurried to his cabin. A moment later he returned with the recorder button of Sophronia Cleer's theories of Otherhood, which Alexia had given to him. He explained where he got it, then put the button on one of the computer's recorder-players while Ranger monitored the wavelengths of its electromagnetic output.

"That's it," Ranger said after a few minutes. "They recorded the directional beam at a subliminal frequency. Lulu might have been able to detect it when it was being fed into her banks, but she had no reason to be suspicious then."

"How could I ha' been so stupid?" Dawnboy angrily accused himself. "Ye warned me what to expect from them, and I still let them trick me into leading them here. Now it could cost ye everything ye own!"

Ranger put a comforting hand on his arm. "Don't be too hard on yourself. This could have happened to anybody, and it'll teach you to be more on-guard the next time. Besides, our situation isn't too serious yet. I still have some tricks of my own in reserve, if they push us too hard."

"But I let her make such a fool o' me!" Dawnboy fumed with humiliation. "She led me on, made me think I was something special to her, and all the time she must've been laughing at me behind my back. Aagh, the shameless two-faced slut! If only I could get me hands on her lily-white throat . . ."

"And don't be too hard on Alexia either," Ranger said. "It was just a military assignment for her. She has nothing personal against you, and probably she really does like you. What you must remember is that she—like everyone else—is a product of her society and its conditioning. She sincerely believes that what her people are doing is good for the advancement of all intelligent beings, just as you believed the clan's codes of behavior were the best rules for anyone to live by. If you're going to be a successful interstellar businessman, the first thing you'll have to learn is to accept other peoples' standards as normal and proper for them, even if they seem weird and revolting to you. We simply don't have the power to make them change their ways, as the IFIB and PHAP expeditionary forces do, even if we could be sure that such changes were for the best. Actually Alexia is—according to her standards—a highly moral and idealistic young woman."

"So was Lucrezia Borgia," Lulu said. "I just wish I were back in my old body and could have ten minutes alone with that little tramp. I'd teach her to toy with the feelings of a young, sensitive boy!"

"I think she already knows how to do that pretty well," Ranger said with a smile at his son. "Mark it up to experience, m'lad. We all have to learn from our mistakes. And at least when a man makes a fool of himself over a beautiful woman, he has the consolation of knowing that he just behaved naturally. If you hadn't been vulnerable to her charms, then I'd really worry about you."

Dawnboy tried to find comfort in his father's forgiveness, but he didn't have much luck. For the rest of the day he was too occupied by their planetary surveying chores to give the matter much thought. But that evening when his father had gone to dine aboard the IFIB ship, he fell to brooding angrily over his depressing feelings of guilt, shame, and bitter self-recrimination. What hurt most was the painful wound his masculine ego had suffered from having been outsmarted and manipulated by a mere woman. It reminded him of how—years before he had been born—his eldest uncle, Rincon-the-Pegasus-Tamer, had betrayed the clan for love of Chief Chatto's daughter, and for his treason had been put to death by his own father, Laird Angus. Was there no way that even the mightiest of warriors could ever be safe from women's deceitful wiles?

When Lulu tried, in her grandmotherly fashion, to cheer him up, she only succeeded in worsening his anguish. For a teen-age boy struggling to become a man, nothing is more humiliating than to be treated as a child who still needs a woman's protection against the harsh world. He had not yet learned that when a man is threatened by something as dangerous as a woman, the only thing that can possibly protect him is another woman.

He tried to salvage his pride by vowing that he would never again let the opposite sex influence him in any way. He would be a confirmed bachelor and fill his heart with hard, cold resistance against any feminine efforts to make him soft and helpless. He'd show the sneaky, double-dealing she-serpents that he was more than a match for their underhanded tactics! For a while he actually believed that he could stick to such a resolve for the rest of his life, and it greatly boosted his sagging morale. But eventually even his youthful inexperience began to doubt the viability of lifetime celibacy, especially when the only purpose of his pledge was to get even with one hateful female. That would be like cutting off his nose to spite his face, and the sharpness of the simile made him flinch.

All right then, he would find another way to avenge the insulting injury that Alexia had dealt to his honor. If he could not live entirely without women, he would condition himself to treat them in the brutal manner of a true Apache raider. The next time he encountered Alexia—and he would meet her again, he swore, even if he had to follow her across the universe and fight the entire IFIB empire to do it—he would show her how a *real* man dominates women and uses them. No amount of tearful pleading for mercy would weaken his determination, and when he was finished with her he would cast her aside with a scornful laugh.

No, on second thought he would take her prisoner and amuse himself by subjecting her to the many gruesome Apache tortures he had heard older braves describe with sadistic relish. How he would savor her agonized screams as he slowly reduced her firm flesh and strong will to bloody pulp! Then, when he had irrevocably destroyed her beauty and strength and she would be begging for the relief of death, he would release her. That way, her grotesque appearance would be a constant reminder to her that she had made a tragic mistake by incurring the enmity of Dawnboy MacCochise.

With those uplifting thoughts in mind, Dawnboy went to bed and slept peacefully.

25

ABOUT THE ONLY news that Ranger brought back from his visit with Autry Lopezov was that Alexia had changed her hairstyle and looked even more lovely. For some reason, that juicy tidbit did not excite Dawnboy or Lulu very much.

Ranger, observing how his son's chagrin had distilled to bitter animosity toward Alexia, thought it best not to mention the many sincere questions the girl had asked about him. Her open fondness for Dawnboy was most flattering, and Ranger did not doubt that it was genuine. Of course, she could feel little romantic interest in a boy so much younger than herself. But she said she thought he had a good mind and showed great potential. Ranger, knowing of her wholehearted dedication to Otherism, didn't have to ask, "Potential for what?" Nor did he doubt for a moment that she would—given another opportunity to be alone with Dawnboy—take up exactly where she had left off in her proselytizing efforts, blithely ignoring his raging urge to strangle her. She was indeed a most formidable young woman.

For two more days they continued their preliminary survey of Dawnworld.

As Ranger had suspected, the large island continent proved to be the planet's only land area, aside from some small islets that were hardly more than barren rocks thrust out of the endless sea. It gave Dawnboy a strange, lonely feeling to cruise along hour after hour with nothing in view but gray-cloud skies and wave-tossed waters teeming with fish and other aquatic life-forms. He felt as if he were a shipwrecked survivor drifting alone in a lifeboat. Not even their occasional sightings of the IFIB starship lazily following behind them did much to relieve his creepy sensation of having been stranded and forgotten on this primeval world.

So he felt considerably cheered-up when Ranger decided to go down to the continent to make a more extensive investigation of its potential for human habitation. Dawnboy was impatient to get his feet on firm ground again, but his father cautiously insisted on analyzing many samples of the land's air, water, soil, flora, and fauna before exposing themselves to it.

When Ranger was finally satisfied that the place held no discernible dangers beyond their capabilities to cope, he steered the ship to one of the lovely green valleys on the middle plateau. For the first time in many months, the *Gayheart* extended her landing gear and settled her full weight down onto the surface of another space-traveling body. But even then, Ranger restricted their first venture out of the air lock to a few minutes' walk in sealed vac-suits.

At last even Lulu's hyperwariness of alien contamination was allayed enough to permit them to step out into the subtropical humidity clad only in light clothing. They both carried synapse disrupters for protection and to take unharmed any interesting animal specimens they might come across. Ranger also had a needle rifle slung over his shoulder—just in case.

Dawnboy wandered off through fields of wild flowers, intoxicated by their heady perfume in the fresh air. He did not need much imagination to fancy himself back in one of the wilder parts of Apache Highlands, although the land here had much more moisture and vegetation. Still, this was an enchantingly primitive and unspoiled world, and Dawnboy felt so pleasantly at home in it that when a small, six-legged reptilian creature scurried away practically under his feet, he did not have the heart to use his disrupter on it.

A patch of crimson and gold flowers caught his attention, but at his approach it suddenly fluttered aloft as a cloud of butterfly-like insects. They had such chubby little bodies that he wondered how their fragile wings could lift them so gracefully; but when he saw they were equipped with horny-tipped tails that might be poisonous stings, he decided he had gotten close enough to them for the time being. He caught one of the creatures in his specimen net and started back to the ship with it, just as his father called out to him.

Ranger had found a spring-fed brook that had cut a winding channel through the middle of the valley. There was just a trickle of water at the bottom of the five-foot-deep streambed now, and Ranger had climbed down to study the exposed strata of soil and rocks. He was scowling uncertainly at something in the bank when Dawnboy came up to him.

"Anything wrong, Dad?"

"That's what I'm wondering. See these shells embedded in the clay? I'd bet my last stellar they're the same species as some samples we took yesterday down at the seashore. And they aren't fossils, either."

"So . . . ?"

"So what are they doing up here at six thousand feet

above sea level? I doubt that one of the native carnivores carried them this far just to enjoy a seafood lunch in the mountains."

"Well, I reckon this area was once part o' the seabed," Dawnboy said with his smattering of geological evolutionary knowledge. "Then volcanic action or changes of pressure on the planet's surface caused it to be raised up here. All stranded life-forms that couldn't escape back to the sea or adapt to living on land eventually died and were buried under layers of material eroded down from the higher elevations."

"You're right, Son, but normally it takes millions of years for that to happen. I'm sure that a carbon dating of these shells would prove they haven't been here more than fifty to a hundred thousand years." Ranger looked around them with growing puzzlement. "The whole ecology of this place is screwed-up. We've seen dinosaur-like reptiles of the early Mesozoic Era grazing on flowering plants that shouldn't have evolved until a hundred million years later. We haven't found a single feathered creature yet, but there are some primitive mammals swimming around out there. And as for the insects—"

"Oh, don't be so anthropocentric," Lulu said in their earphones. "Just because most Earth-type planets have been found to have followed Earth's pattern of development doesn't mean they all do. Just offhand, I can think of at least one perfectly logical explanation for all of this ecological confusion."

"What's that?"

"Well, suppose the tallest mountain peaks here were independent islands for hundreds of millions of years. They would have provided landspace for the evolution of many different life-forms, with a sea barrier to protect them from each other and the marine predators. Then, as land bridges formed between the islands and other aquatic life-forms adapted to surviving with their heads above water, the process would naturally produce overlapping stages of evolutionary development."

"That makes sense," Dawnboy said.

"Yeah, I guess it could have happened that way,"

Ranger agreed. "But I still can't shake off the uneasy feeling that some sort of intelligence has been at work here, helping the planet develop an inhabitable environment."

"I'll buy that," Lulu said. "I never have been convinced that evolution necessarily invalidated the Theory of Divine Creation; and there's no reason why *this* world should be godforsaken, even though it does look that way."

"Maybe this planet *was* visited thousands o' years ago by that race o' superintelligent beings," Dawnboy suggested. "The ones that yer expedition was searching for when ye came out here before."

"Maybe. If such a race ever existed." Ranger vaulted to the top of the streambank and started off briskly toward the ship. "Come on, I want to go upstairs and have a look at something again."

They rose fifty miles above the cloud cover and orbited the planet while Ranger studied its two moons with the electronic telescope and laser beam probes. Dawnboy, finally growing bored with his father's moody preoccupation, was about to go to the galley for lunch when Ranger muttered: "I'd sure like to go up and have a close look at those two hunks of rock, just to set my mind at ease about something."

"Well, then, why don't we go up there?" his son asked.

Ranger pointed at the IFIB ship, hanging off in the distance. "We will, as soon as I can get those nosey snoopers off our backs. Lulu, program another sub-ether torpedo for SSA Headquarters, and adjust its speed to keep it just ahead of a starship."

"Will do, Boss. What's the plan?"

"It's possible that Lopezov still doesn't know for sure if we've registered our claim here yet. So he may think this torp is intended for that purpose and maybe he'll try to chase it down and destroy it. That might take him away from here for a few days, or at least until he gets tired of the game."

"Ye really think it'll work?" Dawnboy asked.

"It's worth a try. Even a smart old spacehound like

217

Autry might not be expecting us to use the same tactic twice in a row. Fire when ready, Lulu."

"Aye, aye, sir. And I'll even put a few extra kinks in the torpedo's course that I'll defy any other computer to second-guess."

A few minutes later, Lulu launched the torpedo and they had the pleasure of seeing the IFIB ship blast-off after it. But that pleasure was marred by the sight of a smaller craft leaving the starcruiser and moving toward the planet's surface.

"Damn! They're leaving a guard party behind to keep tabs on us," Ranger growled. "Follow that boat, Lulu. I want to see just what they're up to."

They trailed the small craft back down through the cloud cover to the island continent. Lulu reported that her sensors detected only three people aboard, but Ranger said that didn't matter; it was obviously a survey boat equipped with much advanced electronic gear. They followed it all the way down to a landing on a high sea-cliff promontory on the continent's west coast, where the day had progressed only to midmorning, and watched two figures disembark and move around the craft.

"They'll probably stay there and track us electronically," Ranger speculated. "That's about the best they can do, since their boat doesn't have the speed to tail us. That won't interfere with our trips to the moons, but still I hate to leave them there with the place all to themselves. No telling what mischief they might try to stir up."

"Then why na leave me down there to keep an eye on 'em?" Dawnboy proposed. "I'm na overanxious to visit a couple o' dead moons, anyhow."

Ranger thought about it for a moment, then shook his head. "No, it could be dangerous. IFIB troops are usually well disciplined, but they have been known to commit some pretty nasty atrocities when there aren't any high-ranking officers around to control them."

"I can take care o' meself," Dawnboy said confidently. "Come on, Dad. We're partners, aren't we? So why na let me do my fair share o' the work?"

"Because he knows you're not old enough to handle so much responsibility," Lulu said. "He wants to keep you under his wing until you've had time to grow up and face the universe on your own two feet."

"Don't try to use reverse psychology on me," Ranger said to her as Dawnboy was about to snap an indignant retort. "I don't need you to help me decide when he's ready to take on more adult duties, and"—he sized up his son's eager expression—"I guess he's as ready for that now as he'll ever be. Go get your gear together, Son, while I stock an antigrav car with the supplies that you'll need to stay a few days down there."

"Yes, sir!"

Grinning broadly, Dawnboy rushed off to his cabin.

"But I want you to promise you'll stay in a defensive position and not take any chances," Ranger called after him. "Understand?"

He may as well have been talking to the wind.

"They grow up so fast, don't they?" Lulu sighed.

"Let's just hope he's grown-up enough for this job," Ranger said worriedly. "Hunting grizzly bears may be fine sport for boys, but he'll soon find out that it takes a man to deal with really dangerous game—other men."

26

DAWNBOY BROUGHT HIS antigrav car down on a cliff across the bay from the promontory where the IFIB party had landed. Some careful scouting from the air had revealed this to be an ideal observation post from which to keep the promontory under surveillance. The sheer limestone cliff face fell away eight or nine hundred feet to a rocky, wave-pounded beach. Several flying reptiles nested in the weathered nooks and crannies, but they all appeared to be small and of harmless varieties.

The only place in the cliff that might possibly accommodate something large enough to be dangerous was a cave about a hundred feet down from the top, and Dawnboy's quick mind had already found a use for that gaping hole. Leaving the car, with his antigrav pack and needle rifle he walked to the edge of the cliff and stepped over. He drifted down to the cavern entrance, holding his rifle cocked and ready, and flashed the beam of the light on his vac-suit helmet into the shadow-darkened interior. Some bat-sized creatures, startled by the light, darted out past him with high-pitched squeals.

When there was no further noise or activity from the cave, he cautiously stepped inside and looked around. The cavern did not seem to have ever been occupied by anything larger than the bat-creatures, although it was dry and fairly well sheltered from the wind. It extended back about fifty feet into the cliff and was some twenty feet wide and fifteen high. Just an ordinary, everyday-type cave—nothing to get very excited about. But it suited Dawnboy's needs nicely, and the narrow entrance looked just about the right size for what he had in mind.

Returning to the antigrav car, he carefully maneuvered the boxy vehicle down to the cave and wedged it into the entrance. It was a tight fit, with just enough space left around the sides and top for good air circulation. By taking the remote-control switches of the hatches of the car inside the cave with him, he had a double barrier against anyone or anything that might try to come in after him. Thus established, he used the car's communication unit to report his situation to the *Gayheart*, which was already far beyond the range of his throat mike. Ranger complimented him on his good work, which reenforced his own rather smug feeling of self-satisfaction.

For a while Dawnboy watched the promontory through his infrared binoculars, but did not observe any discernible activity around the IFIB craft. He therefore decided to devote some time to making his position more secure.

He moved all his supplies from the car to the rear of the cave and built a stone parapet around the area where he would be sleeping. Although Ranger had expected to be away for only about twenty-four hours, he had insisted that Dawnboy take a full week's supply of food, and now even those rations looked pitifully small. Well, he could always do some hunting and fishing if his father's return were delayed for very long. But his meager ten gallons of water would have to be supplemented, in case he had to withstand a siege or hole up in the cave for a while.

Searching along the cliff face, he eventually found some wet streaks that led to a freshwater spring. The water flow was little more than an ooze, but sufficient to fill several of his collapsible plastic containers. When he had them stored away in his stronghold, he took time out for a bite to eat, then did some more spying on the IFIB position. Still not much going on over there. Maybe the three crewmen were taking advantage of the absence of higher authority to 'goof-off'—something that Ranger said was a universal practice among all military personnel.

By then it was midafternoon, and Dawnboy's strong Apache instinct for action—along with his normal boy's adventurous curiosity—made him too restless to spend the rest of the day just sitting around. So, after checking over his weapons and gear, he carefully locked both car doors behind him and headed for the beach. While he was packing to leave the *Gayheart*, he had thought of taking his bow along, but then he realized how poorly armed that would make him for this assignment. Besides, he needed to get in more practice with some of the other weapons that he would probably be using more frequently. For that reason he had selected, among other weapons, the spaceman's old reliable Berlix .057 Magnum needle rifle and a New Aussieland comeback blade.

Soon, stripped to his breechclout and moccasins like

an Apache brave of an even older tradition than the clan's, he stood on the rocky beach and inhaled the cooling sea breeze that ruffled his long black hair.

Ah, this was more like the kind of wild, free life he had always thought he wanted to live! What a relief he felt to be out in the fresh air again, after so much cooped-up spaceship living. The happy surge of energy through his body made him want to run, leap, and yell his carefree young head off; instead, he satisfied the urge by singing odd snatches of songs as he scrambled over rocks and waded in the waves' foamy backwash. Down here out of sight of the IFIB craft, he could easily imagine he was all alone in this world—*his* world.

He was at last a true Dawnboy—the first man on a new world whose future was as bright and promising as his efforts could make it. A man could have a wonderful life here. For a while, the temptation to dream about it even made him forget his longing for a career in space. All he needed was a good wife—or several good wives, if he could support them, since the clan had no laws against polygamy—to help him start a new race to populate the planet. His mind seethed with ideas about how he would organize and govern his tribe to ensure every member's proper development and conduct.

Without being aware of it, Dawnboy was starting to understand why the migratory urge is such a powerful drive in all intelligent species. In every society there have always been some individuals who feel restricted by familiar surroundings and established modes of behavior. They lust to break free of old traditions that their inner discontent reflects as hopeless stagnation for everyone, regardless of how happily progressive others may find the environment. When such dissatisfied people are unable to bring about external changes to improve their opportunities, they often look around for new, unspoiled territories where they can make a fresh start at building an ideal civilization, unhampered by the mistakes of all who preceded them. Usually these adventurous pioneers *do* repeat many of those mistakes, while inventing some new ones of their own.

But if nothing else, the physical migrations of individuals through time and space at least keep a species from going stale; and the great variety of differing societies scattered among the stars increases the odds that eventually one of them may achieve that elusive ideal. The law of averages make success inevitable, given enough intelligently populated worlds in an infinite universe—even if no gambler in his right mind would place a bet on it happening within his lifetime.

Blissfully unconscious of those weighty facts, Dawnboy happily fantasized his future on Dawnworld as he rambled along the surf-washed beach, often sending small reptiles and crustaceans scurrying for shelter under rocks, and glimpsing strange-looking aquatic organisms sporting out in the blue-gray water. As he climbed over a large boulder, he was finally brought out of his daydreams by the sight of a tiny cove niched into the base of the cliffs, a cove complete with a sandy bathing beach free of rocks. It was a lovely spot, and as he hurried down to the beach a brief break in the clouds allowed the sun's rays to paint the sand a soft, buttery golden.

The sun was well down toward the horizon by then, but it was still a warm day and his exertions had made him work up a heavy sweat. For a long moment he stood in the middle of the beach staring yearningly at the inviting cool water and wondering if any of the ugly marine predators swam this close to the shore. His father had warned him against taking any unnecessary chances, but . . .

It took about thirty seconds for two facts—his father was a great distance away, and he was dying for a swim—to add up to their natural conclusion. Dropping his antigrav pack and weapons, he kicked off his moccasins and hit the water with a running dive.

It felt every bit as cool and refreshing as it had looked. He surfaced with long, even strokes, not pausing until he was twenty yards out from the beach. Then he tried to roll on his back and float. But the water lacked buoyancy and had only a faintly salty taste, so he had to tread water while looking around. Nothing else seemed to be sharing the cove with him, but still he could not keep the disturbing thought of powerful jaws closing around his legs completely out of his mind. Not that he was afraid. But since there was no one around to impress with his courage he could not see much point in staying in the water more than ten or fifteen minutes.

Returning to the beach with a sigh, he was about to stretch out on the sand to let the sun dry him, when he happened to glance out over the bay. He thought he saw a dark speck in the sky over the IFIB-occupied promontory.

He blinked, rubbed droplets from his eyelashes, and looked again. Then there were two specks; but they suddenly dropped down below the top of the promontory and were no longer outlined against the sky. Perhaps, he thought, they were just pterodactyls. But he could not afford to take anything like that for granted.

He picked up his rifle and squinted through the telescopic sight. What he saw then made him snatch up his ammo belt and run to the end of the beach: a figure on an antigrav scooter was moving across the water toward him, followed by a trim little scouter.

Dawnboy couldn't guess what business the IFIB crewmen might think they had with him, but if they were looking for trouble he was ready and willing to accommodate them. He climbed to the top of the boulder he had surmounted to find the cove and lay prone on the stone's flat surface. At a touch of the release stud, the rifle's telescoping barrel and stock snapped out to their full lengths and locked into position. He put the butt to his shoulder and peeped through the sight again.

The scooter seemed to be racing toward him at full speed, the rider crouched low over the handlebars to reduce wind resistance. The scouter was some distance behind and above the scooter, but closing swiftly, as if ... That was strange. The scouter pilot seemed to be chasing the scooter rider, instead of just escorting him.

Dawnboy adjusted the sight for clearer detail and focused on the scooter rider.

"Alexia!"

27

"I GUESS WE'VE seen enough here," Ranger said, turning away from the dead, airless satellite pictured on his viewscreen.

"I told you it was just an ordinary natural moon," Lulu said. "The other one has all the mystery."

"I know, but I had to investigate this one first to put my mind at ease. Take us around to the smaller moon, while I get ready to do some spacewalking."

"Do you think that's safe?"

"Is anything ever safe for a starship captain?" Ranger asked, slipping into his vac-suit.

"But if anything should happen to you, with Dawnboy alone down there on the planet with those people . . ."

"You should have thought of that before you talked me into letting him go down there alone," Ranger irritably cut her off. "I'm worried about him, too. But he will never learn to take care of himself if we don't let him get some experience at it. The best thing we can do is remember that he's a smart, courageous, resourceful Apache brave, and then concentrate on our own problems."

"I suppose you're right," Lulu said reluctantly. "But I wish he would call in more often and report that he's safe."

She swung the *Gayheart* around in a tight orbit to come in on the small satellite, as Ranger finished preparing for the vacuum of space. He checked his toolbelt and attached a holstered synapse disrupter to it.

"That's not much of a weapon," Lulu commented.

"I'm not expecting much trouble," Ranger said. "Unless you can tell me something about this strange piece of space junk that I don't already know." He studied the satellite's rocky, pitted surface in the viewscreen.

"I can only confirm your first suspicion: it is an artificial metallic structure of some kind. Its luxium content is too heavily concentrated in one spot to be a natural ore deposit. But I can't get a scanner reading of the satellite's composition. It must have a powerful shielding device."

"That's understandable. Whoever put it here would not have wanted strangers to mess around with it. I wonder what its function is? To observe and record the planet's development with instruments that relay the data to the observers' homeworld?"

"Your guess is as good as mine," Lulu said. "I can't get any response to my attempts to communicate with it, so it's probably fully automated."

"Probably." Ranger started toward the air lock. "Well, I'm not going to learn anything just standing around speculating about it. I'll try to stay in constant touch with you. But if anything happens to me, don't waste time crying about it. Instead, get right down to the planet's surface and pick up Dawnboy. Then you and he can decide what to do next."

"Yes, sir," Lulu said as Ranger stepped out of the air lock. "Be careful not to get too close to that luxium. Your tissue couldn't regenerate from *another* severe radiation burn."

"You tend to your own duties and let me worry about that," Ranger said tartly.

He drifted down until his heels touched the satellite's surface, then set his antigrav pack on Earth-normal and took a few experimental steps in the fine dust.

They were on Dawnworld's night side, but the area was well illuminated by the *Gayheart*'s signal lights. Ranger kicked a boulder as tall as himself and watched it roll a few paces. "Just as I thought," he reported to Lulu, "the staellite's gravity field has drawn in meteors and other cosmic debris until it acquired the appearance of a natural moon."

"It must have been there a long time to accumulate that much junk," Lulu said.

"Yes, there's no telling how old this thing is, unless I can find a way to get inside it. Did your probes reveal any sort of entrance?"

"Not a one. That sphere is as hermetic as an egg."

Ranger looked around at the ragged horizon framed starkly against the blackness of space. The horizon looked close enough for him to reach out and touch it because of the satellite's smallness, but it still had a lot of surface area to cover on foot.

"I'm not going to waste time looking for something your probes couldn't find. Do you see that small depression framed by three boulders, about twenty yards in front of me? Use your laser torch to cut a hole there."

"Yes, sir. Protect your eyes from the glare."

Ranger turned his back to the depression as the torch beam lanced out from the ship and went to work with a sizzling crackle. After a few minutes he asked: "Aren't you finished yet?"

"That is some tough material," Lulu complained. "I'm giving it all I've got, and the torch is hardly making a dent . . . There, it's starting to go now. I guess just the outer layer was the hard part. I think it's just about— Yes, it's all the way through now. Wait a bit for the edges to cool."

Ranger walked to the fused rim of the newly burned hole and flashed his helmet light inside. "Looks like a smooth metal deck of a wide corridor, about twenty feet below. I'm going down to see where it leads to."

"Be careful," Lulu cautioned.

He graved down to the deck and looked around. Nothing but metal bulkheads port and starboard, and curving walkways fore and aft. He guessed it didn't make much difference which way he went, so he started walking in the direction he was facing. He had gone about a dozen steps when it occurred to him that he should mark a trail that he could follow back to the exit hole. He unhooked the aerosol spray can of phosphorescent paint from his belt and retraced his steps. But his lightbeam playing along the overhead revealed nothing but solid unmarked metal.

"It appears that this thing has some sort of automatic repair service, Lulu," Ranger said. "I'm sealed inside, so you'll have to burn me out when I'm ready to leave. But I want to have a good look around first." He waited a few moments, then said: "Lulu, do you read me?"

The silence from his earphone was total.

He tried again to contact Lulu, with no success. Evidently the satellite's covering skin blocked communications beams as effectively as it patched holes. His situation did not look very promising, but he wasn't ready to call it desperate yet. He had several hours' supply of air and was confident that Lulu would wait a reasonable length of time before obeying his order to go pick up Dawnboy. So he might as well use that time to do what he had come here to do.

He turned and walked back along the corridor.

He moved slowly at first, and carefully watched his radiation detector gauge. The needle stayed well within the safe area, which didn't surprise him. The luxium nearby would most likely be a fuel supply, so naturally it would be kept in safe containers.

When he had covered about a thousand meters without seeing anything but deck and bulkheads, he became more confident and quickened his pace. A short distance further he came to a fork, with another corridor turning off to his right. Protruding from the bulkheads on each side of that corridor were several innocent-looking metal knobs about the size of his thumbs.

He stood there a while wondering about the knobs' purpose. They could be part of a sensor detection system, similar to photoelectric cells, to set off an alarm or trigger a defensive weapon against intruders. But in that case they would be redundant, since the act of cutting a hole to enter the satellite would have been an unmistakable announcement of invasion. Then again, however, a hole could be caused by a natural phenomenon, such as collision with a stray meteor. So it would make sense to have some sort of internal security system against an intelligent intruder who might get this far.

Ranger finally concluded it was pointless to try to reason out everything about the satellite when he knew nothing about the intelligence that had built it. The knobs might be no more than artistic decoration. In fact, it was quite possible that the entire satellite was nothing but a toy that had been carelessly abandoned when its owner had grown tired of it. He wouldn't know for sure about that until he had found a control room or some other clues to help him understand the satellite's function. Just the same, he decided not to meddle with the knobs just yet. Instead, he continued down the main corridor.

Another hundred meters brought him to a second fork. But this time the bulkheads of *both* of the corridors ahead of him contained the metal knobs. Ranger shrugged fatalistically. Evidently he wouldn't be able to continue his exploration of the satellite without testing the knobs' function sometime, so he decided he might as well do it now. He took out his photon torch and played the fine cutting beam over one of the knobs. The intensely concentrated discharge of energy left no visible mark on the knob, so Ranger settled back to see what other results it might produce. He didn't have long to wait.

A high-pitched squeal penetrated his helmet with earsplitting force, as his light detected movement far down the corridor. He braced himself with his disrupter in one hand and the torch in the other as an object came swiftly toward him. It was a metal drum about two meters tall that apparently rolled on casters. Multicolored lights blinked in the thing's midsection and what appeared to be several retractable arms or tentacles stuck out of its body. It was probably some sort of robot watchman, Ranger thought with a surprisingly calm mind, while his legs trembled with the more sensible desire to turn and run. Though the squealing sound could be the robot's method of communication, and it might be trying to get him to identify himself as friend or foe, Ranger sadly doubted that any of the languages and dialects he knew would enable him to accomplish that task; nor were his weapons likely to be effective against such a challenger as this.

While he was trying to decide what to do, the machine came to a halt in front of him. Two of its metal tentacles shot out and coiled around the man's body. It was a light embrace that left Ranger's arms free, but the limbs were obviously strong enough to crush him or tear open his vac-suit. Either or both of those fatal events seemed imminent as the robot continued to receive no response to its nerve-grating inquiry.

Desperately, Ranger flicked on his torch and applied it to one of the tentacles. He may as well have tried to tickle the robot with a feather. Probably nothing less powerful than the *Gayheart*'s laser torch could burn through this metal monster's thick hide.

Reflexively, Ranger's right hand leveled his disrupter at the robot's body, before he realized how futile the action was. The disrupter beam could only affect the chemical-electrical impulses of living neurons. The weapon's charge would have no impact on the programed circuitry of a mechanical brain. Or would it? How did he know what sort of a thinking device this alien machine possessed? Maybe its creators had provided it with the brain of a lower animal. Anything was possible, but right now the only thing for certain was that he had to do something before it was too late. Already the tentacles had started to tighten around his body and his squeezed lungs were laboring for breath. He aimed a tight disrupter beam at the robot's blinking lights and fired a full charge.

One of the tentacles holding Ranger suddenly fell away. But the other one retained its grip and whipped wildly back and forth, slamming him against the bulkheads and deck with bone-jarring force. Terrified and battered half unconscious, he was finally released and thrown several meters down the corridor where he lay in a tumbled heap. He had just enough strength to roll over and look back at the robot.

The machine seemed to have gone berserk. It gyrated drunkenly on its casters with its tentacles flailing in all directions. It started to roll toward Ranger, then reversed itself and smashed into a bulkhead. The impact knocked the robot over onto its side and it lay motionless. All of its lights slowly blinked out.

Ranger was too badly shaken to stand, so he used his antigrav pack to get back on his feet. He checked himself over and was relieved to find that he had suffered no injuries more serious than a lot of aching bruises.

Most of the equipment from his toolbelt was scattered around him. As he gathered it up he came across his disrupter, mangled to uselessness by the robot's casters.

The machine had certainly been a well-programed guardian. He wondered just what sort of a brain it did have, but he wasn't interested enough to examine it just then. He only hoped he wouldn't encounter any more of them as he limped on down the corridor.

Evidently there were no other robot watchmen on duty in that area. Ranger wandered unchallenged and aimlessly for another hour through the satellite's labyrinthine interior, before he luckily came upon what he had been looking for. By then he had found so many chambers containing incomprehensible machinery and equipment that at first he did not realize that he had finally entered the satellite's main control room.

He stood puzzling over a complex electronic console, eager to experiment with its many levers and dials but fearful of the disastrous results his ignorant bungling might produce. All at once the familiar sight of a viewscreen caught his attention. At least he felt competent enough to operate this without causing any great damage.

He activated the screen and discovered through trial and error that it was tied in to a computer library of extensive technical literature. The language was unfamiliar to him, of course, but it contained many pictographs that made word and phrase meanings easy to figure out. That, along with the fact that many of the scientific formulae described were based upon universal natural laws, enabled him to make roughly accurate translations of the basic operating instructions to some of the equipment in the room.

After an hour's study, he felt confident enough to make some minor adjustments on the control console. Then he said: "Hello, Lulu. Do you read me now?"

"Boss! Where are you?" Lulu's voice cried in his earphone. "Are you all right? I've been worried sick ever since that awful thing swallowed you up."

"It's a long story that I'll tell you about when we have some spare time," Ranger promised. "I just wanted to let you know that I'm safe and have located the satellite's controls."

"Well, where are you? I'll burn you out of there."

"I don't think that will be necessary, if these controls are as simple as they appear. I've already learned how to let a communication beam get through the satellite's shell. I'm sure that a little more study will tell me how to open an exit from in here."

"Good. Then you can come back aboard and we can get away from this scary hunk of metal and go down to see if Dawnboy is all right."

"Oh, quit worrying about him," Ranger said. "We aren't going to leave here until I've finished figuring out this satellite's purpose for being here. That shouldn't take more than another dozen hours or so, with time out for eating and sleeping."

He cut off Lulu's protests and happily returned to studying the computer's technical library.

28

DAWNBOY STARED IN unbelieving astonishment at Alexia's face framed in the gunsight. Her eyes were slitted against the wind and her long hair was whipped to a tangled mane as she looked fearfully up from her scooter at the scoutcraft following above her.

How could it possibly be she?

But as Dawnboy thought the matter over, he supposed that this could be an entirely normal duty assignment for her. Modern military powers did not believe in coddling their women. But what was she up to now? Were she and her IFIB comrades hoping to catch him off-guard? What happened next did not exactly answer those questions, but it did make the current situation somewhat more understandable.

The scouter was a two-place job, carrying a pilot and observer-gunner—the latter manned the sonic blaster whose coil-wrapped snout extended from a ball turret at the front of the craft. As Dawnboy watched, the gunner activated the blaster. No muzzle flash was visible, but the sudden eruption of water below and behind Alexia could only have been caused by a tightly concentrated charge of sound waves. Since every living cell is an elastic medium that can be damaged by powerful vibrations, Alexia's body would simply have disintegrated if the charge had struck her.

Alexia was surely aware of her danger, for she desperately whipped her scooter into an evasive zigzag course. But the scouter crew knew its business, and stayed right with her, blasting repeatedly to force her closer and closer to the water. Evidently the men did not want to kill her, and figured that once they had her helpless in the sea they could easily fish her out alive. The plan seemed to be working very well. At the rate they were going, Alexia would be driven into the bay long before she reached Dawnboy's shoreline.

Dawnboy wondered what he should do. He had no quarrel with these people as long as they didn't attack him. And he certainly had no reason to take Alexia's side in a fight. Still, she was a woman in trouble, and he was mighty curious to find out just what had gotten her into this predicament . . .

While he was considering Alexia's predicament, her time was running out. She was down to a point where she was nearly skimming the wave tops now, and the scouter was bearing down relentlessly on her.

Another look at her terrified face and Dawnboy made up his mind. He snapped off his rifle's safety and put on the sight's infrared self-adjuster that automatically allowed for elevation and windage. All he had to do was line up the scouter pilot's transparent bubble in the crosshairs and squeeze the trigger.

His first shot was a clean miss. So were the next three, because a moving target is not easy for an inexperienced rifleman to hit, even with the best gun available. But he kept trying, and was rewarded by seeing his fifth shot crack the blaster turret. He put two more rounds into the scouter before the pilot realized what was happening, pulled up, and came speeding straight at him, just as a tall wave hit Alexia's scouter and plunged her into the water.

The scouter was less than a mile from the shore by then, and it seemed to cover the distance in the snap of a finger. Dawnboy kept up a steady stream of fire at it, throwing the blaster gunner's aim off enough to send his charges harmlessly into the water. The shock absorbers in his rifle's stock reduced its recoil to a mere twitch and enabled him to hold a tight bead on the scouter. The Berlix was one sweet little weapon, all right.

But the stalemate could not last forever. Dawnboy was thinking about making a retreat and calling it a tactical maneuver, when the scouter drew up about two hundred yards in front of him. The pilot put her on hover to give the gunner a steady firing platform, also giving Dawnboy a stationary target. Whereupon Dawnboy calmly shot the pilot squarely between the eyes.

Almost simultaneously, he watched the gunner get off a sonic blast that would surely have vibed him if the impact of the pilot's body on his controls had not sent the scouter into a spiraling dive. Instead, the charge hit the boulder, making the thirty-ton rock dance like a water-skipping stone and bucking Dawnboy high into the air. The rifle was torn from his grip.

As he turned a lazy flip-flop in the air he saw the scouter shoot past him and plow into the sand about fifty yards up the beach. It seemed to take him forever to get back to the ground, but even that was much too soon, for he was then slammed down with enough force to break a good majority of all the bones in his body—if the sand had not been such a good cushion. As it was, he only lost some skin and all of his breath.

Never totally unconscious, he was able to experience to the fullest the grinding pain of his battered flesh and the helpless terror of gasping and gasping without ever seeming to get any air into his lungs. Finally he was able to rise panting to his knees, just in time to see a man walking toward him from the wrecked scouter. The man carried a hand blaster and wore an expression that said he was going to enjoy what he planned to do with it.

Dawnboy watched dully as the man raised his weapon. Then instinct took up where his stunned wits left off and, groping desperately, his hands touched the comeback blade sheathed on his belt. He came tottering to his feet with the blade in his hand.

The IFIB gunner halted and smiled, taunting him to go ahead and throw the weapon, if he thought it would do any good.

Dawnboy drew back his arm and let fly. Then his heart sank as he watched the whirling blade veer off to the man's left and miss him by a good dozen feet. The man looked rather sympathetic as he carefully took aim and started to press the plaster's firing stud. Dawnboy's mind started to clear and he thought he had just about enough time to compose himself to face death with the dignity suitable to an Apache warrior—when the comeback blade's airfoil executed a beautiful 180-degree turn and brought the weapon spinning back to plunge full-force into the IFIB gunner's back. The blade split his head so efficiently that he didn't even have time to look surprised as he pitched forward into the sand.

For a moment Dawnboy was too stunned even to express his relief. Then it burst from him in hysterical laughter that went on and on, until he again fell to his knees weak and shaking. He needed several minutes to recover enough of his scattered wits to remember Alexia.

Turning, he could just about see her out in the water swimming weakly toward him. He didn't think she would be able to make it, even if none of the voracious sea carnivores found her. He hurried to his antigrav pack and strapped it on.

She had given up swimming when he reached her, and was merely struggling to keep afloat. Even that seemed too much of an effort for her, and her head slipped under the waves as he reached down and caught her hair. He lifted her in his arms like a limp, soggy bundle of rags and carried her to the beach. She was unconscious and barely breathing by then, so he rolled her onto her stomach and pumped what seemed to be a gallon of water from her lungs.

He was thinking of applying mouth-to-mouth resuscitation, when she opened her eyes and smiled wanly at him.

"Oh, I'm so glad it's you," she whispered hoarsely. "They wanted . . . to come over and kill you in your sleep tonight. My . . . two enlisted techs. They wouldn't obey my orders to . . . leave you alone. So I was coming to warn you . . ."

"Do na try to talk now," he said, although he was glad to learn the reason for her mysterious behavior. "Come, I'll take ye to a place where ye can rest better."

He again gathered Alexia in his arms, and they moved along the cliffs until they came to his cave. She hardly seemed any weight at all, for such a well-developed girl, and even with her wet clothing she felt so nice nestled against him that he hated to put her down when they were inside.

"Get out o' yer wet clothes and wrap yerself in these blankets," he instructed. "When I come back, I'll fix ye some hot soup."

"Please don't leave me alone," she said in a frightened voice.

There was nothing he wanted to do less than that, but duty demanded that he do the decent thing for his slain enemies. "I'll be right back," he promised.

The sun was setting and the tide was coming in as he returned to the cove. He quickly dug shallow graves for the two bodies and chanted the Death Song over them. Then he hurried back to the cave.

Only now did the full impact of what had happened hit him: he had Alexia in his power! The treacherous she-snake who had deceived and humiliated him was completely at his mercy. Ah, the gods were smiling on him at last! And oh, how she would pay the price for trifling with an Apache warrior's honor! For at last he had earned his full manhood by killing men honorably in battle, and he was fully entitled to have his way with a woman. Alexia was—in a sense—his prize of war that he had won in a fair fight. How good it felt to be free of the hateful restrictions of civilization and live like a real Highland Apache again!

He could hardly wait to get back to Alexia and realize his vengeful dreams. Well, maybe he wouldn't torture her after all, since she had already suffered so much on his account. But she would learn who was her master this night—on that he swore his solemn oath. And afterwards . . . ? Well, they would see how things worked out between them. Actually she probably wasn't really such a bad sort deep-down. Maybe all she needed was a good man to give her a beating now and then to keep her out of mischief. Anyway, it seemed ironically fitting that Alexia should be his first woman.

When he re-entered the cave, nervous with anticipation, things didn't quite work out the way he had expected.

Alexia was bundled up in his blankets, sound asleep. When his light fell on her angelically lovely and innocent face, all his lust and vengence melted away, until his heart felt like a great, soppy sponge. He didn't really want to hurt her. He wanted to cherish and protect her. He wanted to take care of her and to win her favor by proving how much he cared for her.

He turned away from the sleeping girl, ashamed and disgusted with himself. What kind of an Apache was he, anyway? There lay his prize, the woman who had been the cause of the most miserable experience of his life—there she was, helpless before him, and he lacked the will to make her pay for it. Oh, damn this rotten, soul-destroying civilization that turned his masculine strength into soft, womanly sentimentality! Though maybe civilization wasn't to blame. There had always been that shameful soft streak in him; it had made him doubt that he would ever really be a great warchief, no matter how often he proved his courage. Maybe it was his fate to be something less than a full man, and he would have to find his satisfactions elsewhere. Maybe a religious or scholarly life would suit him better . . .

Well, whatever the fault was, he was too tired to think more on it now. He took the one blanket that Alexia had not used and drapped it Apache-style over his shoulders. After eating his supper rations cold, he stretched out on the floor across the cave from Alexia and soon drifted off into a sound sleep.

Even then, he couldn't entirely escape the spell that Alexia seemed to have cast over him. He dreamed of them walking together through endless fields of wild flowers, while crimson-and-gold butterflies fluttered about their heads. It was such a charming dream that he hated to awaken the next morning, especially when he opened his eyes and saw Alexia holding a synapse disrupter on him.

29

"THANKS FOR YOUR hospitality," Alexia said with a friendly smile. "It was a lovely evening, but now I'm afraid I have to get back to work. No, don't try to reach for your weapons. I only have this on stun, but you know what a bad concussion headache even that can give you."

Dawnboy halted his right hand's reflexive movement toward his rifle and stared blankly from the girl's leveled disrupter to her guileless face. His mind was still sleep-clouded, but the shock of finding himself in this condition was swiftly clearing it.

"Ye . . . ye tricked me!" he spluttered. "The story about ye wanting to keep yer two men from killing me, and them appearing to chase ye—all lies!"

"Don't take it so hard," Alexia pleaded. "We did it for your own good. If you and your father had been allowed to put this planet up for sale on the open market, you would've just become lazy and corrupted by all the money you got for it. This way, we can use you as a hostage to persuade your father to sign over his claim to the Family, who will see to it that the planet is populated and developed according to the high moral standards of Otherism. And you two will be able to continue your useful lives as honest workingmen, free of the degrading burden of excess wealth."

"I hardly ken how to thank ye for the favor," Dawnboy said sourly, sitting up and pulling on his moccasins. "Ye're a master o' slyness, Alexia, I have to give ye credit for that. But what about the two men in the scouter? Was it necessary to sacrifice them for ye to weasel into my confidence?"

239

"No, that wasn't in our plans," she said with a touch of sorrow. "They were only supposed to chase me to you and make it seem that they really wanted to capture me. But they weren't expecting you to put up a fight, so your shooting must have triggered their combat reflexes. Pity; they were good men. But we are all prepared to give our lives for the advancement of Otherism, and their actions will be duly noted by the Bureau of Heroic Honors."

"I'm sure that'll be a great comfort to 'em," he grunted.

Alexia dismissed further thought of her dead comrades with a slight shrug. "Come along now. We'll use your antigrav car to get over to my ship on the promontory." She held up a small remote-control switch in her free hand. "I've already triggered the comm system over there to send off a prearranged signal to Controller Lopezov, so we should break atmosphere at just about the right time to rendezvous with him."

"Then he was na fooled by our sub-ether torpedo?"

Alexia gave him a condescending smile. "Oh, really now. We knew your father wouldn't waste any time registering his claim. So it was obvious from the beginning that the key to our success lay in capturing you. We computerized several alternate plans for accomplishing that, and the way you voluntarily separated yourself from the *Gayheart* played right in with one of them. Now it's just a matter of tying up a few loose ends, so let's go."

Dawnboy looked around at his few belongings in the cave, decided they weren't important enough to ask permission to take them with him, and started toward the antigrav car. Then he paused and turned back to Alexia.

"One more thing—if ye had that disrupter all night, why did ye wait till now to pull it on me?"

"There was no hurry. Besides, we both were exhausted and needed a good night's rest."

"But were ye na worried about going to sleep alone with me so close to ye?"

Alexia's eyes went wide with innocence. "Of course

not. I've always known that you're a perfect gentleman."

The teasing undertone in her voice made Dawnboy wonder if perhaps deep-down she hadn't hoped she'd been mistaken in her judgment of him. It was one of life's little mysteries whose answer he would never know for sure, but it gave him something to think about while they graved over to the IFIB landing craft.

There Alexia ordered him to strap down on an acceleration couch. It had special straps that could only be released by a switch on her control panel, so he would remain her prisoner until they went into orbit and docked with the returning starcruiser.

Dawnboy's pride was frustratingly humiliated by having been captured by a woman, and the defeat was made even more galling by the realization that she had twice outmaneuvered him. Worse than that, his unforgivable stupidity in letting her get the better of him seemed certain to result in economic disaster for his father. He had to think of some way to get out of this mess! The more he searched his mind for a plan of escape, however, the more hopeless his position appeared.

That fact became painfully unavoidable when he was taken under guard to the starcruiser's bridge to meet Ship-Controller Lopezov. He did not even have a chance to snatch one of the guard's weapons and go down fighting to an honorable warrior's death.

"My dear boy!" Lopezov beamed, clapping Dawnboy on the shoulder. "How happy I am to see you still alive and well."

"Thank ye, sir," Dawnboy replied sullenly. "Wish I could say the same."

"You certainly have your father's stubborn spirit," Lopezov chuckled. "With a strong Apache instinct for survival, too, according to Alexia. She has told me how you vanquished her two men. What a shame that we lost them! But by God, that was a fight I wish I could have seen! I've often told our High Command that we should try to recruit troops from barbarous worlds like

Apache Highlands, and so keep our combat readiness from getting flabby."

"I'm sure my clansmen will be glad to show ye how to fight," Dawnboy said, "if ye ever dare to set foot on their land."

"No doubt they will." The plump officer's smile faded a little at Dawnboy's grim expression. "Well, it's been a great pleasure chatting to you this way, and I wish we could prolong it. But I've already spent too much time on this assignment. Actually, if it were my decision to make, I'd let your father keep this little out-of-the-way planet, as it's of such limited usefulness. But I'm just a military man and must obey my government's orders. We've established communication with the *Gayheart*, so I want you to tell Ranger what he must do to ensure your safe return to him. We have a message all prepared, instructing SSA Headquarters to transfer his claim to the Interstellar Family of Intelligent Beings. It only requires his voiceprint to make it official."

"And if I refuse to do as ye say?" Dawnboy asked.

Lopezov looked sincerely upset at the possiblity.

Alexia, who had rejoined them after going to her cabin to change clothes, said: "Personally, I hope you do. I'd love to keep you with us a while and give you some intensive instruction in Otherism and in the general aspects of our way of thinking."

Dawnboy shuddered, imagining what sort of "instruction" he would receive.

"Let's not waste time on idle speculation," Lopezov said, his voice hard with command authority. "You know you are in no position to bargain with us. You can either make this easy or hard on yourself. The result will be the same. Because of my respect for your father, I'd rather not treat you too harshly, but please don't try my patience."

Dawnboy took a long look into Lopezov's narrowed eyes—as hard and cold as blue ice under a polar wind—and nodded. "All right, I'll do it."

"Good."

Lopezov led him to a photophone and nodded to a

technician, who immediately brought Ranger's image to the screen. He looked anxiously at Dawnboy and said: "Hello, Son. Are you all right?"

"Aye, sir. But I'm sorry to have caused ye all this trouble."

"He has something important to tell you," Lopezov prompted. "Don't you?"

"Aye." Dawnboy took a deep breath and blurted: "Don't give in to 'em, Dad! Fight them! I don't care what they do to me—"

Strong hands gripped him and he struck out with fists and feet as two burly guards struggled to overpower his furious resistance.

"Sorry about that," Lopezov said to Ranger, when calm had been restored to his bridge. "But don't worry; we won't hurt him, as long as you give us what we want."

"It was my fault for not warning you about his unpredictable temper," Ranger apologized. "Gets it from his mother's side. But you've made your point, and I'll do whatever you say to get him back. Son, don't give them any more trouble. It's stupid to go on fighting after we've been beaten."

Dawnboy stopped struggling, and concentrated on holding back angry tears at the bitterness of defeat. In growing shame, he listened to Lopezov dictate his terms of surrender to Ranger.

"All right, I'll do it," Ranger said. "Let the boy go, in his antigrav car. When he's halfway to my ship, I'll send the message to SSA Headquarters. You can keep a weapon trained on him, as insurance that I'll keep my word."

"Agreed," Lopezov smiled, his round face once more the image of innocent good humor. "And I must say, it has certainly been a pleasure doing business with you."

"Just one more thing," Ranger said. "I don't mind so much giving you this planet, but I had to go pretty deep into debt to pay for this trip. So I'd like to cut my losses by taking the smaller moon in tow when I leave. I've found a small deposit of luxium in it. It should process out just about enough to cover my operating expenses."

Lopezov rubbed his jaw thoughtfully for a long moment, then shrugged. "Oh, all right. I guess we can afford to be generous in victory. My scientific section reported that the satellite serves no useful function there, anyway."

"Yeah, and you wouldn't want to bankrupt me and completely drive me out of business, would you?" Ranger smiled. "You never know when you might have another chance to steal a planet from me ... Oh, by the way, Autry—my tractor beam is strong enough to tow the moon once it's under way, but I'll need your ship to help break it out of orbit."

Lopezov laughed heartily. "You capitalists do have to bargain for that last tiny advantage, don't you? Very well. We'll help get you on your way. And I even hope you make a good profit out of it. Since the spread of Otherism throughout the universe is inevitable, the more wealth you contribute to our eventual possessions, the better."

"I'll do my best to see that you get what's coming to you," Ranger promised.

30

DAWNBOY LAY ON his bunk staring gloomily at the overhead. During the three hours he had been back aboard the *Gayheart*, he had felt so dejected and disgusted with himself that he'd hardly moved from the bunk. He had not even had the will to go to the galley for his usual five- or six-course snack, even after Lulu reminded him he hadn't eaten since the previous evening. For a teen-age boy of his size and normal, active nature, that was really a bad sign.

He heard a knock on the door, and Ranger asked: "Mind if I come in?"

"Suit yerself, Dad," Dawnboy grunted.

Ranger Farstar entered, took the chair from Dawnboy's desk and straddled it, facing the bunk. "Sorry I didn't look in on you sooner," he said. "But I was pretty busy making sure the moon is securely in tow and plotting the most direct course to Newtonia. I think the old test-tubers there will be mighty interested in having a look at it. You want to know why?"

He waited, but Dawnboy made no reply.

Ranger grinned at him. "You know, if you let the corners of your mouth droop just a little further, you should be able to shine your shoes with your lower lip. Then at least you'd have gotten something useful out of this experience."

Dawnboy's scowl only deepened at the attempted humor. "Don't waste your breath," Lulu cut in. "I've been trying to cheer him up ever since he came back, and it's as frustrating as spitting in zero gravity. He thinks he has all the guilt of the ages on his shoulders, just because he let a pretty face and helpless smile get to him."

"I let it happen *twice*," Dawnboy said from the depths of his despair. "There's no excuse for that kind o' carelessness."

"Well, I'm not trying to excuse you," Ranger said. "It's up to every man to square his actions with his conscience, so you'll have to learn to live with this the best you can. I just want you to know that I'm not angry with you and that I'm glad we got out of the situation back there as well as we did. We're still alive and healthy, and we're leaving with fair payment for our work. Of course, it's disappointing to have lost the big prize, but when you've been in business as long as I have you become philosophical about that sort of thing. You either get philosophical or you get drunk, and philosophy's cheaper."

"As Plato said, win a few, lose a few," Lulu philosophized.

"Thanks," Dawnboy said, with no noticeable change in his expression. "At least I'm glad to know that ye forgive me. I just wish I could do the same for myself."

"I think the trouble here," Lulu said, "is that his spirit is crushed by the way he reacted to Alexia's treatment. Or failed to react."

"If that's what's bothering you," Ranger said, "then it might make you feel better to know that she didn't just use her own little brain to outsmart you. She's a highly trained cyberpsychologist and I'll bet she fed every known detail about you into her computer, then studied the results as carefully as a general plotting a major campaign. Even a man far more experienced with women than you wouldn't have stood much of a chance with her."

"Ye think so?" Dawnboy's dull eyes seemed to light up a bit as he grasped at the offered straw of hope. "But even so, that's na reason for me na being mon enough to settle the score with her when I had the chance."

When Lulu pressed him for an explanation, he haltingly told them about spending the night alone in the cave with Alexia, blushing at his shameful confession of weakness.

"You feel guilty for not being able to force yourself on her?" Lulu demanded. "As if that would have proved your manhood? Believe me, Grandson, by not taking advantage of her you proved yourself to be far more of a man than if you had. A special kind of man."

Dawnboy sat up interestedly. "Maybe ye're right. Maybe the Apache ways are na always the best ways for a mon to behave. What do ye think, Dad?"

"Well, let me put it this way," Ranger said slowly. "You are my son, and I doubt if anything you could possibly do could make me want to change that. But what you did this time makes it a lot easier for me to say that."

For the first time in many hours, Dawnboy managed

to smile. Then he frowned uncertainly. "But I still canna understand her, or the whole system she represents. For instance, so many things about Otherism and the IFIB system seem to make good sense and seem to help people. Yet they can just come along and take our planet away from us and commit I-don't-know-what other crimes, and they don't feel they've done anything wrong. How do ye explain people like that?"

Ranger shrugged. "I don't know, Son. I've told you that the universe is filled with many strange things that we can't understand and just have to accept as they are. Having always been a capitalist individualist myself, the collectivist societies are a mystery to me. The nearest I can make out is that some people must have a deep-rooted compulsion to submerge their own personalities in a crowd. Maybe they're too lazy to do their own thinking. Or too frightened to accept responsibility for their own actions."

"I think that's about right," Lulu agreed. "There is good and bad in everyone, but some people can't bear to face their own wickedness. So they try to hide it behind some noble idealism, such as pretending to care more about others than themselves."

"They must be terribly miserable people," Dawnboy said pityingly.

"Or very happy ones," Ranger suggested. "Who are we to judge? Now, about that satellite, let me put your mind at ease if you're worried about the IFIB using your planet as a penal colony. As I started to tell you before, in a few days Dawnworld won't be very comfortable for any kind of human habitation."

"Why not?" Dawnboy asked curiously.

"Because gigantic tides caused by the moon and sweeping around the planet without resistance will cover most of the sole continent's surface. That's how it was in the planet's ancient past, and that's how it will be now that we have taken away the counter-force that maintained an Earthlike tidal balance on it."

"Ye mean the small moon diminished the large moon's gravitational pull on the planet's waters?"

Dawnboy asked skeptically. "But how could it? It's so tiny."

"Tiny for a natural moon, but not for a manufactured one," Ranger said. "As I had suspected, and soon learned through exploration, it is really a superpowerful, luxium-powered antigravity generator. Its makers obviously placed it there to alter the planet's ecological balance and to make possible the evolution of an environment more hospitable to intelligent beings. Fortunately the satellite's deactivation controls were simple enough for me to figure out before we pulled it out of orbit, or we'd be chasing it over half the galaxy."

Dawnboy jumped up excitedly.

"But how . . . what . . . when . . . who put it there? Was it that superintelligent race ye mentioned before? The ones that ye didn't know if they ever even existed?"

"Well, it had to be *some* superintelligent race," Ranger answered. "I don't know of any existing technology that could build something like that. A rough dating of the half-life of the luxium fuel in it indicates that it has been there for at least fifty thousand Earth years. After such a long absence, it's most unlikely that the people who put it there will ever be back, so I don't think we have to worry about taking something that's still useful to its original owners."

"Fifty thousand years!" Dawnboy whistled. "But, then it must be very valuable, isn't it? Much more than for just the small luxium deposit that ye told Lopezov ye wanted it for."

"Is that what I told him?" Ranger asked innocently. "Just shows how my memory's slipping in my old age. Yes, I think the Newtonian scientists will be willing to pay a good price for an antique like this. Maybe enough to pay off our mortgage and outfit us for another expedition. What do you think of a lost-treasure search this time? There's an old legend about a cargo ship loaded with gold and precious stones that got trapped in the tail of a comet in one of the Magellanic Clouds . . ."

A faraway look came into Ranger's eye and Dawnboy caught his breath.

"Let's go after it, Dad! If we find it, we might get enough money to build a clinic for organ-transplant research on Newtonia, and then . . ."

Father and son exchanged meaningful glances, and Ranger laughed, rising to his feet. "Let's talk about it in the galley. I could use a sandwich."

"Me, too."

Dawnboy suddenly discovered that his appetite was back with a vengeance. He eagerly followed his father out of the cabin.

"Hey, don't you two get so involved with your boy talk that you forget to check in at the bridge," Lulu said. "I can't be expected to do everything around here."

"Why not?" Ranger asked. "Didn't you once tell me you could fly this tub, beat me at 3-D chess, and carry on a conversation all at the same time?"

Dawnboy only half listened to them fall into their endless, meaningless light bickering. He was too preoccupied thinking about their next cruise and, more importantly, about what he was going to eat. His spirit was so overflowing with happy anticipation that he wondered how he could ever have felt so downhearted about Alexia and about losing Dawnworld. Why, the whole universe was out there just waiting for him. All he had to do was reach out and take it. How could he ever have doubted that he wanted to be a spaceman? Or that he might lack the ability to become one? Sure, he still had a lot to learn, but—he glanced at his father—he couldn't have found a better teacher.

He wondered if they should look back to see if the satellite was still safely in tow. Then he remembered: you can't look back in a starship.

He looked forward instead—to the stars.

ABOUT THE AUTHOR

Bill Starr was first inspired to write many years ago while working on the San Francisco docks with Eric Hoffer, the "longshoreman philosopher." His published work to date numbers several hundred short pieces of fiction, nonfiction and poetry and five books—the latest being *Chance Fortune,* an acclaimed historical novel about Los Angeles.

Bill's decision to make Dawnboy MacCochise, the young hero of the Farstar & Son Books, an Apache brave grew out of his lifelong interest in Indian affairs. In 1982 he founded Americans for an American Indian Day, a letter-writing campaign that has been at least partly responsible for the introduction in the U.S. Congress of H.J. Res. 459, a bill to honor our Indian citizens with a commemorative day, and similar proposals in several state and local governments.

Arizona-born and California-reared, Bill lives in a Los Angeles suburb with his wife Veronica and two ornery cats.